DISCOVERY

DESIGNER CHILDREN: BOOK ONE

NAN DIXON

Loved it. Thrilled to see this is a start of of a new series. I am eager to see what happens next in the family. The story flowed and kept me turning pages.

DANCE WITH ME
DANCE WITH ME by Nan Dixon is a heartfelt, emotional and well-written story that truly fits the description in the book—a journey of healing, hope and love.

STAINED GLASS HEARTS
STAINED GLASS HEARTS by Nan Dixon is simply absolutely incredible. It's one everyone MUST READ.

INVEST IN ME
I fell in love from the beginning and didn't want it to end. It has an excellent and spellbinding wonderful plot and in-depth characters.

SOUTHERN COMFORTS
…is a book about learning how to give and receive without any strings attached. It's about caring and trust and loyalty; and relying on those you love to help make your dreams come true.
RT TIMES - Page Turner

THE OTHER TWIN
Nan Dixon will become a favorite author. Part of series but can read as a stand alone. Fun story that's hard to put down. "One more page…just another chapter…" until soon you've reached the end.
A complicated story that reflects the many threads of real life that so often includes knots of problems in addition to the gradual unraveling of past hurts when placed in the light of love and real caring. A story I couldn't put down.

UNDERCOVER WITH THE HEIRESS
So much more than a romance novel.
This was definitely a book I was not able to put down! I took the tablet with me everywhere! **Fabulous Brunette Reviews**

THROUGH A MAGNOLIA FILTER
…a heartwarming story that showcased the importance of family, following your dreams, and true love. I thoroughly enjoyed this tender heartwarming story. **LAS Reviewer**

A SAVANNAH CHRISTMAS WISH
FRESH PICK
…is a book that has you frolicking in gardens, battling storms and falling in love…A book of warmth and love. It will leave you smiling.

TO CATCH A THIEF
Not your everyday Contemporary genre, a little suspense, a little love and definitely entertaining… **Our Town Book Reviews**

A SAVANNAH CHRISTMAS WEDDING (novella)
Another winner. Love this series

COPYRIGHT

eBook ISBN **979-8-9861407-3-5**

Print ISBN **979-8-9861407-4-2**

Copyright © 2022 by Nan Dixon. All rights reserved.

No part of this book may be reproduced in any form or by any electronic or mechanical means, including information storage and retrieval systems, without written permission from the author, except for the use of brief quotations in a book review.

DISCOVERY is a work of fiction. Characters, names, places, brands, media and incidents are either products of the author's imagination or have been used factiously and should not be construed as real. Any resemblance to actual persons, living or dead, events or locales is entirely coincidental. This book is licensed for your personal enjoyment only and may not be re-sold or given away to other people. The scanning, uploading, and distribution of this book via Internet of other means without the permission of the publisher is illegal and punishable by law. Please purchase only authorized electronic editions, and do not participate in or encourage electronic piracy of copyrighted materials. Thank you for respecting the hard work of this author.

Grinning Frog Press - September 2022

Editor: Judy Roth. Cover Design: Covers by Dana Lamothe of Designs by Dana

Copyrights - Cover photos ©Opolja Adobe Stock, DNA ©David Carillon Adobe Stock

CHAPTER ONE

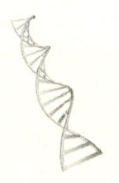

Thirty-three years ago

Andrew, two more of our precious embryos died today. With each loss, my heart breaks. Our children! It didn't matter before you died, but now these few small embryos are all that's left of you. We created these children together, not in the ordinary way of procreation, but our *way.*

Each day another piece of my heart breaks. I have to save what's left of you, but I'm not foolish enough to implant all eight remaining embryos. What can I do?

My love always, forever and beyond. Lainie

The private journal of Elaina Harrison Ashland, MD, PhD

HOUSTON
Present day

"I heard a rumor you're thinking about running for governor?"

Harris Torrington smiled at his mother's question. Apparently her Saturday brunch invitation hadn't been casual. Outside, the Houston sun sparkled off the swimming pool.

He took more huevos rancheros, anything to avoid her question. Besides, his mother's cook made the best breakfast in Texas. "Who have you been talking to?"

She flashed a cheeky smile. "I never reveal my sources."

His mother's informant list was better than the CIA's.

He'd been thinking about running for governor for months but hadn't breathed a word to anyone until yesterday. "Did you bug my office?"

"How can you think that of your own mother?" She slapped a hand to her heart. "The years it took to have you. All the sleepless nights you gave me. I swear you were colicky for your first twelve months."

"You remind me of your struggles every birthday." He exhaled, worried she wouldn't support his ambitions. "What do you think?"

"Governor. It's a big step." She traced the flower on her china teacup. "If you fail, it might affect your future choices."

"Fail? You and Dad never let me *think* the word."

His mother pushed away her tea and placed her palms on the table. "You might consider a smaller step."

"The timing on running for governor couldn't be better." His fingers flexed around his fork. He needed his mother's support.

She broke off a piece of blueberry scone and popped it in her mouth. "Why don't you follow in your dad's footsteps and run for the state legislature?"

"He would have taken this opportunity."

She tipped her head and her blonde hair shifted and settled into place, curving around her elegant face. An eyebrow arched above eyes as bright as a Texas bluebonnet. "Your father and I always want you to aim high, but running for governor is a big step."

"I thought about running for United States senator, but the old geezer who holds the honorable seat from Texas can't be beat."

Her laugh warmed his heart. "When I head to D.C. tomorrow, I'll tell your father you called him an old geezer."

"I talked to him on my way here. He sends his love."

"And he didn't call to warn me." She sighed. "What did he think about you running for governor?"

He imitated his father's deep voice. "'What the hell are you thinking, boy?'"

"What are you thinking?" she asked. "You're thirty-one and single. There aren't many unmarried governors."

He lined up his arguments, ticking off the salient points. "One, I'm getting more media attention than any possible candidate. Two, Governor Patrick isn't running again and three, the lieutenant governor's retiring from politics." He nodded. "It's like the planets are aligned in my favor."

"When someone asks you why you're running, *never* mention planets aligning. That's a sure way to lose votes." His mother's lips pinched together. "What about attorney general? It's a natural step."

"Yes." He'd considered every office. But he could do more good as governor of Texas.

When he'd run for Houston's Harris County district attorney, his motto had been *Back to Basics*. As DA, he'd streamlined the office and staff. Now his team maintained a higher conviction rate than any previous district attorney. He would use his strong record to carry him to the governor's mansion and maybe beyond.

"I believe this is the right step." He straightened. As governor, he wanted to mend the deep political division in the state. If he succeeded, maybe he could do the same for the country.

He poured coffee into his cup and added a dollop of fat-free cream. After Dad's heart attack, Mom had eliminated all fats from his diet. With stents in place, the man would probably outlast him. Unless Dad kept sneaking cigars and steak.

"Us Texans like our governors to be married—with children." His mother pointed her finger. "We trust a man with roots."

"I have you and Dad. No one could have better roots than that."

"Of course." His mother shifted in her seat. Odd. She didn't usually fidget. "Being a bachelor could hurt your candidacy."

"Jason and I discussed my image." Jason had run his campaign for district attorney. "He thinks it's worth the risk. Single people are elected to office."

"Jerry Brown, Janet Napolitano, Corzine—wait—not a good example." Enthusiasm flared in his mother's eyes. "I'll talk to their campaign managers."

"I'm only in the exploration stage," he reminded her.

"You do what you're best at; analyzing, planning and focusing on your goal. I'll do what I'm best at, working in the background." Mother nodded. "If this is what you want, we're behind you."

Her acceptance lifted a weight off his chest. "Your support means everything to me."

"You need to date a wholesome conservative young woman." She drummed her fingers on the table.

Her shook his head. "I don't have time to date."

She tipped her head. "How about Kat?"

"She's a friend."

"Y'all look good together." She mussed his hair. "Such a contrast. She's blonde to your dark, both of you are tall. Kat's getting a lot of television airtime too."

"She's a friend. And she conned me into playing at a golf tournament Monday for Big Brothers and Sisters."

"Excellent." She tapped her lip. "Make sure the reporters get a good soundbite. Jason can pull one together."

"This is a charity."

"Multi-task dear." She smiled. "I'll find you the perfect conservative woman."

"Not happening."

Mother pointed a finger at him. "Whatever you do, stay scandal-free."

"This isn't my first rodeo." She didn't have to warn him. "I've lived under a microscope all my life. No reporter will find anything on me. I'm spotless."

New York City

"Sunee," Grandmother hissed over the clinking of glasses and the hum of conversation. "You're breaking out in hives!"

No! Sunee clasped her hand on her neck. "Is it bad, Po Po?"

"Terrible. Do something." Grandmother waved her away. "Don't embarrass your father."

Sunee inched into the hallway and scuttled toward the back stairs. Darn heels and tight skirt. She longed for her clogs. At the hospital, she could run all day.

That was where she'd rather be, either in her lab or treating patients. Not spending Saturday night surrounded by strangers. But Father had badgered her into flying home to New York for this party. He didn't understand she had important work back in Houston.

Slipping off her heels, she ran up the stairs and into her bathroom.

Angry welts covered her neck and chest. *Damn!* She took a deep breath and exhaled, but deep breathing wouldn't stop this reaction.

She had two options. Stay away from the crowd or take an antihistamine. How she longed to choose option one.

But she couldn't. Even though she despised small talk and political discussions, her father wanted her at this party.

Sunee pushed out a pill and swallowed the antihistamine. Then she waited. Paced. Her bare feet whispered against the tile. Each pass by the mirror showed the welts hadn't change.

She needed to head back downstairs. Maybe she could cover the welts. She pulled the pins from her French twist, but her straight black hair didn't camouflage her neck.

She hadn't brought much home with her, but there were plenty of clothes in her closet. She dug through her mother's silk scarves, letting them slip through her fingers. Her mother had been so beautiful.

Since she wore a black sheath, she selected a deep red and purple scarf. Burying her nose in the silk, she tried to find a hint of her mother's perfume. Maybe it would give her a little of her mother's poise.

Her shoulders slumped. Mother's scent had disappeared.

She took a few more cleansing breaths and checked her skin again. The welts weren't as bright red as before. She draped the scarf across her neck and chest, closed her eyes and imagined warm waves washing over her. Her breathing and heart rate slowed. Finally.

She headed downstairs. Maybe she could fade into the background and let the antihistamine work.

She hadn't even gotten to the bottom step when her father's voice boomed out, "There she is."

Michael Miller, her father, waved her over. Couldn't the self-designated kingmaker leave her alone for a few minutes?

Sunee straightened her shoulders, forced her fingers to relax, took another breath and pasted a smile on her face.

"Sunee, I'd like you to meet Representative Stephens." Her father wrapped an arm around her shoulder and grinned. "If I have my way, he'll soon be Senator Stephens."

She held out her hand to the distinguished man whose gray hair gleamed in the lights. "It's very nice to meet you."

"It's nice to meet you, Doctor Doctor Miller." The man chuckled at his joke. "Your father brags about how smart you are."

What could she say to that? Under the scarf the welts itched. "Thank you. Sunee is fine."

"Come now, you spent all those years in school. You should enjoy using what you've achieved." The candidate stared at her. "Although you look too young to be an MD and PhD."

"Thank you again." Uncomfortable when people commented on how young she was, she shifted the silk so it pressed against the itch.

"She'll be working with me soon." Her father set a hand on her shoulder. "Eventually she'll run my investment firm."

"I'm happy where I am," she murmured.

"And where is that? I hope in one of my voting districts," Representative Stephens said.

"Sorry," she murmured. "I live in Texas."

"That's too bad. But knowing your father, he'll have you back in New York before the next elections."

Her father grinned.

She didn't say a word.

Representative Stephens pointed at her neck. "Are you all right?"

She touched her throat. "Umm, I'm fine."

Her father glared, his jaw jutting out. He'd never understood her anxiety.

She adjusted the scarf, her face filled with heat. "I ... reacted to something."

"Oh." The man backed away like she had an STD. "It was nice meeting you but I should mingle."

"Why can't you control this?" her father whispered in her ear.

She could give him the psychological and physiological reasons behind her anxiety attacks, but that wasn't what her father wanted. "I took an antihistamine."

"How will clients ever trust you?"

She lifted her chin. "I'm happy at MD Anderson."

He closed his green eyes. They were the same color as hers. "As my only child, you'll take over the firm."

"But I c-c-can..."

Her father hurried after Stephens.

"I can do more good with my research," she whispered. But he was gone.

Sunee slumped against the newel post. A waiter came by with a tray of champagne flutes. She shook her head, wanting to hide. Mingling and making small talk was a waste of time. She knew her strengths—research and patient care. Her experiments never asked her about the weather or politics.

"You're still covered in hives," her grandmother whispered. "You're mother never got them, and she was in front of cameras and people constantly."

Oh how she wished she'd gotten a tenth of her mother's confidence. "I know, Po Po."

"You need to return to New York. Live here. Then you'll stop reacting." Po Po pulled on her elbow. "Come. There's someone your father wants you to meet."

She followed, wishing she had the backbone to say no. Wishing she'd told her father she couldn't fly home. Milling around a political cocktail party wasn't helping fight the battle against cancer that had taken her beautiful mother.

But Father and Grandmother were her only remaining family. "Yes, Grandmother."

Houston

"I don't want you to worry." Monday morning, Sunee had come straight from the airport to the hospital. She squeezed Jasper's hand and glanced at the eight-year-old's mother. Her phone vibrated in her pocket, but she ignored it. Calming Jasper was her number one priority. "I don't want either of you to worry. We're going to kill these cancer cells, right?"

Jasper nodded, chewing his lip.

"Dr. Miller, will the chemo make him sick?" Jasper's mother bit her lip.

Sunee should have talked to the mother—again. Outside of Jasper's room.

On Thursday Jasper's mother had been confident about the treatment plan. Apparently the mother's fears were back. Jasper's mother wasn't soothing her son, she was making him worry. "I've already ordered an antiemetic."

"Anti-what?" Jasper's dark eyes went wide. "Will it hurt like when they take my blood from my bones?"

"No." Sunee held his hand. "The medicine stops you from throwing up."

Worry filled his eyes. "You'll check on me right, Dr. Sunee?"

"I'll be in and out of your room all day." She smiled, trying to instill calm. "You'll get tired of me asking how you're feeling."

Jasper twisted his ID bracelet. "Okay."

"Can you close your eyes for me?" Sunee asked.

Both Jasper and his mother did.

She talked him through deep breathing exercises. His thin shoulders and face relaxed. So did his mother's. It had been her mother's technique as she'd gone through chemotherapy. Sunee's heart ached at the memory.

Jasper's father came in, followed by one of Sunee's favorite pediatric nurses.

"Hey Jasper," the nurse said. "Are you ready to go into battle?"

The boy swallowed. "I guess."

"No guessing here. I have your Captain America bandages, as ordered," his nurse said. "But you have to be brave like your favorite hero."

"Captain America?" The father ruffled his son's hair. "What happened to Thor?"

"Dun' know. I like Captain America now."

The dad looked at the nurse. "Let's get this show on the road."

Sunee nodded and they moved Jasper to a wheelchair. If only the father could convince Jasper's mom to be positive.

"I'll see you later," Sunee said.

As she headed down the hall, her phone vibrated in her pocket. It wasn't her hospital phone. It was her personal phone. Shoot.

Ashe: I'm in the lobby

Ashe: Still waiting

Ashe: Where R you?

Shoot. She'd forgotten Ashe was coming to say hi to the kids.

On my way.

She whipped off a quick text to her assistant and hustled to the lobby.

Ashe paced next to a group of chairs, his fingers drumming on his thigh. She hurried over and hugged her best friend. "I'm sorry I made you wait. I was with a patient."

"No problem." He grinned.

She took a step back. In a polo shirt and khaki pants, he looked like an executive on his day off. "Don't you look respectable."

"Stop." Ashe rolled his eyes.

"Seriously, I only see you in workout clothes or a football uniform."

He bopped her gently on the head. Easy for him. Ashe was six-foot-six, almost a foot-and-a-half taller than her.

He plucked at the Texans' team logo over his heart. "I think of this as a uniform. It makes it easier to spend the day in it. Besides, I'm playing golf after this. My manager wants me to improve my image."

"Poor Ashe." He'd whined about the tournament in their last phone call. "You couldn't get out of it?"

"I don't mind doing this for charity." His fingers rattled against his leg. "But does the game have to be so slow?"

"You'll survive." She gave him another hug. "I'm sorry I wasn't in Houston when you arrived. I'd been called *home*." Her teeth snapped together.

"Po Po still predicting she's dying?"

"Yes." She shook her head. "I've told her she's fine, but she won't believe me. How did you guess?"

"Something about the way you said *home*—like pestilence and plague rolled into a ball."

"That describes my trip home to a 'T,'" she said. "Po Po doesn't understand why I live in Texas. She thinks I can do my *little* research in New York. And my father insists I'm his heir apparent."

"I thought you loved working here?"

"I do, but Dad thinks this is a detour in my road to becoming an investment banker."

"You need to say no to your family." He straightened her shoulders. "Where's your backbone?"

"It was only a weekend." She shrugged. Well, three days. "Dad wanted me at his fundraiser for Representative Stephens."

"So he could show off his brilliant daughter. Bet you loved that." He looked closer. "I don't see any hives."

"Oh, they were there." She shuddered. "Representative Stephens moved away rather quickly after noticing the welts."

Being around strangers made her anxious. Anxiety triggered her hives. Her father knew this.

"Wish I could help." Ashe rubbed her back.

"My dad spent the rest of the weekend insisting I'll have fun working for him." She shook her head. "Instead of research, he wants me to look at other people's discoveries and decide whether to invest in their companies."

"He doesn't know you at all."

"No." She sighed. "Come on, I'll take you up to the kids."

She led him to the elevator bank.

"Did you tell your father you didn't want to join his firm?"

She punched the up button a little harder than needed. "I ... I said I'd think about it."

He frowned. "You have to say no."

"I will." She crossed her arms. But this was her father.

"Your dad should come see you here." He held his hands up, encompassing the hospital entrance. "Look at you, Double Doctor. You're wearing a lab coat with your name on it and everything."

"They give us jackets instead of pay." She linked her arm with Ashe and guided him into the elevator. "Thanks for coming. My assistant got the box of goodies you sent. The kids will be ecstatic."

"They probably won't know my name," he said.

"You'd be surprised. The sportscasters have been talking about the Texans' new quarterback for weeks."

"The sportscasters are probably reminding everyone that when I was in college, I ruined the Longhorn's chances for a national title." He squeezed her elbow.

"I think I might have caught that." She laughed as the elevator doors opened. "Come on."

"How's the research going?" he asked.

"I love working on this team."

"What are you studying?"

"The molecular mechanics of DNA damage and repair in conjunction with cell cycle checkpoint mechanics." She squeezed his arm. "It's exciting."

"You're such a warrior."

"I'm just one warrior in this battle." She inhaled. "I want to eradicate cancer. No more deaths. No more heartbreak. If we can stop defective DNA from replicating, we might stop the mutations that lead to tumor growth."

"You always planned to cure cancer." He rubbed her shoulders. "Now you are."

"I'm part of a team." She'd set her goal at age fifteen. "We're years away from a breakthrough, but I plan on being part of the victory."

"You'll do it. You're the smartest woman—correction—*person* I know."

She sighed. "Not in time to help the kids you'll meet today. They're gathered in the social room on the pediatric floor."

Her doctorate might be in biochemistry and molecular genetics, but her heart was in pediatric oncology. A year ago, a position had opened that combined both loves; pediatric oncology and genetic research. She'd jumped at the chance to move to Houston and the University of Texas.

"When can you introduce me to your lady friends?" Ashe held the door for her.

Sunee bit her lip. Since moving to Houston, she hadn't made many friends.

"You promised you wouldn't become a hermit." He raised black eyebrows over his steel-gray eyes. "You can't live in your lab."

She almost pushed him into the room holding a dozen kids. Some were playing games, some were in wheelchairs, and a couple who couldn't sit up, lay on gurneys.

"No time to talk," she muttered. She wouldn't discuss her non-existent social life.

He shook his finger. "This conversation isn't over."

"My assistant, Laura, is in the pink scrubs," she said. Time to check on Jasper and her other patients. "I'll be back."

"Hey guys, anyone like football?" Ashe bounced into the room.

She could almost hear his body click into performance mode. No hives for him.

He chatted with each child, handing them balls and T-shirts.

The kids perked up like he'd given them a blood transfusion. He even dropped back and threw nerf footballs to the children.

God, what she wouldn't give to study his DNA—the fittest and most confident man she'd ever met. Maybe she could figure out how to inject his confidence into her own genes.

"I HOPE the grounds crew can repair the divots I left on the course." Harris rotated his shoulder. "That was a work out."

"You survived the round." Kat handed her putter to her caddy. "And our score is respectable. We can hold our heads up as we walk into the clubhouse."

Harris didn't care how they'd played, but Kat did. She was so competitive. Not just in sports but every facet of her life. She might be one of his oldest friends, but she was ambitious. She would probably throw him in front of a charging bull to beat her competitors to the perfect story.

"Make sure our scores don't become part of tonight's broadcast," he replied, only half joking.

She pulled off her visor and fluffed her blonde hair. "I'm off tonight."

Thank goodness.

Her blue eyes zeroed in on his. "I wouldn't mind an interview on Maryanne Barney's upcoming trial. I need something to catch the network's attention."

"Kat," he warned.

"Sorry, I promised not to work if you played in this tournament." She wrinkled her nose. "I need a great story."

"I don't think covering Barney's trial will get you a job on the national political coverage team." Even though he was counting on it to give him a leg up in campaigning for governor.

"A girl can hope." She grinned. "Don't forget, they've got a dinner buffet set up."

"I'll drop my clubs at the car." Then he'd press the flesh and act like Texas' next governor.

Harris swung by the locker room before heading to the dining room. There was a richness to the furnishings; cherrywood lockers, travertine floors. The artwork looked like Old World masterpieces, dark and heavy with paint. He spotted a sauna back by the showers.

When another man entered the bathroom, he was standing at the urinal.

"I'll be right up. Save me a chair," called the man.

Harris glanced sideways. Not anyone he knew, but there was something familiar about him. Weird. The man was as tall as he was. Unless they played for the NBA, Harris usually towered over most people.

The stranger swore.

What was wrong with the guy? Harris's head jerked up and he glanced to his left.

The guy stared. "Uh ... uh ..."

Harris's mouth dropped open. The stranger looked *just like him*. His heart hammered so hard it might break his ribs.

The man standing at the sink had gray eyes and curly black hair. *Like his.* Prominent cheekbones jutted out, *like his. Exactly* like his. The same wide shoulders, maybe even wider. *What the ...*

"Who the hell are you?" the guy asked. Lord, they *sounded* alike.

"Mind if I put my dick back in my pants?" Harris's mind spun like a twister on the panhandle. He shook and zipped, his heart pounding, his thoughts swirling.

"Who are you?" the stranger asked again.

"Give me a minute." He had to process.

They ... looked like twins. How? He had no known relatives. Nothing would explain running into a man who looked *exactly* like him.

Harris moved to the sink and meticulously washed his hands.

A shiver raced down his spine. The man wearing his face gaped at him in the mirror.

He dried his hands. "Harris Torrington."

"Ashe Bristol."

"The Texans' new quarterback?"

Ashe nodded.

Harris hadn't seen a picture of the new quarterback without a ball cap or a helmet. No one had hinted they looked alike. His nostrils flared. Was he the only one to see the resemblance? *No way.*

Harris stared. There were differences. For one, Ashe had more muscles in his chest and arms. Two, his hair, imprinted by his ball cap, was longer than Harris's own. Three, a small scar above his eye bisected his forehead.

"I don't understand." Ashe's face paled under his tan. "Why do we look alike?"

"Maybe we're ... related?"

Ashe shook his head. "Not that I know."

Harris took a couple of deep breaths. His parents had tried for years to get pregnant. The same mother who'd warned him to stay scandal-free.

He swallowed. Had his parents done something illegal years ago when they'd had trouble getting pregnant? Before Dad had gone into politics?

"Are you adopted?" Harris asked.

"No." Ashe paced along the sinks. "Are you?"

"No." Harris pushed on a sharp pain behind his eyes.

Last year his team had successfully prosecuted a black market baby ring. The ring would snatch children, sometimes right out of the hospital and sell them to desperate parents. The adopting parents had thought they'd been legit. Although the ring had been based in Houston, it had operated throughout the country.

Had he ever seen pictures of him and his parents in the hospital? A chill zipped through him. Could his parents have been that desperate?

Whatever reason he and Ashe Bristol looked like twins *could not* be good for his career. Or his father's.

A shower shut off. The man who'd been singing headed toward the lockers.

Harris didn't want anyone to see the two of them together before he understood the ramifications to him and his father. The sinking feeling in his stomach might be his political career heading into the toilet.

"We can't be seen together," Harris whispered.

Ashe leaned against the sink. "Agreed."

"Can we meet?"

"Until I find a house, I'm staying at a hotel," Ashe said.

"Too public," Harris said. "My house?"

"Sure." Ashe's voice shook. "You want to head over now?"

"Absolutely." If they could get out of here undetected.

Ashe straightened. "You got beer?"

"This might call for something a lot stronger."

CHAPTER TWO

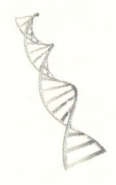

Harris waited as Ashe entered his home address into a GPS app. Ashe was driving a Porsche. Nice. "I'll see you there."

Ashe nodded.

Harris slid into his Ford 150 King Ranch truck. American made. He could afford a Porsche, but buying American was better for his career.

Ashe followed him to the interstate.

Twins. That was the obvious explanation. But it didn't seem possible.

Harris had seen his birth certificate. But the only video he'd ever seen was after his parents had brought him home. *Was there a reason for that?*

Wait. His mother had said they'd had a water pipe break at their first home. It had ruined a couple of years of pictures.

He hoped that was the truth.

He dialed Kat's phone and got her voicemail. "I had to leave. Enjoy the banquet."

What a mess. Thank goodness no one had seen him and Ashe together. But eventually someone would wonder why they looked alike. They'd better have answers before the media got their hands on this and made up their own explanation.

One step at a time. His high school track coach had told him to stay in the moment, in the race. Concentrate on the next step. Your body could always push itself to take another step—don't think beyond that step—because it screwed with your mind.

But he could still remember the tortured birth parents testifying at the black market baby ring trial.

He pulled into the security gate of his development.

"Hey, Steve, how's it going?" Harris asked the young guard.

"Great, Mr. Torrington." Steve pushed the button for the gate.

"My friend is right behind me. Leave the gate up, please." It might not be security protocol, but Harris didn't want Steve taking too close a look at Ashe.

"Sure, Mr. Torrington. Have a nice night."

Not going to happen.

Ashe pulled into the driveway as Harris stepped out of his vehicle.

"Nice neighborhood," Ashe said. "I'll mention this development to my realtor."

Harris blinked. Having someone who looked like him move into the development would have the neighbors talking. "I like the security."

He'd learned something from his life as the son of a United States senator. His house wasn't the biggest on the block, but it backed up to a nature reserve. The driveway wrapped around the back of the house. If a photographer somehow got through the gate, they couldn't identify cars or peek into the garage.

Harris nodded at Ashe's car. "Nice ride."

Ashe grinned. "Bought this baby when I signed my first contract."

A shiver ran up Harris's back. It was eerie having his grin plastered on someone else's face.

Ashe followed him into the house through the garage. They walked down the hall past the laundry room and into the kitchen.

Turning, he stared at Ashe. It was his own face—with a deeper tan, longer hair, but his features. Harris's hand clenched into a fist until he forced it to relax.

Ashe shook his head. "This is too weird."

"I need a drink." Would his roiling stomach reject anything he put in it? "What's your pleasure?"

"Beer."

Harris pointed him toward the beverage refrigerator and then poured a shot of bourbon over ice.

They took their drinks into the media room. Ashe commandeered an armchair. It was strange to see someone bigger than he filling one of his chairs. Ashe must weigh twenty or thirty pounds more than he did—all muscle.

"I can't get used to looking at you." Ashe scrubbed his hands over his face.

Harris took a swallow of bourbon. It burned a path to his stomach. "This is—unbelievable."

"They say everyone has a double ..." Ashe waved his hand between them.

"Not like this." Harris didn't know probabilities, but someone looking exactly like you seemed highly unlikely.

"Do you think we're brothers?" Ashe asked.

"I can't imagine how." This was his parents they were talking about. The people who had instilled in him right from wrong.

But maybe water damage *wasn't* the reason there hadn't been any hospital photos of him adorning the walls in their house.

"Cousins?" Ashe's leg bounced up and down.

"Identical cousins?" Harris couldn't keep the doubt from his voice.

"Where were you born?"

"Houston," Harris said. But the black market baby ring had forged birth certificates.

DISCOVERY

"I was born in Minneapolis." Ashe rocked back and forth. "My dad played for the Vikings back then."

"I don't have any pictures of mother and me in the hospital, but she said water damaged their photo albums," Harris said. "What about you?"

"Not that I remember. But I never looked for any." Ashe rubbed his chin. "Mom was the one who took pictures or movies. Dad was only interested in football film."

Was it a coincidence neither of them had evidence of their birth? Hell, he'd never seen pictures of his mother pregnant. Again, the explanation was the water damage, but what if it had been something else? Harris took another swallow of bourbon, but it threatened to come back up. "My mother says she tried for years to have me."

Ashe cringed. "Did she go to a sperm bank?"

"I don't know." He ran a hand through his hair. "I don't look like either of my parents."

"Maybe we have the same sperm donor as a father." Ashe exhaled. "Sounds farfetched if we were born so far apart. Don't you need to donate sperm on site?"

Harris couldn't help but laugh. "Hell if I know. Never in my craziest dreams did I imagine having this conversation."

"Neither did I." Ashe raised a dark eyebrow.

Harris tapped a finger against his glass. "When's your birthday?"

"September 30th."

"October 5th." Harris rubbed his upper lip. This didn't sound good.

"I'm thirty-one." Ashe stood and paced across the room. "How old are you?"

"Thirty-one."

"How do you get twins who have different birthdates?"

Black market? Adoption? Harris couldn't say the words aloud. Not his parents. Everything he'd learned about honesty and truth, he'd learned from them. They were his moral foundation.

"Let's try our families," Ashe said. "Maybe there's a connection we don't know about."

They drew their family trees.

Harris shook his head. "Nothing matches."

"This doesn't make sense." Ashe pushed away from the family trees they'd created and paced. "I guess that six degree thing doesn't always work."

"Did you think it would?" Harris drained his glass. He should have brought the bottle into the media room. "There has to be a connection. We just haven't found it."

"This is fucking bizarre." Ashe blew a breath out. "Maybe our moms were impregnated by aliens."

Harris's stomach lurched. He could see the headlines. *Candidate for Governor Believes Father was an Alien.* That would thrill the voters.

"What else do you know about your birth?" Harris asked.

Ashe paced to the sliding glass doors that looked out to the reserve. "My mom had trouble getting pregnant too. They'd tried fertility treatments and started adoption proceedings. Then she got pregnant with me. They'd been living in Minnesota for a couple of years by then. She never said she went to a clinic anywhere else."

Harris nodded slowly. "My mother always called me her miracle." He didn't know enough about fertility treatments. Was that kind of thing done in people's hometowns or did they travel?

"Christ—do you think we're looking at some weird fertility doctor who implanted bunches of women with his sperm?" A look of revulsion sprinted across Ashe's face.

"There was a doctor a while back." Harris couldn't recall where or when. "I don't know what to think. I don't have enough data."

Almost in the same breath, they said, "DNA tests."

DISCOVERY

They stared at each other. The only sound in the room was their breaths.

Harris broke the silence. "We can't let the press make a connection between us. They'll speculate when we don't have any answers." He held up a finger. "My father's a US senator. I'm the district attorney, a public office. Any hint of a scandal could derail both my and my father's careers. This is not good."

Ashe returned and sat, but his fist bounced on his thigh. "I wonder why my dad never said anything. He's lived here a couple of years."

Here was one connection Harris understood. "Coach Bristol is your father?"

Ashe nodded. "You must get a lot of news coverage if you're the district attorney."

"It comes with the job." And the pending trial would be well-televised.

"Coach was never big on watching anything but football." Bitterness laced Ashe's tone.

Harris tried to remember everything he'd heard about the Bristol family. Father and son both college stars at The Ohio State. Ashe had played for his father. He might have even been a Heisman Trophy candidate. Bristol had personally snatched the national championship title from the University of Texas—Harris's alma mater.

"What do we do now?" Ashe asked.

"We keep this quiet." Harris didn't want speculation erupting from a reporter. "No public meetings. I don't want to be asked questions I can't answer."

"Agreed." Ashe's leg bounced up and down like a jack hammer. "The citizens of Texas don't like me as it is. My publicist tells me I must maintain a sterling image. This won't help. And it definitely won't help you or your dad."

"I'll need to wait until my mother gets back in town to ask her any questions," Harris said.

"My mom's dead, but I could ask my dad what he knows."

"Only if you do it in person," Harris warned. "Don't bring this up in phone calls or emails."

"Agreed."

Harris pushed his hand through his hair. Ashe did the same. Harris's stomach flipped at the similarities. "We have to find out if we're related."

"Back to testing?" Ashe stood and started pacing again.

"I suppose we can use one of those DNA tests they advertise. Wonder if that would work."

With their luck a clerk would ID Harris or Ashe and sell the story. Harris could almost feel the heat as his dreams of running for governor went up in flames. "We need another solution."

"I've got something better." Ashe smiled. "Friend of mine does genetic research for the University of Texas."

Harris bet his smile looked exactly like Ashe's. Scary. "Can he keep his mouth shut?"

"Absolutely." Ashe nodded his head. "And he's a she. She's always wanted to test my DNA. Now she can check out mine and my clone."

"Oh, crap—do you think we were cloned?" Harris rolled his shoulders, but the crawling feeling wouldn't disappear. "That's illegal, isn't it?"

"Let's have her tell us."

A clone would never be elected as governor of Texas.

Boston

Victor Giuseppe's assistant burst into his Boston office. The possible uses for Elaina's latest drug discovery evaporated at the interruption.

"What Brian?" Victor snapped.

"Did you know Ashe Bristol was traded to the Houston Texans?" Brian asked.

Victor waved his hand in a get-on-with-it motion at his assistant. "Texans?"

"The football team. The Houston Texans." Brian turned red. "This is the search programs you have me run each month. The one for Ashe Bristol. The quarterback. This change popped up with a red flag."

Victor reclined his chair into his favorite thinking position. Houston. A kid from Elaina's long-term study lived there. He hadn't thought about that study in years.

"What's the name of the kid who lives in Houston?" he asked Brian.

"Torrington. Harris Torrington."

"Right." When Elaina had done the embryo implantation, the kid's dad had been a lawyer or something.

Victor hadn't been interested in the long-term work Elaina had done. Once she'd proved the DNA modifications had worked, he'd licensed her amazing protocols for millions to the Mendel Foundation. The Foundation's biggest stipulation had been lifelong secrecy.

Brian edged toward the door. "Should I do anything with this information?"

Victor spun his chair and gazed out on the Charles River. "No."

Bristol and Torrington were two of the initial embryos. Now they would be living in the same city. His fingers formed a steeple. He needed to refresh his memory on the two subjects. He didn't think both Bristol and Torrington being in the same city created a problem, but he'd rather be prepared. The Foundation didn't like surprises. And he didn't want an expensive legal battle if their experiment was exposed and the confidentiality clause was broken. He rubbed his stiff neck. They were not the forgiving type.

He'd used that to his advantage once.

Victor pressed a button on his phone.

"Good afternoon." Elaina's beautiful voice filled his office.

He closed his eyes and let the sound comfort his soul. "Hi."

"What can I do for you, Victor?" she asked.

"Come up, please. And bring the Torrington and Bristol files with you."

She hesitated, the silence crackling over the speaker. "I'm in the middle of a very critical experiment."

God, you'd think she could be less formal. They'd known each other for almost forty years. He'd loved her all those years.

"Get an assistant to finish whatever you're doing," he said.

"I'm afraid that's not possible. I could free up time tomorrow."

"Fine." Victor stomped down the frustration he'd lived with for... forever.

He heard her flipping through her calendar. "How much time do we need?"

A lifetime. "Thirty minutes."

"I'm open at three," she said.

"I'll make myself available."

She hung up without saying goodbye.

Victor clenched his teeth and slammed down the phone. Obviously he had to work around her schedule. He'd been accommodating Elaina all his life.

Boston

Elaina Harrison Ashland dropped the phone into its cradle. She took a sip of water, but her hand shook so hard she splashed the papers on her desk.

Why was Victor asking about Ashe and Harris? Once she'd determined the DNA modifications had worked, Victor had never asked about the boys. She slapped her quaking hand on her mouth. Had he figured out she'd lied about using separate anonymous donors for the embryos?

No. Victor would have screamed at her.

She inhaled, trying to keep her heart from pounding out of her chest. Victor could never find out Harris and Ashe were her children. He couldn't discover she'd broken protocol and used her and Drew's embryos.

Why now?

Piper peered into her office. "Everything okay, Mom? You're as white as a ghost."

Elaina's hands clutched the edge of her desk. "Just ... dizzy. I missed lunch."

Piper rolled her chair and blocked the doorway. Concern painted her lovely face. "Do you want me to get you something to eat?"

"Would you?"

"Sure." Piper pulled her long curly black hair into a knot and clipped it to the back of her head.

Seeing Andrew's hair on Piper's head, Elaina's heart ached. Her daughter unfolded her willowy figure from the chair, and Elaina bit her lower lip. She'd gotten her father's height.

"I'll be right back." The lab door swung shut behind Piper.

Elaina dashed to the file case. Why had she kept the files and her private notes in her lab? She shoved her hair off her face. Sweat beaded on her forehead. Anyone could have walked in and reviewed the information. She ripped out the boys' files.

At her desk, she poured through years of accumulated material. A sound in the hall made her glance at the door. Pictures fell to the floor. *No!* If Victor saw the photos, he would know Ashe and Harris were her and Drew's children.

She shoved the photos into her briefcase. Tonight she'd find other pictures on the internet. Strangers. She would cover her tracks. No. She would eliminate all the pictures.

She flipped open Harris's file. Each piece of paper, each note drew her further into the past. Thirty-one years. She relived her sons' lives through her records, lost in memories. Victor would never figure out what she had done.

"The only soup left in the cafeteria was potato." Piper walked in with a bowl, crackers and a cup of tea balanced on a tray. She started to slide it on the desk. "Oh, do you need help with anything?"

"No thanks, sweetheart." Elaina shut the folders. Pain gnawed at her stomach, fiery embers of acid eating at the lining. Not again. "I decided to clear out old files."

Piper pointed at the file label. "Wow, this is from before I was born."

Elaina forced a smile on her face. "Don't make me feel ancient."

"You're not." Piper waved at the food. "Eat something before you fade away."

"You always take care of me." Elaina swallowed back tears.

"Don't cry." Piper ripped open the packages of crackers. "You just need someone to remind you about the basics in life; eating, paying bills and taking vacations."

"And you ended up taking care of your mother. I'm sorry I'm a burden."

"You aren't a burden. Without you, I would never have fallen in love with genetic research." Piper rubbed her back. "I think it's romantic, carrying on my father and mother's work."

Elaina loved working with her daughter, loved and admired the sharp analytic brain behind Piper's gray eyes. But right now she wanted her hovering daughter to go away.

"Could you check on the test we set up this morning?" she asked.

"On it." Piper headed to the lab next door but called back, "Eat."

Elaina took a spoonful of soup, barely able to swallow the lukewarm cloying mass.

Then she went back to sanitizing the files.

Victor could *never* know Harris and Ashe were her sons. *Never.*

Houston

"Nice house," Sunee muttered as she pulled up to the address Ashe had sent her. "Very secure."

Ashe had told her to give her name to the security guard. The guard had let her into a very swanky gated community. Getting to his house was harder than getting onto the hospital's psychiatric floor.

She hated the reason Ashe had called her. He wanted a DNA test. Was this for a paternity test? He'd always sworn he didn't sleep with the groupies. Had he lied?

She sure hoped her best friend hadn't gotten someone pregnant. Idiot. Maybe he'd taken too many hits to the head.

Ashe's sample could be sent in with those she'd gathered from her newest patient and his family. Abraham was the second family member diagnosed with hepatoblastoma. The incidence rate of liver cancer was so low in children this couldn't be a coincidence. Hopefully they'd find something in the DNA analysis. If not, they would do an environmental study.

She pushed on the doorbell a little longer than necessary.

Ashe opened the door.

"What a relief. It's cool in here." She stepped into a marble foyer. "It's a hundred degrees outside and my Volvo's air-conditioning quit."

"Ummm..."

"Look at you all dressed up in a suit." She stood on her tiptoes and kissed Ashe's cheek. "You changed your aftershave. I like it."

"Umm..." he muttered again.

"What *are* you doing in a suit?" She wrapped her arms around him.

He patted her back, two perfunctory pats. His body felt different, as if he'd lost weight. Had his knee really healed?

Sunee stared up at him. His steel gray eyes heated up. Her breath caught in her throat. It was like looking at a stranger. A hot, good-looking stranger. She stepped away, chills crawling up and down her spine. "What's wrong?"

Ashe looked—serious. Then she remembered the tests he'd asked her to perform. He must be worried about his upcoming paternity test.

"Hey, Sunee, thanks for coming." Ashe's voice came from her right.

She glanced at the doorway. A second Ashe sauntered out from a room carrying two beer bottles.

"Ashe?" Her knees wobbled.

"I see you've met Harris," Ashe said.

"Who?" She took a quick step back.

The man she'd hugged held out his hand. "Harris Torrington. Sorry for the confusion. This is my home."

She'd known Ashe was looking for a house. It had seemed logical to conclude the house was his. Shame on her. She would never make assumptions like that while treating a patient.

Sunee's gaze bobbed back and forth. She categorized the obvious similarities. Gray eyes—recessive. Widow's peak—dominant. Dimples—dominant. Black hair—indecisive. Wavy hair—indecisive. Their facial structure. My lord, she could barely tell them apart.

"I ... what? How?" She couldn't form a coherent sentence. "Are you twins?"

"We don't know, but we need to find out." Harris *sounded* like Ashe, but a Texas twang flavored his vowels.

"I don't believe it." Sunee stared at the two men. Her hand covered her mouth.

"Neither did we." Ashe wrapped an arm around her shoulders and tugged her down a hallway. "We met yesterday. Spooky, isn't it?"

She couldn't find words so she nodded.

They entered a kitchen as clean and sleek as her lab. Sunee headed to the black granite counter and rested against it. Ashe and his look-a-like stood in identical poses, legs spread, arms crossed over their chests. Standing six-foot-six inches, the two dark-haired males formed a wall of masculinity.

"I thought you wanted a paternity test done on the sly. Ashe, I'm …" she didn't finish her sentence. Again she'd taken a few facts and jumped to the wrong conclusion. How could she call herself a scientist?

"You thought that of me?" Ashe closed the distance between them and pulled her into a hug. "You know me better than that."

"I'm sorry." Heat filled her face.

Harris didn't say a word.

She stepped away from Ashe and pointed at Harris. "So that's what you'd look like in a suit." Harris's dark gray suit looked tailored for his lean body. Gorgeous. "You should try it sometime."

"And wear a necktie? No way," Ashe told her, giving her another hug.

"Are you related?" She couldn't stop staring, but she wouldn't make any more assumptions. She'd already made two blunders.

"We can't find a connection between us." Harris's jaw clenched so hard she worried he would crack his molars. "That's why Ashe called you."

She'd bet her electron microscope these two men were closely related. How close was the question.

Harris headed to the fridge. "Can I get you something to drink?"

She'd like a strong drink. "Water."

He filled a glass from a separate spigot in the sink. The man moved with the grace of a big cat. He was leaner than Ashe and reminded her more of a panther while she'd always thought of Ashe as a wolf.

"Is it possible you're cousins?" she asked.

"Not that we found," Harris said.

"Okay. Give me the facts you know." She took a seat at the table because her legs were shaky. Harris took the chair across from her.

Ashe paced.

Harris pulled out crudely drawn family trees. No connection. Then they produced copies of their birth certificates.

"You were born in different cities five days apart," she said.

"That's what the birth certificates say." Harris pushed his fingers into his temples. "I picked this one up today. Just in case …"

Her eyes widened. "In case?"

"My parents falsified my birth certificate." Harris's voice was flat.

"Oh." Wow.

Ashe pointed at the paper on the table. "I had to go down to Hennepin County and pick up a copy of my birth certificate before I went to college."

She wouldn't jump to any conclusions, even though her eyes were telling her they were twins.

"Let's see how closely related you are." She pulled DNA sample kits out of her purse. "I'll snip a little hair and then swab your mouths." She tugged a hank of Ashe's thick hair. "You need a haircut."

"Yeah," Ashe murmured as his leg bounced up and down.

"I have scissors near your handsome face," she warned. "Sit still."

"You've always wanted to get your hands on my genes," Ashe joked, but his face didn't break into his normal grin.

"Open your mouth." She swabbed his cheek. "Let's see what makes you tick."

After repeating the process with Harris, she sealed and labeled each bag and tucked the samples in her purse.

Then she took the chair between the two men. They were a genetic puzzle. Excitement bubbled up in her chest. She shouldn't be excited to solve the mystery, but she was.

"Have you talked to your mother? Asked her any questions?" she asked Harris.

Ashe's mother had died two years ago. Even now, a shadow of grief crossed her best friend's face and she reached for his hand.

"Not yet." Harris shook his head. "Nothing makes sense. I've evaluated all current data points. I want more information before I confront my parents."

Confront? Not something she'd ever done with her own father. "I'll make sure the samples are submitted tomorrow, but it might take a week or more."

"Keep us posted." Harris's eyes shone with a steely light that made her shiver. "This has to be totally confidential. You're the only person who knows about us."

"I'd never do anything to hurt you." She touched Ashe's hand again. "Your names won't be on the samples. Everything is coded. I have four other samples heading to our testing lab tomorrow."

Harris blew out a deep breath and for the first time since she'd walked in his door, he smiled. Warmth spread through her body like a wildfire. How could a man who looked like her best friend make her insides melt?

There were differences between them. The first was obvious. Ashe couldn't sit still and Harris was an island of calm.

Sunee loved Ashe. He was her best friend, but spending too much time with his frantic energy was like listening to nails on a chalkboard.

She valued peace and quiet.

Harris checked his watch. "I planned to throw chicken on the grill and I've got plenty. Can you stay for dinner?"

"I have a command dinner with my dad and I'm late." Ashe stood, leaned down and kissed her forehead. "I'll call you later."

"Okay," she said. "Say hi to Coach from me."

Before she could even gather her things, Ashe was out the door.

"I'll get going too." She didn't know this man, didn't belong here. As much as he looked like Ashe, being close to Harris filled her stomach with butterflies. Now that Ashe had left, her neck was heating up. Next there would be an outbreak of hives.

"The chicken's already defrosted. You haven't eaten, right?" Harris's smile warmed his eyes from ice cold to as sizzling hot as a Houston summer sidewalk. "I've a fair hand with the grill."

Standing this close, Harris's face was thinner, more refined. His build was slender, if a six-foot-six inch tall man could be considered slender. A small scar, possibly from chicken pox, near his right mandible marred his perfection.

Sunee wrapped her arms around her waist. She should head home, or back to her lab. She could check on her patients.

"Please stay," he said in his deep calm voice.

She should leave. But after enduring Ashe's energy, she wanted to immerse herself in Harris's stillness. "I'd love dinner."

HARRIS SHOULDN'T HAVE ASKED Sunee to stay for dinner. She and Ashe had—something going. The guy had hugged her a half dozen times. But logic outweighed his conscious. Sunee might hold the key to his and his father's political careers in her hands. He wanted to know if she could be trusted.

If his parents had unknowingly used a baby ring and Sunee leaked the fact she'd taken DNA samples from him and Ashe, nothing would stop the ensuing scandal. *Senator Buys Baby? Twins Separated at Birth?* And what if Sunee became a women scorned? She'd thought Ashe had fathered a child. What girlfriend would be okay with that? If Ashe dumped her, would she retaliate by notifying the press?

The third reason he wanted her to stay for dinner was personal. He loved looking into her moss green eyes. How did a woman of Asian descent end up with eyes the color of the forest? He wanted to know the answer to that question and more.

She whipped her long, silky black hair back into a ponytail and wrapped something stretchy around the tail. "How can I help?"

He pulled out the marinating meat and a packet of potatoes, peppers and onions his housekeeper had prepared. Now all he had to do was start the grill.

"Would you make a salad?" he asked.

"Of course."

He left her searching through the crisper and flipped on the grill. The thermometer still hovered around one hundred degrees. He headed inside and changed into a shirt and shorts.

Back in the kitchen, he said, "I'm having a glass of wine. Would you like one?"

She looked up from chopping lettuce. "A half glass would be nice. I want to stop back and check on a patient."

"I thought you did research?"

"I have a hospital practice too. Besides being a molecular geneticist, I'm a pediatric oncologist."

"I didn't know molecular genetics was part of med school." Of course he'd been studying over in the law library.

She chopped the peppers into small squares with surgical precision. "No, I have a doctorate from the University of Texas."

"You have an MD and PhD?"

A peachy blush washed over her golden skin. Ashe must love

touching her skin. It looked so soft. Shit. Harris had to stop thinking about Sunee's skin and eyes.

"Tell me about your research," he said.

"I'm looking into the genetic etiology of human cancer using an epidemiological approach to identify the most likely models to account for the distribution of tumors in kindreds." Her green eyes burned with fire. "We're searching for families whose genetic etiology can be included in a collaborative study using cytogenetic, biochemical and molecular markers to localize the gene. With the family's cooperation, we'll investigate the role of radiation, chemotherapy, and host predisposing factors and then we'll analyze the risk of subsequent tumors in childhood cancer survivors."

He slouched against the counter, the barrage of terms almost knocking him on his ass. "I have no idea what you said, but it sounds impressive."

"I'm sorry, I get carried away." Her exquisite golden cheeks turned peach again. "I'm part of a team of doctors and scientists doing genetic research in families with cancer."

"Way to hide your light under a basket, doctor." He needed to get the potatoes on the grill. "I'll be right back with your wine. Shiraz okay?"

"That would be lovely." She kept her eyes focused on the counter. Was she shy or regretting she'd stayed for dinner without Ashe?

After tossing the potato packet on the grill, he poured Sunee's wine. "Here you are."

"Thanks."

"Cheers," he said.

She tipped her glass to his, still not looking him in the eye. "Cheers."

An awkward silence filled the room. She moved their salads to the table. Maybe if they talked about something familiar, like her boyfriend, she'd relax.

"How did you meet Ashe?" he asked.

"We met on campus at a Walk for the Cure event."

A cancer walk? "This was at Ohio State?"

"Yes. Ashe was walking with his mother." Her smile was sad. "Mrs. Bristol had just been diagnosed with breast cancer."

Now their meeting made sense. "So, where did you attend med school?"

"Oh, I was in med school when I met Ashe." She picked at a nonexistent thread on her slacks.

He tried to do the math. She would have been young. "Child genius?"

There came the blush again, painting her cheekbones.

"I started school when I was four and skipped third and sixth grade. Then finished my undergraduate in three years and went straight into med school." Long dark eyelashes hid those green eyes from him as she took a sip of wine.

"Overachiever."

Her arms were crossed, her hand tucked under her chin. Damn, she looked uncomfortable.

"Was the cancer walk a requirement for med school?"

"Oh no." She shook her head. Her eyes lost their glow. "My cousin died from leukemia when she was eleven. Then I lost my mother to breast cancer when I was in college. Fighting cancer became … my purpose in life."

A jolt of electricity sizzled through him. Sunee's passion for her work matched his enthusiasm for truth and justice.

He'd never met a woman like her in his life. He'd heard they were out there, but he'd found her in his kitchen, sipping wine.

A weight settled on his shoulders like a bucket of water on a campfire. Ashe had found Sunee first.

"Thanks for staying for dinner. I was glad for the company." Harris had enjoyed trying to break shy Sunee out of her shell.

"Thank you for dinner." She wiped down the table and set the salt and pepper shakers back on the shelf. "I'd better head to the hospital."

At the front door, they both reached for the doorknob, their hands brushing against each other. Heat poured between them.

Harris wanted to take those tiny, competent hands and lace their fingers together. "Let me get that for you."

He cursed Ashe for leaving and letting him find out how truly enchanting his girlfriend was. He'd never coveted anything before. Now he wanted to spend more time with Sunee and couldn't.

Walking out to her car, he asked, "This may be rude, but I've been wondering all night. How does an Asian-American end up with green eyes?"

"My father's Irish and has red hair and green eyes. But my mother must have carried a recessive green-eyed gene."

"Of course." He smiled at her answer. "I enjoyed dinner."

She stopped next to her vintage Volvo but didn't open the door. "Thank you for having me." With a big sigh, she added, "It was nice. And calm."

"You don't get a lot of calm?"

"Oh yes, but it's hard to watch children who are sick." Pain crossed her face.

How could she deal with children with cancer every day? "That must be tough."

He patted her shoulder in comfort. She stared into his eyes and attraction flamed inside him.

"Good night." Sunee slid into the car.

Harris released the breath he'd been holding since he'd touched her.

She turned the key, and there was a clicking sound but no engine roar. She stopped. Then tried again. Nothing.

"Pop the hood." Harris moved to the front of the car and peered into the engine.

Sunee joined him. "This car spends more time in the shop than out."

He tested the connection to the battery and played with the carburetor. "Try it again."

Nothing ignited.

"We'll have to call for a tow," he said.

Sunee handed him napkins and he wiped his fingers.

She pushed at the wisps of hair blowing around her cheek. "My mechanic is across town. It'll take forever for him to come get this beast."

"I know you want to get to the hospital. Why don't you borrow my car," he suggested. "I'll call my garage and see if they service Volvos."

She shook her head. "I can't take your car."

He wanted to stroke away the furrow forming between her delicate eyebrows. "Sure you can, I have two. No one's fixing your car tonight. Unless you'd rather take my truck."

She shook her head. "I grew up in New York City. I don't think I'd be comfortable driving a truck."

"Okay." He eyed the position of her car in the drive. "We need to move your car farther to the right."

He pushed as she steered. Then he ducked inside and grabbed his extra set of keys. She was twisting her hands in front of her as he backed up a Tahoe.

"That's not a car. That's an SUV." Distress laced her words. "I can't borrow this."

He wrapped his hands around hers. "Yes, you can. No arguments."

She tipped those dazzling eyes up and stared into his for a long moment. "Thank you."

They exchanged phone numbers. Then he gave her a quick

lesson on the vehicle. Anything to spend a little more time with her.

She punched on the engine and put it into gear. Through the open window, she said, "You're a very nice man."

Standing in the driveway, he waved as Sunee drove away.

She was wrong. Harris wasn't nice. How could he be nice when he lusted after Ashe's girlfriend?

CHAPTER THREE

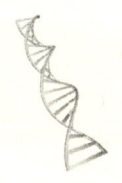

oston

B   Elaina flipped through the files one more time in the elevator. They were clean. She'd been up until one making sure.

She walked into Victor's office without knocking. Plush carpet muffled her footsteps. Ebony and glass furniture and bookcases filled the room. A spotlight shone down on a sculpture and another on a new painting filling one wall.

The décor made her shiver. Where had the dedicated molecular engineer gone? She was the only partner still in the research lab.

After graduating from Harvard, she, Drew and Victor had planned to discover medical miracles. They'd arrogantly assumed they would set the bio-medical world on fire.

She clenched the file tight. The financial foundation of the company had come from the genetic modification protocols she and Andrew had developed. When she'd stopped that line of research, her battle with Victor had been ugly. No one should play God. No one.

Victor spun away from his computer.

"How's your day, Victor?" she asked.

"We've almost concluded the negotiations on the marker kit you finalized last year."

"Who was the highest bidder?" She hoped the recipient had the money to continue the research she'd started.

"Genesis Corporation."

"If they need assistance in the tech transfer, let me know."

Victor shook his head. "They didn't negotiate for your services."

"I'll meet with them," she chided. They'd had this conversation too many times over the years. "Not every task needs to have a dollar sign attached to it."

"Those dollars pay for your expensive lab equipment."

She held up her hands and turned, taking in his office, the artwork, the statues and his thousand-dollar suit. "They also pay for a lifestyle we never imagined when we first dreamed of working in genetics."

Victor abandoned the barricade of his massive desk and waved her to the easy chairs set in front of a coffee table. His office furniture cost more than her and Drew's first house.

"I always dreamed of wealth," he said. "I wasn't as altruistic as you and Andrew."

"We dreamed of making the world a better place. Finding cures, discovering the causes for diseases."

"And we have," Victor responded. "But we've also reaped the benefits of our discoveries."

She'd never win this battle. She just hoped she hadn't sold out.

"Here are the files you requested." She set them on the coffee table. "Why did you need them?"

"Bristol was traded to the Houston Texans."

Her body froze. Ashe was in Houston? With Harris?

Victor frowned. "Are you all right?"

She sat. "I … I haven't paid attention to the participants since the longitudinal study ended."

She'd been so wrapped up in training Piper, she'd missed this. She would have caught it next month, but next month might have been too late.

She had to meet with the boys. Soon.

"I want to know if we're vulnerable to exposure with Torrington and Bristol living in the same city," Victor said. "There's no expiration date on the Mendel Foundation's confidentiality clause."

Her throat tightened. They *were* vulnerable. Her embryo editing had been illegal and unethical. Plus, the Mendel Foundation didn't know the boys were related. They'd specifically requested each embryo be differentiated to ensure the babies didn't look alike.

She'd ignored that requirement.

"I'll look through these later." Victor thumbed through the top file but didn't look at anything.

"If you let me know what you're worried about, I can scan the files," she volunteered. She didn't want Victor thinking about the original experiments. Her hands formed fists in her lap. What if Victor did the same internet search she'd done last night. It was obvious Harris and Ashe were related.

"You monitored the children personally?" Victor glanced up. His salt and pepper eyebrows drew together.

"In the beginning. You were copied on my findings." God, she'd lied so often in her reports. "By the time they hit college, it was evident the DNA engineering had succeeded. Should I have continued the study?"

"No." Victor waved his hand.

"I'm glad we stopped that line of research. We started with the best of intentions, but we were heading down a path mankind should not take." She regretted playing God, but she didn't regret she'd implanted her and Andrew's embryos in other women. Now her research focused on correcting genetic abnormalities, not on creating super beings. "What right did we have to manipulate Mother Nature?"

"*You* forced us to stop the research." Victor's voice carried the irritation of losing the battle they'd fought years ago. "We no longer manipulate anything but genetic flaws. We could have made millions, but Saint Elaina said no."

Victor always chose money over science. "It was illegal. And we do make millions."

He rifled through the file pages. "Who donated the eggs and sperm?"

"The sources were confidential." She swallowed, lacing her fingers together. She forced her eyes to meet his, forced them not to blink. "We vetted them as healthy sperm and egg. You haven't heard of any problems, have you?"

"No." He pushed the file away. "There isn't any way to trace the embryos back to Legacy, is there?"

"We worked through a national fertility clinic chain."

"No distinguishing characteristics, that's what we specified?" Victor was looking down when she jerked.

"None." That was what she had promised, but not what she'd delivered.

The boys were identical—but their genes had been edited.

"I need to get back to work." She gathered up the files like lost sheep.

Victor set a hand on hers. "Leave the files. I want to take a deeper look."

"Sure." She placed the files back on the table and walked to the door, longing to run.

"Elaina." Victor followed and caught her between the door and his body. "Let me take you to dinner."

She shivered. "Don't you know what today is?"

"Wednesday, June 15th."

"It's my anniversary." She forced the tears back.

"Oh Christ, Lainie." His fingers tightened around the back of her neck. "The man's dead. It's time to let him go."

When had he gotten so close? She elbowed him back. "You were his best friend. You were best man at our wedding. How can you say that?"

"Me? I'm not the person who sanctified her husband. The man is dead! He'd want you to live a full life." He kissed her cheek. "I'm here. Andrew's gone."

Elaina pushed him back. "Stop."

"Give us a chance."

Shaking her head, she escaped to the comfort of her lab.

Tonight she would mourn her loss. Tomorrow she'd plan a trip to Houston.

It was time to tell her sons the truth.

HOUSTON

The bell on the restaurant door jingled and Harris's head snapped up. Again.

"You look like a Bobblehead doll." Charlene topped off his coffee, her smile as wide as the Rio Grande. "Are you waiting on a lady?"

Harris nodded.

"She must be some kind of special if she's got the mighty DA flustered." Charlene fluffed her poufy blonde hair. "I thought you promised to marry *me*."

He grinned. "I couldn't survive you."

"You got that right." Charlene winked and left his booth.

Had he been that obvious? He was waiting for Ashe's girl-friend. How sad was that?

Like an anxious teen on his first date, he'd arrived fifteen minutes early. Wouldn't his adversaries love to see him twisted up like a pretzel over a woman who was dating his lookalike.

The bell jangled. Sunee stopped in the doorway, a slim finger resting on her lip. Half-standing he waved, worried the grin splitting his face made him look idiotic.

Sunee spotted him and a hesitant smile flickered across her lips. She hurried to the booth, her lab coat flapping.

"I'm sorry I'm late. I was with a patient." She smiled again, and the room lit up as bright as a Friday night on a Texas high school football field.

He wanted to greet her with a kiss and wrap his arms around her. Instead they exchanged a fumbling handshake.

She looked down as she slid into the booth. Her face went red. "I forgot to take off my lab coat."

She wiggled, slipping her arms out of the coat embroidered with her name, Dr. Sunee Miller, stitched on the pocket. He enjoyed the show.

Charlene stopped at their table. "So you're the lady who has Mr. DA all flustered."

Sunee frowned. "Me?"

Harris shot Charlene a look that frightened harden criminals.

Charlene laughed. "What can I get you, honey?"

"Water to drink." She flipped open the menu. "And a ... BLT please. No mayo."

"Got it." Charlene turned to him. "Your usual?"

"Please."

After Charlene left, Sunee grinned and asked, "Come here often?"

"Ever since I could drive. They serve the best Denver sandwiches in town."

"That's nice." Sunee looked at him expectantly. "How much do I owe you?"

Owe him? Oh yeah, the excuse he'd used to get together for lunch. If he suggested payment in kisses Ashe would pound his face.

"They charged your battery and replaced a belt." He shifted in his seat. "It didn't even cost twenty bucks. Forget it, we're even."

"But they had to tow my car."

"Don't worry about it."

"Thank you. I saw my car in the parking lot." A wistful expression crossed her face. "I did love driving your Tahoe."

"It was the least I could do for the favor you're doing me—us." What the blazes was wrong with him? She was doing this for Ashe.

"I've always wanted to get my hands on Ashe's genetic material." Sunee's eyes twinkled, her joy ripping a hole in his stomach. She probably planned to marry Ashe and have a true exchange of DNA material by making kids.

He could have driven Sunee's car to the hospital and exchanged keys with her there. Well, he'd keep his thoughts businesslike for the rest of lunch. "How was your patient last night?"

Her smile drooped. "He was still throwing up. The chemo drugs we use to reduce the tumor burden are lethal. We need a better system." She leaned toward him, her hands clasped on the table. "The good news is, we've rehydrated him and he kept down breakfast."

Her eyes shone with a crusader's passion. He almost reached for her clasped hands, but stopped. Business—only.

He tried to keep from staring into her eyes. "Where did you grow up?"

"New York City." A faint smile slipped over her face.

"And you're an only child?"

She nodded, her silky hair sliding across her chest. "Yes."

He tried not to look, but damn, his eyes darted down to where her hair flirted with her breast. *Ask something else. Anything!* He yanked his gaze up. "What was your childhood like?"

She sighed. "There was a lot of pressure to succeed. But that was okay. I loved school. Loved learning."

He fed her questions and she answered. Her soft voice was as soothing as a warm shower. The tension in his shoulders eased. His mind cleared. Had he ever been around someone so tranquil? "You must be good with patients."

She blinked. "What?"

Before he could explain, Kat's voice carried to him through the café's clatter and hum.

"I thought that was your Tahoe." Kat barreled down the aisle.

"Kat?" He stood and gave her a hug. "What are you doing here?"

"Denver sandwiches, what else? You're the bad boy who made me an addict." She jerked a thumb over her shoulder. "Harris, this is the best cameraman in the business. Brent, meet the honorable Harris Torrington, District Attorney keeping Harris County free from evil."

Brent stuck out his hand. A leather strap held back his long hair. "It's nice to finally meet you. I've taken plenty of video of you."

"I hope you got my good side," Harris joked.

"I'll keep working on that."

Kat rolled her eyes and held out her hand to Sunee. "Hi, I'm Kat Phillips."

"Sunee Miller."

"Sunee, what an interesting name."

"I was named for my maternal grandmother." Sunee chewed her lip.

"It's lovely." Kat looked at the table. "So, are you finishing lunch?"

"Waiting on our order," Sunee said. "Join us?"

"Sure!"

Before Harris could disagree, Kat hip bumped him farther into the booth. "What are you having?"

"The usual," he said.

Harris would have preferred to sit next to Sunee. Instead

Brent, the bohemian, had the pleasure. Sunee looked shell-shocked.

Charlene took Kat and Brent's order. Before she left, Charlene added, "Nice piece on Maryanne Barney the other night, Kat."

Kat preened. "Why thank you."

Sunee's eyes opened as wide as the saucer under her mug. "You're on television. On ..." she tapped her fingers on the table, "... channel five."

"That I am." Kat nodded.

"What story brought you out this way?" Harris asked.

Brent snorted. "Kat mouthed off at the staff meeting today. Guess who's covering the zoo's newest baby elephant?"

"Kat, Kat, Kat." Harris shook his head. "When will you learn?"

"When I'm old and gray and can't hold a microphone anymore." She scrunched her lips. "Sometimes I wish I had a rewind button on my mouth."

Kat took a gulp of Harris's water and turned laser blue eyes on Sunee. "What do you do?"

Sunee blinked and pointed a finger at her chest.

"Yes you," Kat said.

"I work at MD Anderson Cancer Center."

"University of Texas." Kat waved a hand between her and Harris. "Our alma mater. "What do you do there?"

"Pediatric oncology and genetic research." A blush filled Sunee's face.

"Wow. And how do you know Harris?" Kat asked.

Harris jumped in. He loved Kat, but he refused to tell her about Ashe. The potential for scandal was too great. He couldn't get the idea of black market babies out of his head. And with both parents now in DC, he refused to call or send an email on the issue. And he didn't trust his friend. She was too good of a reporter.

He had to sidetrack Kat. "Sunee had car trouble, so I lent her mine. We're exchanging vehicles."

Kat elbowed him in the stomach. "You're such a Dudley Do-Right."

They talked about the current heat wave, and Harris kept Kat from interrogating Sunee.

Charlene dropped off plates filled with sandwiches and fries. "Anything else I can get y'all?"

Kat nodded. "A to go box, please."

Sunee looked confused, but Harris had witnessed Kat's routine before.

"Do you have to leave?" Sunee asked.

"Oh no. This way I only eat half my sandwich. Otherwise I'll eat everything on the plate." Kat stared at Sunee and sighed. "You're so tiny, you probably devour everything and never gain a pound."

"Oh, I forget to eat and the hospital food ..." Sunee winced. "If I were a patient, I'd try to get healthy very quickly."

Everyone laughed. Sunee asked about Kat's job, and the conversation stayed away from how he'd met Sunee. Thank goodness.

As Kat bit into her half-sandwich, she bumped her head on Harris's shoulder. "Can I interview you next week?"

"I'm not talking about the Barney trial."

"Not that. I'm doing a one year follow-up on the black market baby brokers." Kat took another bite of her sandwich.

Harris froze. "I don't know how much time I'll have next week."

"Try and fit me in." Kat stole a French fry off Sunee's plate. "It could be good for your image."

Not if his parents had taken advantage of a baby broker. "I'll see."

"Your mother called last night," Kat said.

"From DC?" What was Mother up to? He looked at Sunee who had her head bent over her BLT.

"She invited me to her dinner party. I'm your date."

Harris snorted. "I haven't agreed to attend."

"The guest list is a Who's Who in Houston." Kat wiggled her eyebrows. "If you're running for governor, you need to show up at your mother's party."

Harris took a bite of his sandwich. He would not confirm or deny Kat's suspicions.

"I asked your mother if I could bring a film crew," Kat added.

"I'm sure she declined." Lunch was spinning out of control. Nothing unusual when Kat was around.

"She said no, but I love to pull her leg. Can you confirm you're running for governor?" Kat nearly bounced out of the booth.

"No comment."

Sunee's eyes met his. "Governor?"

He shook his head, unwilling to say anything in front of Kat.

"Got to run." Kat heaved an exaggerated sigh. "Must make my Edwina the baby elephant story shine." She and Brent dropped money on the table. "Nice meeting you, Sunee."

Kat kissed his cheek before dashing away. Brent sauntered behind her.

"Is she always like that?" Sunee wilted a little in the booth. "Like she consumed five hundred espressos?"

"Pretty much."

"Wow. She uses up all the oxygen in a room." Sunee shook her head and hair drifted around her face.

Harris almost stretched across the table to push back the silky mass.

"It's nice to decompress with you. You're easy to be with." Sunee sighed. "I need..."

"Quiet." Kat's frantic energy wasn't always on high, but sometimes his chest hurt from being around her. "I get it."

"She's a female Ashe." She reached across the table and touched his arm. "They both have more than their share of energy."

He hadn't seen Ashe sit still for more than a few minutes at a time. "Kat's the last person I want knowing about Ashe and me."

She nodded. "Understood."

They both looked at her hand still touching his arm. Did he see something else in her eyes? Desire?

Wishful thinking on his part.

He picked up the check and the money Kat and Brent had left on the table.

"Oh, how much was my lunch?" asked Sunee, opening her purse.

"I got it."

She blinked green eyes that had kept him awake last night. "That's not necessary."

"Not a problem. Remember, you're helping us out."

They moved in tandem to the cash register. When they exchanged keys, the brush of her fingers sent a little chill up his arm.

Too bad about her and Ashe. Really, really too bad.

CHAPTER FOUR

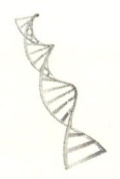

Harris opened his front door and Ashe shoved two bags into his hands.

"Dinner as instructed. Sunee asked for Thai," Ashe said. "I thought we weren't getting together until next week?"

"Something happened that I couldn't share on the phone or through email." Harris peered outside, anxious to see Sunee again and experience her island of calm for an hour or two. It would be a nice way to spend a Friday night. "Where's Sunee?"

"Five minutes behind me."

"I'll keep these warm." Harris led the way into the kitchen and slid the containers into the warming drawer. He pulled a couple of beers out of the beverage fridge, handing one to Ashe. "Someone asked if we were related."

Ashe pushed away from the counter and paced to the sliding doors. "A reporter?"

"Opposing counsel. It's why I wanted to meet." And to see Sunee, but he wouldn't share that with Ashe.

Ashe rapped his fingers on his beer bottle. "What did you say?"

"I lied." Harris's shoulders slumped. He hated how this was changing him. "I said we hadn't been introduced."

"Not *really* a lie." Ashe paced to the counter and fiddled with the napkin holder, finally bringing it over to the table. Then he prowled the kitchen. "No one *has* introduced us."

"Semantics." Harris shook his head.

"If someone asks me, I'll ... say it proves everyone has a double." Ashe rapped the counter with his knuckles. "Maybe that's all this is."

Harris stared at the face he saw every day in the mirror, a face that wasn't his. "Do you believe that?"

"No." Ashe sighed. "Did you talk to your mom or dad?"

"They're still in DC. I want to talk to them in person." Harris wanted the facts before he approached his parents. "You?"

"Didn't get a chance."

They set the table as they waited for Sunee. When there wasn't anything else to put in place, Ashe crossed his arms and leaned against the counter, his foot tapping some weird beat. "Did you grow up here or in DC?"

"Mom and I stayed in Texas. The senator came home on weekends." Harris smiled.

He'd been the man of the house, tasked by his father to take care of his mother. Even though they'd had servants, it had been his first taste of responsibility. He'd loved it.

"Unless there was a big event in DC, we spent the school year in Houston. Then we'd head to DC for some of the summer." Harris looked at him. "How about you?"

"When I was young, Dad played for the Vikings. After he blew out his knee, he became a coach." Ashe rubbed his own knee. "When I was twelve, he took the coaching position in Ohio and we moved to Columbus. I ended up playing for my dad."

"That was quite a championship game my senior year," Harris said. "I was there."

Ashe's eyebrows went up. "This is too strange."

"The senator hooked up box tickets. It wasn't quite like being in the student section, but we got better replays." Harris sat at the table. "The sportscasters kept rerunning your victory touchdown. Heartbreaking."

"Thrilling." Ashe grinned. He pulled a chair out and spun it around to straddle. "It was a great way to end my college career."

"Well, the fans got their money's worth. I'm surprised you weren't lynched after you moved to Texas. Longhorn memories are … long."

"My publicist wants me to maintain a high positive profile. Birth scandals probably aren't what she wants." Ashe finished his beer. "That's why I was at the golf tournament. She was upset I didn't stay for dinner and schmoozing."

"My campaign manager said the same thing," Harris said.

"I thought you were already elected? District Attorney is an elected position down here, right?"

"Yes, but I'm … thinking of running for another office."

"What office?"

Harris hesitated. It might not happen. "I'm exploring the possibility of running for governor."

Ashe's leg bounced up and down, rattling the silverware on the table. "I've never known someone running for governor. Aren't you too young?"

"I thought the timing was perfect until I ran into you in the locker room." Because if their parents had bought black market babies, careers would be jeopardized.

"This waiting is painful." Ashe's chair screeched as he stood and headed to the beer fridge.

The doorbell rang. *Sunee.* Harris hurried to the entry and tugged open the door.

She smiled up at him, still wearing her lab coat. "Hi, Harris."

"Hi." His voice was low and intimate. He couldn't help it. "Any trouble with the gate attendant?"

"Nope." She bit her lower lip.

He ushered her into the entry and slipped her coat off her shoulders. Under her lab coat, she wore a white blouse and slim black skirt. Conservative—and sexy. "Let me hang this up."

"I did it again," she moaned. "Why can't I remember to leave my coat at the hospital?"

"You're thinking big thoughts." He chuckled. "How was your patient?"

"Oh." She blushed. "My patient's ... better. He just needed some reassurance. It's his mother. She can't seem to stay positive."

He set his hand at the small of her back and guided her to the kitchen. "I'm sure having you there calmed them down."

"I hope so."

He knew so. Seeing her, touching her, had already quieted the racket in his head.

Sunee hurried over to Ashe and hugged him. "Hi."

Jealousy twisted Harris's stomach. His hand dropped to his side, but apparently not quick enough. Ashe caught it and frowned.

Sunee kissed Ashe's cheek. "I could tell you apart."

"How?" Ashe asked.

"Harris's face is thinner. But the easy way to tell you apart is your hair." Sunee looked at Harris and blushed.

"You're flushed." Ashe looked at Sunee and then back at Harris. "Are you okay?"

Sunee glanced back at Harris. "It's hot outside."

Harris hated being a third wheel. He turned away from the couple and pulled the food out of the oven. They sat and dished food onto their plates.

"Thank you again for lunch and the use of your SUV." Sunee handed him a container with noodles. When their fingers touched, warmth flashed through his body.

"You had lunch?" Ashe's gaze snapped up to meet Harris's. "When?"

"My car wouldn't start the other night." Sunee opened small containers of sauce and passed them out. "Harris lent me his car, and we had lunch together when he returned it."

"That was nice of you." Sarcasm rolled through Ashe's voice. He jumped up and headed to the counter, pulling chopsticks from one of the bags. "Here."

"For Thai?" Harris asked.

"Sure." Sunee snapped them apart and tasted her spring roll. "This is good."

Harris broke apart his chopsticks. He'd never been proficient with them. Give him smoked ribs any day. He tried to pluck up a pot sticker and it skidded across his plate.

Sunee's sparkling laugh filled the kitchen. "Let me help."

Standing next him, she wrapped her hand around his. His world narrowed to just her. Her touch. Her scent. Her.

After readjusting the pieces of wood in his fingers, she helped him pick up and guide the pot sticker into his mouth. It wasn't the food making his mouth water, it was her.

He looked over his shoulder and stared into her hypnotic eyes. If he moved, their lips would meet. "Thank you."

She smiled. "You're welcome."

"Will you help me too?" Ashe's voice interrupted the moment. His tone could have set the wooden chopsticks on fire.

Sunee jerked away, breaking their connection and returning to her chair. "I taught you years ago."

Ashe glared at Harris.

Never in his life had he forgotten who was in the room with him. Never. As a politician's son and as an elected official he couldn't.

But he had with Sunee.

"Why are we meeting?" she asked.

Because I wanted to see you again. "Since I don't want conversations via phone or email, I needed to tell you someone asked about Ashe and I looking alike."

"Oh." She frowned.

Ashe's legs bumped the table as he stretched out. "That probably didn't call for a dinner meeting."

"You're the only two people in the world I can talk to about this," Harris said.

"I understand." Sunee set her fingers on his fist. "It's nice having dinner."

Comfort rushed through him.

Ashe's gaze zeroed in on their hands. Harris relaxed his fingers and slipped them away from her.

"Do you have any news?" Harris asked Sunee.

She stared at her plate. "I called the techs, hoping they'd run your samples, but they're queued for Tuesday."

"Can you push them?" Ashe suggested.

"I can't." Sunee chewed her lip. "I'm sorry."

Harris patted her hand, and then yanked his away. She was too touchable. "Tuesday will be fine."

She blushed again.

Ashe's stare burned through his chest.

He had to shut down this attraction to Sunee. "Can we get together again Tuesday?"

"Are you okay with that?" Sunee asked Ashe.

"What?" Ashe still glared at him.

"Are you okay with getting together on Tuesday night?" she asked again.

He shook his head. "I have a press conference Tuesday, then meetings and dinner with Coach. You'll have to call me."

"We've already agreed to no phone calls, texting or emails. We don't want any—leaks until we understand what's going on." Harris rubbed between his eyes. "We need to figure out a better way to communicate. You never know who could be watching or listening in."

"Politics sure has made you paranoid." Ashe tipped back his beer bottle.

"Ashe," Sunee scolded.

"Cautious," Harris said quietly.

Ashe shook his head. "Semantics."

"Do you have any theories?" Harris asked Sunee, trying to diffuse the tension crackling around the table. If Ashe would leave, he'd be able to enjoy Sunee's tranquil presence.

She swallowed the pad thai she'd put in her mouth. "Until I see the DNA readouts, I don't want to speculate. As an attorney, I'm sure you don't predispose yourself to an answer."

Harris nodded. "Makes sense, but the waiting is killing me."

"At least we have each other." Ashe's mocking words had them all concentrating on their food. He emptied his second beer and grabbed a third from the beverage fridge. He was making himself right at home.

"Is having another beer wise?" Sunee asked. "You're still taking pain meds for your knee."

"I don't need a doctor." Ashe slouched and took a long gulp. "I have plenty already."

"And they think drinking on pain meds is fine?" she snapped.

"I don't need a mother either," Ashe shot back.

"But I care about you," she whispered. "You're important to me."

Harris should leave. Let them work out their problems.

Ashe set his bottle down with a crack.

Sunee's phone buzzed. She shook her head and slipped it out of her bag. After reading the text, she said, "I'm needed at the hospital."

She'd barely eaten. Harris grabbed a bag and stuffed in containers. "Take these with you."

"Thank you." Sunee shook her head at Ashe and pushed away from the table. "I'll let you know if the timing for the tests changes."

Harris said, "Just don't—"

"—I get it," she interrupted Harris, then sent a disgusted look at Ashe. "Don't drink and drive. Remember what happened your senior year."

She walked out.

"You're an ass," Harris said to Ashe, scrambling to see her out.

He tugged her lab coat off the hanger in the closet and ran outside with the bag of food. "I'm sorry."

Sunee yanked open her car door. "Why are you apologizing?"

"He's upset." Because of the way he had looked at Sunee.

"Obviously." She tossed the coat and food onto the passenger seat. And inhaled. "But you can't apologize for him."

The front door opened and Ashe rushed out. "Don't go away mad."

She crossed her arms and stared at him.

Ashe ran his hands up and down Sunee's arms. "I'm sorry."

She touched his face. "I don't want you to end up like Darren."

Who the hell was Darren? He should turn away, but it was like a bronco ride. Sixty seconds of hell that you couldn't stop watching.

"You're right." Ashe set his forehead against hers. "You've always been my conscience. Always there to ground me."

"I try," she whispered.

Ashe crushed her to his chest. "I can't live without my moral compass."

Harris's dinner threatened to come up. He backed away from the couple. "I'll ... good night."

In the entry he sank against the door. He needed to corral his attraction for Sunee and tuck it away.

Her car started.

Would Ashe follow Sunee to the hospital and then home? He'd be able to wallow in her serenity. Inhale her floral scent. Stroke her silky skin. Make love to her.

Ashe pushed through the door.

"Sunee said I needed to apologize for being rude." Ashe's voice didn't hold any regret.

Harris ignored the non-apology. As they headed back to the kitchen, he asked, "Who's Darren?"

"My college roommate." Ashe closed his eyes. "He was my center. There was a party back in Columbus after the national championship. I'd gone back to the apartment, but Darren kept celebrating. Ended up drinking and driving."

This didn't sound good. "And?"

"The accident was so bad, they amputated his foot. He would have been drafted."

Harris swore. Ashe and Sunee had history.

Ashe crossed his arms. "What do you think you're doing with Sunee? Having lunch. Lending her your car?"

"She needed help." He tossed garbage away.

"She could have called a cab. She could have called me."

"I was here." Harris would not confess his attraction to her.

"Stay away from Sunee. Don't smile. Don't flirt." Ashe jammed a finger into Harris's chest. "And don't touch."

Harris shoved Ashe's hand away. "Got it."

He would leave her alone. But he couldn't stop his body from reacting every time they were in a room together. He didn't have that kind of control.

Ashe headed for the entry, turned and snarled. "You'll be sorry if I find you've been messing with her."

TUESDAY MORNING, Harris looked around his office conference table at the Maryanne Barney prosecution team. Pretrial motions would be argued next week. He refused to let a guilty woman pollute the streets of Houston. "Anything new, Marta?"

"Thanks to the lead detective," Marta nodded at the woman across the table from her. "We have a neighbor willing to testify she saw Mrs. Barney and Mr. Lucas together numerous times.

She's the perfect witness. She actually noted *suspicious activities at the Barneys* in her personal diary. We have dates."

"Can she identify Lucas?" he asked.

"Yes." Marta grinned. "She'll be hard to shake in cross."

"Excellent, what else do we have?" Harris asked.

"One more pharmacy has video of Barney buying prescriptions under a false name. The recording's pretty grainy, but you can hear the conversation and identify her. The pharmacist even cautions her on narcotic use."

"So we have a wife having an affair and buying prescription narcotics. She's young, her husband is old, rich and now dead. An apparent drug overdose that the grieving widow says was a suicide."

His staff continued with their discovery material updates and review. Harris didn't have a smoking gun in Mrs. Barney's hand, but by the end of the meeting their case was solid.

"Thanks, everyone." He pushed away from the table. "We'll meet Friday for a final review."

Deborah, his assistant, came in as the team filed out, holding a handful of green slips. "Here are your calls. I'm heading to lunch. Do you want me to pick up anything for you?"

"A sandwich would be great."

"Will do. Anything you need before I head out?"

He stared at the slips, not seeing the names or numbers. "I'd like to refresh my memory on a trial from last year."

She laughed. "Which one?"

"The black market baby ring." He wanted to see how far back the victims went. And if there had been any reported around his birthdate.

"I remember that one." She shivered. "It's awful what those people did."

"A reporter wants to do a follow up. I'd like to see the list of parents who were victims."

"I'll find the information."

He waved the stack of slips. "Anything important?"

"The mayor wants an update on the Barney case. And a man named Ashe, no last name, said your meeting was pushed off until tomorrow. Same time? There's nothing on your calendar."

"It's personal." Had something come up with their DNA results?

Deb held up one more slip. "Also a Dr. Elaina Ashland called."

He hadn't heard Dr. Ashland's name for ... wow ... years. The doctor had run some long-term study on nutrition and IQ or brain development, and he'd been a participant. "What did Dr. Ashland want?"

"She'll be in Houston and wants to catch up."

"Did she say when?"

"No. You had another call coming in, so I didn't get a chance to ask." Deb held out her hand for the slip. "I can call her back."

"I'll call."

Harris sat at his desk. He should call the mayor first.

Instead he called Dr. Ashland. She had a Boston area code. Had he known that?

The voice on the recorded message was familiar and warm. The doctor had visited him four times a year up through high school and then once or twice a year until he was twenty-one. She was a nice person.

After the beep, he said, "Dr. A? Sorry I missed your call. Let me know when you're in town. I'd love to catch up."

Boston

Victor pushed open the lab door. He wanted to slam it, grab Elaina by the shoulders and shake her. How could she?

"Elaina?" He headed to the glass-enclosed office set in the corner of the room. Keeping her office down here was ridiculous. Over the years he'd offered her one on the building's executive level. She'd always refused. A partner deserved an office with all the trappings of their success. Instead Elaina was down with lab rats, unwashed beakers and Bunsen burners.

Movement at a lab table had him turning.

"She's not here." Piper slipped off her protective glasses and set down a pipette.

He checked his watch. It was four o'clock. On Tuesday. Elaina never left the lab before six. "Is she sick?"

"Oh, she went to …" Piper closed her eyes, gray eyes just like her mother's. With her thick curly black hair, she might be a male version of Andrew, but she'd inherited her mother's silver gray eyes. And Elaina's smile. "I think she said Houston. Or was it Minneapolis? You know how she took those trips every quarter. Maybe San Francisco?"

He wanted to shake the girl out of her haze. Piper was too much like her mother, always focused on work. "What exactly did she say?"

"I can't remember." Her eyebrows pinched together. "She'll be back by Saturday or Sunday. Maybe our pilot knows?"

He dialed the corporate pilot's number. If he'd been in the air, the call would roll to voice mail.

"What can I do for you, Mr. Giuseppe?" the pilot asked.

"Did you fly Dr. Ashland anywhere? Or plan to?"

"No. I'm in Chicago waiting for the clinical trial director. Then we're returning to Boston. Do you need me?"

"No." He hung up.

Damn Elaina. She was running to warn the boys.

He'd found their pictures this morning. She hadn't used random donors for the experiments. The two boys looked exactly like Andrew. But they had Elaina's eyes.

"What's wrong, Uncle Victor?" Piper stripped off her gloves and laid a hand on his arm.

He let the frown relax off his face. He wouldn't upset his goddaughter. She might contact her mother. He wanted to see

Elaina's face when he accused her, the queen of medical propriety, of breaking protocol. She'd implanted her own babies in other women. She'd put everything at risk by using her own children.

"I need to talk to your mother about ... something. Do you have her itinerary?"

Piper frowned. "She didn't give me one. Let me see if she sent it to my email."

Piper's desk was piled with books and files. She was the heir-apparent of a multi-million dollar corporation, and like her mother, she hid herself in a basement lab.

Piper jiggled the mouse and then typed in a complicated password too fast for him to catch more than a few keystrokes. She scanned her emails as he looked over her shoulder.

Tipping up her face, her long black ponytail slipped over her shoulder. "I don't have anything. Do you want me to send her an email? Or call?"

"No, that's fine." He patted her back.

In the hallway he scrolled through his phone. He hadn't used this number in years. What if his contact didn't answer?

"Yes?" Mark Dell's voice hadn't changed.

"We need to meet," Victor said.

"Why?"

"Not over the phone." Victor exhaled. "Six at Delmonico's."

"JAMESON NEAT," Victor told the waiter.

Elaina had used her own *children*. Elaina never violated protocol.

He exhaled and took a deep breath, but nothing eased the tension in his shoulders. The protocol had called for cloning zygotes from anonymous donors. Instead she'd used embryos from two parents with IQs off the charts. And the genetically modified men were both in the public eye. What other rules had she broken? Was anything in the file she'd handed him accurate?

When his drink arrived, he let the alcohol burn a path down his throat. He yanked at his tie, but the strangling sensation didn't disappear.

Finally Mark slipped into the chair Victor had left open for him. The chair let Mark watch everyone in the restaurant and kept his back to the wall.

Victor only made a mistake once.

Since the last time they'd met, Mark Dell's hair had gone silver. A black tailored suit clung to his still fit body. It was almost ninety degrees, but Mark wouldn't take off his suit jacket, ever. It hid his gun.

"Why are we meeting?" Mark asked. No chit chat. No hi, how are you.

"Do you remember the first grant the Mendel Foundation gave to Legacy?"

"The long-term study on the boys. The modifications were cognitive thinking and physical skills."

Victor nodded. "We followed the boys until they turned twenty-one."

"We didn't need to follow them after they were five. The gene editing experiment was successful."

Victor swallowed. "There might be a problem."

Mark's already dark eyes turned black. "Problem?"

The waiter interrupted. "Are you ready to order?"

Victor ordered a prosciutto and melon salad, and linguine with clams.

"I'll have the same." Mark hadn't opened his menu. "Coffee to drink."

Even though he hadn't finished the first, Victor ordered a second Jameson.

Mark laid his arm along the top of his chair, and his coat gaped enough to see his gun. "Talk."

Sweat broke out on Victor's upper lip, and he swallowed the last gulp of his drink. He flipped pictures of Torrington and Bristol across the table to Mark.

It was almost a relief when Mark's intense dark eyes left his face and he stared at the photos. Too soon his gaze flashed back up to pin him like a cobra hypnotizing its prey. "Twins?"

"Bristol is the Texans' new quarterback. Torrington is Houston's district attorney and son of Senator Torrington. The two are now in the same city and both will have media coverage."

"Where and who is the third?"

His stomach twisted. "I don't have that name right now." He couldn't believe he'd gone to this meeting unprepared. He'd gotten lax since the days when he'd meet with Mark at least twice a month.

His only excuse was the lash of Elaina's betrayal. *He'd* wanted a child with Elaina. Once Andrew was gone, she should have been his.

"They're two of the original three from the first experiment?" Mark pointed at the pictures with a long thin finger.

"I didn't realize whose eggs and sperm had been used. The protocol called for anonymous donors. We assumed students would donate."

"If we're meeting, apparently that wasn't the case."

"Doctors Elaina and Andrew Ashland were the donors."

"Andrew?" Mark hissed. "The *Andrew* you had us eliminate?"

Victor glanced at the other diners, afraid they'd heard Mark, but no one was pulling out cell phones and calling the cops.

"Yes," he whispered, the S slithering to silence between them. "I asked her some questions, and now I think Elaina's going to warn them. Hell, she might tell the world what happened."

"No." Mark's eyes narrowed. "You know the rules. Nothing can be traced back to the Foundation."

Victor waved at the photos. "I didn't expect Elaina to do this."

"I'll take care of it." Mark pushed away from the table, already pulling out his cell phone. "Don't talk to her. Don't talk to anyone. The Mendel Foundation will not be exposed."

Victor slumped back into his chair. At least the problem had been kicked to Mark.

"THE OFFICE," Mark Dell barked to his driver. He placed a call. "Simon, where are you?"

"At work."

"I'll be there in fifteen." Mark expelled a breath.

Simon was everything Mendel had programmed him to be. He'd been in the first modification wave and had lightning reflexes and was agile in both body and mind. That group was now turning twenty-nine. Their features were nondescript. The initial donors' facial features hadn't been handsome, but not ugly either. Theirs were the faces people had trouble describing because they didn't stick out. The Foundation had designed the perfect spy with Dr. Ashland's unknowing help.

Simon's talents might be wasted as his assistant, but Mark relied on him.

Now the damned woman who'd pioneered the protocols could lead to their exposure. That would not happen. Not now. They were too close to their objective. If they were discovered, he'd be blamed. Age wouldn't save him. Mendel did not have a retirement plan. People weren't put out to pasture—they were buried.

How could he have believed Victor had everything under control? The man had always been a soft spot in the trio forming The Legacy Group.

As the car pulled up to the innocuous building housing the Mendel Foundation's Boston office, Mark said, "Wait for me."

At the door he placed his ID against the reader. There was a beep and the lock released. The security guard looked up. "Good evening, sir."

Nodding, Mark headed to the elevator. He punched the button for the top floor and waited for the retinal scan.

When the elevator opened, Simon stood next to his desk and followed Mark into his office. The Boston office matched the ones in Washington DC, Iowa and LA. The only thing that changed was the view.

"What do you need?" Simon asked.

"The background information on Elaina Ashland, Harris Torrington and," what the hell was the football player's name? He sank into his chair.

"Yes?" Simon jotted down names.

"He's a quarterback." Mark snapped his fingers. "For the Texans."

Simon typed in a query on his iPad. "Bristol."

"Yes. Dr. Ashland may be on her way to Houston. She needs to be stopped."

"Any limitations on how we stop her?" Simon's tone was robotic.

"None." Mark tapped a finger on his desk. He was not taking the blame for this. His bosses would never know they were close to being exposed. "Any means necessary. Just don't let it lead back to us."

CHAPTER FIVE

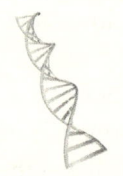

Houston

Sunee checked her hair in the car mirror before grabbing bags from the passenger seat and heading to Harris's front door.

She'd finally gotten the DNA results. A day late. Now she could tell Harris and Ashe together. Unfortunately the results didn't make sense.

At the massive double doors, she took deep breaths, trying to slow her heart rate. She even closed her eyes. No good. She couldn't wait to see Harris. Science couldn't explain why a man who wore the same face as her best friend made her pulse leap.

One more exhale and she pushed the doorbell, trying not to squirm.

Harris pulled open the door. "Hi."

"H-h-hi," she stuttered. Great. She was such a social misfit. Her face heated like a wok. *Please no hives tonight.*

"Come in where it's cool." Harris waved her into the house.

She followed him, unable to think of anything to say. And she hadn't shaken his hand either.

"Let me take those bags." He slipped them off her shoulder, his fingers sliding across her bare shoulder.

She shivered. If only he were touching her because he wanted to and not because he was being a gentleman.

She followed him into the kitchen. "This is such a great room."

"Thanks. But I bought it this way."

They emptied the bags, the silence between them only broken by the crinkle of cellophane and the slither of plastic.

"What did the DNA tests show?" he asked.

"You're related." She rubbed her head. "But something is—off. Can I wait to explain that to both you and Ashe?"

Harris's lips formed a straight line. "Sure."

Now what? What did people talk about?

"You didn't have to bring the fixings for dinner." Harris refolded the empty bag.

"I don't cook often, but I like to," Sunee said. "And this meal is fast."

"What are we making?" he asked.

"Chicken piccata." He'd said *we*. "I thought … you don't have to help. I can—"

He placed his finger on her lips. "I want to help."

She got lost in his warm eyes. She'd always thought gray eyes were cold, but a fire blazed in his.

He jerked his finger away. "Sorry."

Right. He and Kat were together.

"I'll need …" her mind went blank. Her mouth hung open.

He chuckled. "Cutting board? Something to cook in?"

"Yes." This was worse than high school. She'd always been three or four years younger than her schoolmates. She'd had crushes, but the guys were older so they ignored her. "I'll need a large fry pan. Cutting board. Pie tins or something flat to dredge the chicken. A juicer if you have it."

Harris pulled things from the cupboards. "What else can I do?"

She had him beat the egg as she pounded out the chicken. She'd already mixed the flour, salt, pepper and paprika. "Did Ashe say when he would get here?"

"He had an appointment to look at a house. Hoped to get here by seven."

She swirled olive oil in a fry pan and then dropped in a pat of butter.

He opened a drawer and ended up caging her between his body and the counter.

"Oh." She looked up. There was that fire again. She bit her lip and his gaze dropped to her mouth. Her breath came out in a whoosh.

"Sorry." But he didn't move.

She froze. Her heart rate had to be over one twenty. If she kept up this shallow breathing she would hyperventilate. "Harris?"

He smiled. "I like the way you say my name."

She smiled too. "It's a nice name."

"So is Sunee." He tucked strands of hair behind her ear.

The space between their bodies was heating up like a boiling pot of water. "It means capable."

"That's nice." He sniffed, then frowned.

So did she. "The pan!"

Grabbing a towel from the counter, she pulled the blackened pan off the range. "I'm sorry."

"My fault." He dug into the cupboard and hauled out a cast iron pan. "Will this work?"

"Yes." No more distractions. If she wasn't careful she'd burn down his house.

She drained the artichokes and sliced the mushrooms. He rolled and squeezed lemons, snapped asparagus and put on a pot of water for the noodles.

As he opened a bottle of wine, he asked, "How was your day?"

"Good." They set the table while she talked about her patients. Tension disappeared from her shoulders, her fingers.

He relaxed her. Harris listened as she talked about her patients and work. She asked about his work, and his legal cases were fascinating.

"Everything is set." She washed her hands.

Harris's phone buzzed. "Ashe will be here in twenty minutes."

She calculated cooking times. "I think we can get started."

She let the oil and butter melt. Tossed a few drops of water in the pan to make sure it was hot enough. Then dredged her chicken and set the first piece in the hot pan.

"You need an apron so you don't splatter your clothes." Harris set one over her head and tied the strings around her waist.

As she set the next chicken breast in the pan, he tugged her hair out from under the ties around her neck. His hands lingered as if he were stroking her hair.

She wasn't going to get distracted and burn their dinner. She hip-checked him and kept adding chicken to the pan. After browning both sides, she asked, "Can I have something to put these on?"

He grabbed a platter from the cupboard over her head.

She set the chicken on the plate. "Can you put this in your warming drawer?"

After adding wine she scrapped off the pan and let the wine reduce. Then she added chicken stock, capers, mushrooms and artichokes.

Harris leaned over her shoulder. "Smells great."

She swallowed. Harris smelled great too. "The water's boiling. Could you add the noodles?"

"Sure."

After returning the chicken to the pan, she said, "Now all we need is Ashe."

He handed her a glass a wine. "I grabbed a white, figuring if you were using white wine in the dish, this would work."

She looked at the label. Pinot Grigio. She sipped. "Perfect."

He held up his glass and toasted her.

"Oh, I forgot the asparagus." Looking at him did that to her.

"I'm on it." Harris slid the baking sheet into the hot oven, bumping his hand against the upper rack. "Damn."

He nudged the oven closed with his shoulder.

"Are you burned?" She grabbed his hand and tugged him to the sink, running cold water. The side of his hand was red. "You are."

"It's fine."

"Do have burn cream? Aloe Vera?" She scanned the kitchen.

He caught her hand. "It's not bad."

She examined the red skin. "No blisters. That's good."

"I'm fine."

"It should be cleaned and covered with ointment. Vaseline will do." She looked up into his eyes. He was laughing. "What?"

"It doesn't hurt." With his uninjured hand, he turned her so they stood face to face. "You're amazing."

She'd always believed a good doctor touched her patients. It was important. That had to be why she cradled his cheek with her hand.

He stared into her eyes and her breath stalled. Hunger replaced the laughter in his gray eyes. His gaze dropped to her mouth, and her lips tingled as if he'd caressed them with his tongue.

She tried to pull her hand away from his face, but nothing moved. His sandalwood scent locked her in place.

"Sunee." He stepped closer, their legs now pressed against each other.

Her pulse pounded. She was lightheaded.

He tugged her so she couldn't see anything but his lips, nose, mouth, and the dark shadow of his evening beard.

"Sunee." When he whispered her name again it sounded like a prayer.

Harris's lips brushed hers. His hand slid into her hair, and he pulled her the last millimeter closer. Energy arced between them, like a charge from a defibrillator. His tongue stroked the seam of her lips and she inhaled, taking him into her mouth.

Harris groaned. His arm circled her waist and he tugged her to her toes. He licked the roof of her mouth and heat pooled between her legs.

Her fingers pushed into his hair.

He angled her head and matched their mouths together. She felt vulnerable and female. The palm of his hand scraped against her nipple and it came to attention.

"Wait, wait." The man she'd thought about kissing for almost a week shouldn't be doing this. "What about Kat?"

"Kat?" Harris planted kisses in a line from her ear to the sensitive spot right on her neck.

She shivered. "Stop."

Harris dropped his forehead to hers. "Why? I've wanted to kiss you, to touch you ever since you walked in my door and hugged me, even though you thought I was Ashe."

"I like Kat. I can't do this to her." She pushed away from him.

"What does Kat have to do with us?"

Sunee stood, hands on hips. "She's your girlfriend."

"No." Harris shook his head slowly. "Oh shit. Ashe."

"Ashe?"

"Aren't you and he …?" He stopped.

She grinned. Relief bubbled up, and she thought her head would explode with the effervescence of champagne. "No."

"But I thought …" he said. "He acts …"

"I thought …" she said.

He grinned and curled her head into his shoulder with a sigh. His chin rested on the top of her head. "This is the best news I've had in weeks, months."

"Absolutely."

His heart thrummed under her ear. His hand stroked her back. Comfort flowed through her, and she felt cherished for the first time in her life. She didn't have to get the best grade in the class, she didn't have to skip a grade. She just had to breathe.

Dinner. She jerked away from his warmth. "I need to check on our food."

The doorbell rang.

"That must be Ashe." Harris cupped her face. "He already warned me away from you. Maybe we should keep this to ourselves."

"Oh." Why would he want that? Her insecurities crashed around her. She wasn't pretty enough. Sophisticated enough. She'd never been enough. "Sure. Whatever you want."

"I don't want a fist in my face." He headed to the door.

She added the lemon juice, stirred the chicken and then set it on the trivet in the center of the table. Did the same with the asparagus. Then she finally checked the pasta. Maybe a little softer than she liked it, but it was a small price to pay after Harris had kissed her brainless.

She peered out to the hallway but couldn't see Harris or Ashe. There was the drone of their identical baritones. What was taking them so long? Were they talking about her?

They finally entered the kitchen.

She set the wine on the table. "Everything's ready."

Ashe kissed her cheek, then sniffed. "I love your chicken piccata."

Harris stared. Was he jealous of her and Ashe's friendship?

Ashe took one side of the table, which left Sunee sitting across from Harris.

"I told Harris the test results show you're related." She passed around the dishes.

"Harris said there was something strange about the results," Ashe said.

"There is." The reports didn't make sense. "When we're done eating, I'll show you the graphs."

Ashe nodded. "Fine. I'd rather not spoil this great meal."

Harris's foot bumped hers under the table. And stayed there.

Her face heated like she was standing over a flaming Bunsen burner.

"Are you all right?" Ashe asked.

"Why?" she asked.

"Your face is flushed."

Harris's mouth quirked into a smile. His foot rubbed against hers.

She waved her hand. "From slaving over a hot stove."

Ashe frowned. He stared, first at her and then at Harris.

The silence almost had her confessing she'd kissed Harris. But Harris didn't want anyone to know about them.

Harris held up his fork. "This is fantastic."

"Thank you." His compliment had perfect timing, diffusing the tension that had settled over the table like a cloud of water vapor.

"At yesterday's press conference, someone mentioned we looked alike." Ashe pointed between himself and Harris, then added more chicken to his plate.

"Damn." Harris set his fork down with a clang.

"I gave him the *everyone has a doppelganger* answer." He sipped his wine. "The reporter didn't follow up."

"But we don't know if anyone will do more checking." Harris rubbed his chin.

"Hell, my dad didn't say anything." Ashe dug back into his meal. "But he's pretty clueless unless it has to do with football."

Sunee patted his free hand. "I know."

Ashe threaded their fingers together and glanced over at Harris. "Maybe when I'm no longer playing football he'll see me as a son and not a quarterback."

Now it was Harris who frowned.

"I hope so." Sunee slipped her hand away from Ashe's.

It was like Ashe and Harris were laying claim to her. She said, "You deserve a father who can see what a good man you are."

Ashe shrugged. His *go to* reaction whenever his father came up.

The conversation died as they finished their meal. Normally that wouldn't bother her, but tension crackled between the two men.

After clearing the dishes, Harris opened another bottle of wine and led them into his game room. Or maybe it was his family room. There were so many rooms in this house.

"Break it to us." Ashe flopped into an armchair.

Harris sat on the sofa with her. She twisted a hank of hair, twirling the strands into a tangle. "You're definitely related. We might say you're twins."

Harris leaned forward. "Might?"

"Everything matches up too perfectly for you to be only siblings." She handed printouts to each man. "Probability is 99.99% you're related. But with identical twins the DNA should match almost perfectly, and you and Ashe do not."

Ashe flipped through the papers. "So we're … fraternal twins?"

"That's what I don't understand. You're *too* closely linked to be fraternal." She shook her head. When that didn't clear her thoughts, she got up and paced. "You should be identical, but there are sectors that are different."

"Sectors?" Harris asked.

She flipped the pages and pointed at the graphs. "These."

She went to Ashe and flipped to the correct page for him. "To be identical, they should match almost exactly."

"But they don't?" Ashe asked.

"No. And the data doesn't make sense. It's why they re-ran the results."

"So we're twins, but not." Ashe exhaled.

"Our birth certificates say we were born from different mothers, on different days in different states."

"Yes," she said.

Harris's eyes locked on hers. "What do you think?"

"I don't know." She had suspicions but not enough data to confirm. "What's worse, I don't know where to find more answers."

Harris and Ashe stared at each other.

"I'm sorry," she whispered. She'd failed to give them any closure.

"Let's recap," Harris said. "We're related."

Sunee and Ashe nodded.

"Our DNA is too closely matched to be long lost cousins," Harris said.

"Much too close," she said.

"If you'd just seen the DNA results, you would have assumed twins, but there are—" Harris searched for the word she'd used "—sectors that don't match."

"If you were identical, your DNA should be almost a perfect match," Sunee said. "If you were fraternal, approximately fifty to seventy-five percent of the sectors should match, depending on what kind of fertilization occurred."

"But we're higher."

"Ninety-four percent." Sunee twisted her hair.

"We're back to clones—or alien birth," Ashe said.

"Stop." Sunee frowned. "Clones. I hadn't thought about that. Was anyone doing clonal research thirty years ago?"

"When was that sheep in England?" Ashe's foot jerked up and down.

Harris wanted to put anchors on Ashe. He was so restless.

"That's something I can work on. I ... I'll start tugging on that thread." Sunee jotted notes on a piece of paper.

Harris swallowed. "Whatever you do, don't let anyone see any notes or searches you're performing."

"I won't." Sunee touched his arm. "I understand your concern."

Concern? This was his career. His life.

"If this was a black market baby ring, would these results makes sense?" Harris asked.

Ashe stopped jiggling. "What?"

"There was one operating out of Houston for over twenty years. We prosecuted them last year."

"Twenty years ago?"

"That's as far back as I found victims." Harris grimaced. "But they might have started a decade before that."

"No." Sunee shook her head. "It wouldn't explain the DNA results."

The doorbell rang. Ashe and Sunee looked at him.

There were very few people on Harris's permanent list of authorized visitors. His parents, a couple of attorneys and a few friends. Could be a neighbor, but that wasn't likely. He pushed off the sofa. "I'll get rid of whoever it is."

Harris took a deep breath and pulled open the door.

"I left you a message but decided to drive over." Kat Phillips pushed past him and headed down the hall.

Shit, she was heading to the media room.

"This isn't a good time." Harris hurried after her. No way did he want a reporter, even Kat, seeing him and Ashe together. "Wait!"

"I'll only stay for a few minutes." Her heels clicked in the hall. "Well, for a beer. I just spent time with *Mommy Dearest*."

Harris reached out, but she evaded his grasp. "This isn't a good time."

"I'll only be a minute." Kat burst into the room.

Sunee stood at the far side of the room. Ashe slouched in his chair, barely noticeable.

"Sunee, right? Hi!" Kat grinned and winked at Harris. "After I was at my mom's house, I needed to be around someone normal. Harris was the first person who came to mind. It's nice to see you again, Sunee."

"Not a good time." Harris tried to pull her out of the room.

"Harris," Kat tugged her arm away. "We need to talk about your mother's party."

"We can talk—tomorrow." Since Kat's back was to Ashe, Harris frantically waved him into the hallway.

Ashe nodded. Crouching, he slipped around the chair and stumbled.

Kat turned at the sound. Her blue eyes flared open along with her mouth. She stared at Ashe. Then Harris. Then Ashe again. "Who are you?"

CHAPTER SIX

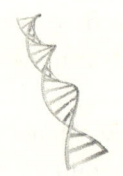

Harris gritted his teeth. Kat was the last person they needed here.

Kat stared at Harris and then Ashe. "I'll ask again, who are you?"

"Kat, leave," Harris insisted.

She looked at Ashe and then Harris. "Are you kidding? I want to know what's going on."

"We don't know." Exasperation filled Harris's voice. He took a breath, but he'd lost the calm he'd gathered from being around Sunee.

Kat's eyes were huge. "Now you have to tell me."

"You can't tell anyone." He pointed a finger at her. "No one. Swear to me on your palomino."

"Sure, bring up my horse. Fine, I swear. But only because we're lifelong friends." Her bright blue gaze locked on Ashe. "Who are you?"

"This is Ashe Bristol," Harris said. "Ashe, Kat Phillips."

Kat's eyes widened. "The Texan's new quarterback?"

Ashe nodded.

Kat's eyes gleamed, a definite sign of trouble. "You look like Harris's twin. Why?"

"We're—" Ashe started.

Harris shook his head. "Kat, I want you to leave."

"No way. Someone catch me up." Kat grabbed a beer from the beverage fridge. "Anyone need anything?"

Sunee and Ashe looked at Harris. He nodded, and they made requests. Kat grabbed a beer for Ashe and water for Sunee. Harris poured bourbon. A double.

Kat sat on the coffee table. "Start talking."

He wanted to wipe Kat's memory. Stuff the genie back in the bottle. But that wasn't reality. Instead maybe they could use Kat's investigative skills. *If they could control her.*

"This is not a story." Harris closed his eyes. "You can't tell anyone."

"If you say no story, I won't report on this." Kat made an X over her heart. "But I need the deets."

"And you won't use them?" Harris asked.

"Not unless you give the go-ahead." She was almost bouncing on the table.

"You may never get that." Harris waved a hand between him and Ashe. "We don't know how we're connected."

Ashe added, "We have separate birthdays and were born in different states."

"I tested their DNA," Sunee said. "They're related. But the results don't make sense."

"Wow." Kat tapped her lip.

They'd increased the people who knew by another twenty-five percent. This had disaster written all over it.

"OMG. Do you think you were snatched as babies?" Kat squealed. "The black market baby ring?"

Damn it. She'd made the connection too fast.

"No!" Harris spit out.

Kat tipped her head. "Are you sure?"

He wasn't. But he would never reveal that to Kat. It would be like throwing chum into the bay and not expecting the sharks to feast.

"You know most of those kids ended up with new birth certificates." Kat looked between the two men. "What do your mothers say?"

"My mother is in DC." Harris's fingers drummed on his tumbler. "I won't discuss this on the phone."

"I could call Leah," Kat volunteered.

"No." Harris didn't want them talking. "I'll wait until she returns."

"My mother died of cancer." A shadow crossed Ashe's face.

Sunee set her hand on Ashe's shoulder.

Harris ground his teeth, even though he knew she and Ashe were only friends.

"The results of the Twin Zygosity DNA test are—unexpected," Sunee said.

"Unexpected." Kat waved her hand between Harris and Ashe. "They're related, right?"

Ashe jerked to his feet and paced to the window and back.

Sunee looked at Harris. Letting Kat know what little information they had was probably a mistake, but he nodded.

"They're related," Sunee said. "But there are anomalies."

"Anomalies? Explain," Kat prompted.

"If they were identical twins—almost everything would match. If they were fraternal, they should share fifty to seventy-five percent of their DNA. But Ashe and Harris share more than expected for fraternal twins and less than expected for identical twins. I can't explain the difference."

Sunee twirled her hair with a finger. She seemed to do that when she was thinking. It was a wonder her hair wasn't one big knot.

Kat's eyes narrowed. "Were you born here, Harris?"

"In Houston, according to my birth certificate, Ashe in Minneapolis." He gave their exact birthdates.

"I need to write this down." Kat's foot bounced a mile a minute.

"No," Harris said. "I don't want anything in writing."

"I don't have your memory. I need to see it, hear it and touch it." Kat straightened her shoulders. "I can help with your research."

"Tactile or kinetic learner," Sunee murmured. "Uses all her senses. Can't sit still, easily distracted."

"That's me." Kat grinned.

"Drove everyone crazy in school," Harris murmured.

"I'll bet you're as smart as Harris," Kat said to Sunee. Then she glanced at Ashe. "Do you have a genius IQ too?"

Ashe smiled. "Close."

"Come on Harris, let me take notes," Kat pleaded. "I've already sworn on Buttercup."

"All right." Harris closed his eyes, afraid he would regret a decision to let her document this problem. "But the notebook stays in my house."

"Fine, fine." Kat rushed into the foyer and came back with her bag. Stopping in the doorway, she bounced up and down.

"Are you all right?" Sunee asked.

"Releasing energy." After one more bounce and a deep breath, she exhaled, headed to the coffee table, sat and flipped to a blank page in her notebook. "How did you two meet?"

Ashe gave a half smile. "We met in the locker room at a golf tourney. Harris was..."

"Enough," Harris interrupted.

Ashe winked at Kat. "I'll tell you later."

"That's why you left the tournament?" Kat nodded at Harris. "So how do you think you're related?"

"I was hoping Harris was my doppelgänger," Ashe said. "But Sunee disproved that theory."

"The black market baby ring has to be a possibility," Kat said.

"Maybe." Harris sure hoped that wasn't the case. If he'd been adopted through the baby ring, what voter would believe his parents hadn't known? It could be the end of his father's career, and by connection, his own. If his public service career ended, what would he be? Just another attorney? He needed to be more. He needed to make a difference in the world.

"Ashe and Harris being taken at birth wouldn't explain the DNA results," Sunee said.

Kat tapped her pen on the notebook. "I can work backwards from your birth certificates. See if the doctors were named in last year's baby snatching case."

The bourbon in Harris's stomach churned. "Okay."

Kat jumped up and paced. "Get me the names and I'll see what I can find out."

Ashe joined her pacing, their paths crossing in the middle of the room.

"Can we make them stop?" Sunee bumped Harris's shoulder. "I'm getting dizzy from watching them."

He leaned close, inhaling her scent and drawing in her tranquility. "I wish."

"Having you do the research is a good idea." Ashe laid a hand on Kat's shoulder as they walked almost to the door and turned in tandem to cross to the fireplace. Ashe looked at Harris. "Having a reporter on our side might work out."

"I'm handy to have around." Kat batted her eyelashes at Ashe.

Was Kat flirting? Harris would have to warn Ashe that Kat didn't do long-term. Although after Ashe threatened him about Sunee, maybe Ashe didn't deserve the warning.

"I don't know what the truth will be, or if we can even find the truth. But it could hurt Harris or Harris's father if we don't control the release of information." Ashe rubbed his neck. "And my dad has an ethics clause in his coaching contract."

"What about you?" Sunee asked.

"I don't think they could screw with my contract. This wasn't something I did." Ashe looked at Harris. "This is about our parents. But I refuse to ruin my dad or mother's memory."

"So we're agreed. Kat will find out more about the doctors. Sunee will research what type of DNA manipulations were happening thirty plus years ago." Harris held everyone's gaze. "And we keep our lips zipped."

Sunee, Kat and Ashe nodded.

And Harris would dig through the trial and discovery materials from the black market baby ring, just in case.

ELAINA CHASED her suitcase along the baggage claim belt. It was the last bag at baggage claims. The Houston airport was eerily empty. Creepy. She didn't want to wait for her bag to go around again. She wanted to get to the hotel and sleep before contacting the boys and explaining what she'd done.

She'd taken the first flight out of Boston and been routed through Chicago. That was where the problems had started. She'd tried to board her next flight but somehow her ticket had been cancelled. The airline staff couldn't explain the snafu. And they couldn't get her on another flight that night. She'd gotten to a hotel at two in the morning.

After getting a few hours of sleep, she'd booked another flight, but the only tickets available were for late evening. It was one in the morning back in Boston. Midnight here. Exhaustion was closing in on her. Was it Tuesday or Wednesday? Had to be Wednesday.

"I'll get that for you," a deep voice said from behind her.

She stopped. "Thank you."

The young man wore a dark suit. And he was big. Not as big

as her sons—but bulked out like a weight lifter. He hauled her case off the belt like it weighed little more than a beaker of water.

"Thanks again," she said.

He pulled up the handle. "I've got it, Dr. Ashland."

She stumbled. "You know me?"

"When Victor discovered you hadn't taken the corporate jet, he asked me to pick you up." He waved a hand toward the exit. "My car is in the ramp."

She froze. "Victor?"

"I think it was Victor." His smile didn't reach his eyes. "Maybe he said something about your daughter? They asked me to pick you up."

Her body clenched. She hadn't given out her flight itinerary. How did Victor even know she'd flown to Houston? She snatched the handle of her case. "I don't need help. I rented a car."

"The rental car counters are closed." He shifted the bag out of reach and took her arm, prodding her to move. "Let me help you."

A chill raced down her spine. Who was this man? Her spine crawled. "I'll ... take a cab."

"I'll get in trouble. Come on." He led her out the doors.

"I can—" she started.

"—I'm in charge." He hustled her across the nearly deserted street. "Don't make a scene, Dr. Ashland. Piper might have an accident in your lab."

Piper? "Who are you?"

"Doesn't matter."

She tripped, hoping someone would come to her aid. Someone other than the man dragging her to the parking ramp.

He yanked her arm up hard enough that her feet dangled in the air. "Watch your step."

She pulled on her arm, but he towed her toward the stairs. Where were all the people? "Hel—!"

The hand crushing her arm, covered her mouth, his fingers

digging into her cheek. He hauled her into his shoulder and tucked his head close to hers. "Shut up."

Any passengers who could help her were too far away or glued to their phones.

He let go of her arm and pushed through a door, shoving her up the stairs. He tugged her purse off her shoulder and stuffed it in a trash can.

Escape! She ran. Stumbled up to the first door and tried to push it open.

Footsteps pounded behind her. She was jerked back and shaken. "One phone call and your daughter's dead."

"No!" She couldn't let Piper be hurt.

Was this a kidnapping? Victor had warned her years ago that she ignored her safety. She was worth millions. He'd suggested she travel with a bodyguard. Had Victor been right?

"What do you want?" She pulled on her arm, and his fingers ate deeper into her biceps. Stars flickered in her vision at the pain.

"Stop talking." He pushed through the door and jammed her carryon into another trash can. Then he hauled her toward a car.

She took deep breaths. No way would she get into the car. He had to let go of her at some point.

He stuffed her bag in front of the car parked near the stairwell, never letting her go.

She was going to die.

Opening the driver's door, he shoved her across the seat. "Buckle up."

She would not walk meekly into her own death. She scrambled to open the passenger door, but he slammed down the locks.

"Why?" she pleaded, hoping he wouldn't notice her searching for her cell phone in her jacket pocket.

"You fucked up, doc." He backed up the SUV. "You shouldn't have exposed us."

"Us?" She oriented the phone and fumbled to turn the volume

down to mute. Then as she buckled her seatbelt, she set the phone on the door side of the seat. "Who is us?"

"Guess you knowing it doesn't matter." When he glanced at her his eyes were cold. Lethal. "The Mendel Foundation. I understand you created the protocols."

Her breath caught. The DNA modification protocols. "That research was stopped years ago. Gene editing is wrong."

He laughed as he slipped the parking ticket and then a credit card into the kiosk. Why didn't they have attendants anymore? At least she would have been able to scream.

He exited the airport.

Each breath hurt. Tears streaked down her face. She would never see Piper fall in love. Get married. Never see the boys again.

Maybe she could convince him not to hurt her. "I thought the Foundation was disbanded."

"I'm a modification." The car accelerated onto the interstate. "Modification wave two."

"What?" Modification waves?

"I was in the second wave."

What had she done? "They used my protocols?"

"Used?" He laughed. "They're still using them. They've refined them."

"But why are you kidnapping me?"

"I'm following orders."

"Please. I have a daughter." A tear slid down her cheek. "Do you have children?"

"Quiet," he hissed.

She couldn't. This was her life. "Where are we going?"

He shook his head.

She had to do something. *The phone.* Pretending to cough, she swiped her password, wishing she'd used fingerprint security.

It took her two tries but it finally opened. She punched in 9-1-1. *Let them find me.*

She couldn't hear anything, but it looked like the phone had connected. "Please let me go. I don't understand why the Mendel Foundation is kidnapping me?"

Maybe the police would be able to track whoever had taken her.

"Shut up!" He backhanded her.

Stars blinded her. She whimpered, trying to hold in the tears. Was anyone listening?

Elaina waited for sirens. For rescue.

No one came. There were fewer and fewer cars on the freeway, and she didn't know this part of Houston. She had to do something.

She coughed and carefully released her seatbelt. They were approaching an underpass. Hopefully the operator was on the line. "Tell Piper I love her."

"Stop talking," he growled.

She took a deep breath, lurched and grabbed the steering wheel, pulling it toward her.

"Damn it!"

The tires squealed. The car jerked. Bounced. They spun sideways.

He peeled her fingers off the wheel.

Too late. They were riding up under the bridge. Brakes screamed.

The world revolved. She went airborne as the car rolled. Airbags battered her. She smashed into the window. Then the roof. There was the screech of metal. Shattered glass.

Still she flew until her head smacked something solid. Pain rushed through her. Red hot. Angry. She couldn't see. She reached for her head. But her hand wouldn't move.

The world shuddered to a stop. A hissing filled the car. Blood covered her kidnapper's face. He wasn't moving.

She had to run but couldn't. Something pressed against her chest.

Sirens sounded.

She tried to stay awake. Talk to the first responders. But darkness overwhelmed her.

Andrew. Piper. Boys. I love you!

CHAPTER SEVEN

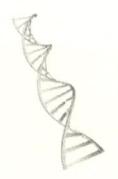

Sunee rushed to the ER nurse's station. "I'm looking for Rosa Carlos? She presented with a severe nose bleed."

The on-call pediatrician could have handled Rosa's case, but she was *her* patient.

And after the kiss she and Harris had shared before dinner, sleep would be elusive. Unfortunately there hadn't been a repeat. Ashe had escorted Sunee to her car.

Maybe Harris regretted their kiss in the kitchen. She hated his world of politics and politicking. It wasn't any different than her father's world.

The hospital was her environment. The hospital and lab were the only places she was comfortable.

The admin's fingers danced over her keyboard. "Room 7."

"Thanks." Sunee picked up the patient information, found the nurse assigned to Rosa and followed her to the room.

Rosa's leukemia had responded to treatment. She'd been in remission for almost a year. Hopefully this was a false alarm. After scanning the chart, she knocked and entered.

Twelve-year-old Rosa looked too tiny for the hospital bed. Her olive skin was gray and her little nose was packed with tubing taped to her cheek. Rosa's father sat next to the bed, clutching her hand.

"Mr. Carlos." Sunee set her hand on Rosa's foot. "Rosa."

"Dr. Miller." Relief rushed across Mr. Carlos's face. "I didn't think you'd come tonight."

"How could I not?" She tweaked Rosa's toe and got a small smile. "I was on my way home when I heard my favorite patient was in the ER."

The nurse checked Rosa's nose. Even though the notes were in front of her, Sunee said, "Tell me what happened."

"I was dizzy." Rosa's voice was nasal from the packing material. "My nose started bleeding."

"She stood and it gushed out." Mr. Carlos squeezed his daughter's hand. "We applied pressure and then ice, but it wouldn't stop."

"When did it start?"

"About an hour ago." The father looked desperate.

Rosa's lip trembled. "Is my leukemia back?"

"Let's not jump to any conclusions." Sunee ordered additional coagulation tests. Then took a more thorough history, catching up on Rosa's life.

A phlebotomist drew more blood. As the young man left, Sunee told Rosa, "Rest while we figure out what's going on."

She headed out the door and talked to Rosa's ER doctor.

"I think we should cauterize her nose," the ER doctor said.

"I agree." She would wait for Rosa's test results, but she was afraid the little girl would be checking back into the hospital.

Sunee grabbed coffee from the staff lounge, then waited at the nursing station.

Red and blue lights flashed. Sirens squealed and then cut off. Two teams of gowned and gloved staff scrambled to the ambulance bay.

"What happened?" Sunee asked the nurse next to her.

"Car accident. SUV versus a bridge underpass." The nurse shook his head. "Concrete always wins."

Sunee stepped aside as two gurneys rushed past her. There was blood. Everywhere. A man and woman, both with IVs running were strapped onto the gurneys. Glass chunks scattered on the floor as they flew by.

Sunee shook her head. The couple didn't look good.

Two officers stopped at the nurse's station. Sunee couldn't help overhearing the conversation.

"Do you have any identification information for me?" the intake nurse asked.

"Nothing on the woman. The man had ID." An officer read out the information he had. "We found a phone but couldn't get anything off it. It must have shattered when the vehicle rolled."

Sunee swallowed. As a resident, she'd survived her ER rotation, but the adrenaline was too much. Car accidents had been the worst.

"We haven't had a Jane Doe for a while." The nurse's fingers clacked on the keyboard. "Here's hoping they both regain consciousness."

There was a frenzy of activity in the two exam rooms. The best thing Sunee could do was stay out of the way and wait for Rosa's labs.

A nurse in a blood-spattered gown ran out of an exam room. She ripped off her gloves, grabbed the phone and requested an OR surgery suite. Not good. Was the patient even stable?

The gurney with the woman rushed down the hall, heading to surgery.

"Dr. Miller, here are the prelim results on your patient's bloodwork." A tech handed her an iPad.

Sunee looked them over. Rosa's white blood cell counts were high. Too high. Her hemoglobin too low. She sighed.

She couldn't worry about accident victims. She had to tell Rosa and her father she was being admitted.

THE NEXT AFTERNOON Sunee waited in her lab for the results of Rosa's bone marrow biopsy. The little girl had been so brave. Sunee hoped her leukemia wasn't back, hoped her blood work was wrong. If they got good news, she wanted to tell the family as soon as possible.

Might as well work on the Ashe and Harris puzzle while she waited. She poured through thirty-five year old papers on cloning and genetic modifications and editing.

"This one's familiar. I read it for my dissertation." She'd been fascinated by the explosion of knowledge that occurred once DNA sequencing had started.

Here was a paper on how a researcher successfully split a salamander embryo by using their own hair. "Embryo twinning? Is that a possibility?"

She flipped from one manuscript to the other. "Yes. That makes sense."

Footsteps echoed in the hall outside the lab. A knock interrupted her.

"Darn it." Sunee pushed away from the desk and headed to the door.

Kat stood outside the locked lab.

Sunee opened the door. "Kat?"

"I'm shocked I found you." Kat's heels clicked on the floor as she moved into the room. "This is a maze."

"Most people don't look for me in my lab."

Kat stalked into the room. "What do you do down here?"

"Research."

Kat rolled her eyes. "What kind?"

"Families with cancer." It was the simple explanation. "And I'm trying to isolate proteins in the blood to help develop a blood test for cancer screening."

"You're a medical hero." Kat stared at the papers spread on Sunee's desk. "Is this part of your research?"

"No." Luckily they were alone. "I'm looking at research from thirty to thirty-five years ago. I found something interesting on embryo twinning."

Kat scanned the top paper. "You understand all this?"

"It's what I do." Sunee raised her eyebrows. "I even write papers like this."

"You're such a geek." Kat laughed, but it wasn't a demeaning laugh.

"That's me. Geek in a lab coat," Sunee admitted. "Why are you here?"

Kat tapped a beautifully manicured nail on the stack of paper on Sunee's desk. "I need a favor."

Sunee tucked her hands behind her back so Kat wouldn't noticed her ragged unpainted fingers. "From me?"

Kat nodded. "You remember Harris's mother invited me to a dinner party."

Sunee nodded. She hated the idea of Harris dating this polished woman.

"That's why I was at Harris's house last night, but we got sidetracked, big time. I can't go to the party." Kat blew on her nails and polished them on her jacket. "I'll be subbing for the news anchor that night."

"Is that a good thing?" It sounded terrible to Sunee.

"It's fabulous." Kat walked to the microscope and peered through the lens. "It's not national news, but it's a step up from reporting. Like you curing a patient but maybe not finding the cure for cancer?"

Sunee hurried to the workbench and guided Kat away from the expensive equipment. "I love it when a patient goes into remission."

Kat grinned. "That's how I feel about being an anchor."

"But, what does this have to do with me?"

"You should attend the party with Harris." Kat pointed at her. "They always have the most interesting people. All the movers and shakers of Texas politics will be there."

Sunee pressed on her stomach. "Oh, I couldn't."

"Why not?"

"I'm not good with—crowds." Her belly twisted at the idea of enduring another political party. "I freeze. Get hives. Sometimes I throw up."

Kat frowned. "Last night you were fine with Ashe and Harris. And me."

"Ashe is like my big brother. Harris makes me nervous, but he's—" Sunee gave her a weak smile. "Kind. Calm. And logical."

"Since you're comfortable with Ashe, think of Harris as an Ashe clone."

"Oh, I don't think they're clones, although it has crossed my mind. But Ashe's musculature is different." Sunee pushed her hair away from her face. "That paper on embryo twinning was intriguing. I wonder if there was more work done on it."

"Hey, hey. Stay focused." Kat snapped her fingers. "We're talking about you attending this incredible party with Harris."

"I'm terrible at parties." Harris wouldn't want her there anyway.

Kat waved her hands around the lab. "Don't you have to get funding for your research?"

"Yes. I hate it." Sunee grimaced. "I'm much better at research than schmoozing."

"Well, this dinner party will give you practice. Plus, the net worth of the attendees will probably rival the hospitals' endowment funds. If you snare any money, you'll be a hero."

Sunee bit her lip. "Does Harris want me there?"

"He loves the idea." Kat's gaze darted to her left.

"Have you talked to him?" Harris didn't want anyone to know they'd kissed. Why would he take her to a party?

"Okay, I didn't ask him." Kat waved her hand. "But he'll love having you as his date."

Sunee itched her neck. Were welts forming at the *idea* of this party? "Why do you want this?"

Kat sighed and patted her hand above her heart. "I've seen how Harris looks at you."

This was the part of high school she'd never had. Talking about boys with a friend. "How does he look at me?"

"Like you lassoed the moon for him." Kat tipped her head. "His smile is different when you're around. It's not his politician smile. It's real."

"Oh." A chill coursed down her back. An involuntary reaction she needed to ignore. "I'm sure Harris doesn't want me to tag along."

Kat pulled out her phone and placed a call.

"What are you doing?" Sunee whispered.

Kat waved her to keep quiet.

This wasn't happening. She would embarrass Harris with her social ineptitude and anxiety.

"Harris," Kat said. "I can't make your mother's party. You should take Sunee."

Heat burned Sunee's cheeks. Did she want him to say "no way" or "sure"?

"I thought you'd like that idea. I'm with her now. I'll let her know." Kat grinned. "You owe me an interview of my choice."

Sunee shook her head. This was awful. She didn't want to go. But she didn't want Harris taking another woman. "I don't have anything to wear."

"No cocktail dresses?"

"Not here. I have things in New York." Cocktail parties weren't part of her life in Houston. She'd left that stress back in New York. "Heels don't go with my lab coats."

Kat laughed, then looked her over. "I'd lend you something,

but you're four or five inches shorter than I am. Time to go shopping."

"Now?" Sunee asked.

"Now."

"I've blocked out this evening to work on Ashe and Harris's research."

"I have research to do too." Kat's blue eyes narrowed. "But this has held for over thirty years. I don't think another ten hours will hurt anyone. Shut everything down, honey. We're going to The Galleria."

HARRIS DUMPED the bag of salad in the bowl and tossed the salad fork on top. Then he set everything on his kitchen table. Good enough. Ribs and cornbread were in the warming drawer. He'd covered the basic food groups.

The news droned in the background as he set out plates and silverware. Sunee, Ashe and Kat were arriving soon. With everyone's crazy schedules, Saturday night was the only time they could connect.

It had been three days since he'd kissed Sunee, so why did it feel like it had been weeks?

The doorbell rang. Let it be Sunee. He wanted to kiss her again. See if he'd imagined how incredible her mouth tasted. How her body fit with his.

He yanked open the door and his smile fell. "Hey, Ashe."

Ashe narrowed his eyebrows. "What's that face for? I haven't pissed you off yet, and I brought beer."

"Sorry." Harris stepped away from the door and Ashe walked inside.

As he was shutting the door, another car drove up. *Sunee.* A grin filled his face. "Go ahead and put the beer away."

Harris walked down and opened her door. "Hey."

Sunee smiled and the tension melted from his body.

"Am I late?" she asked.

"No." He held out his hand to help her out of the car. "You came from the hospital?"

She frowned. "How did you know?"

"I have impressive powers of observation." He slipped off her lab coat.

Her hand covered her mouth, and a blush raced across her face. "I'm an idiot."

"You're brilliant." He stroked her silky hair down her back. He wanted to feel her hair sweeping across his bare skin. Instead he folded the jacket and handed it to her. "There."

"Thank you." She set it on the passenger seat. "I brought clothes to change into."

"Good idea." He set his hand on the small of her back and guided her to the door. "Maybe we can eat on the patio tonight."

"Wait. I brought wine." She hurried back to the car and pulled out a cloth wine carrier.

He rubbed his hand up and down her back. Assuming Ashe had gone straight to the kitchen, he wouldn't spot them. He bent and kissed her. "Hi."

Her smile and blush bloomed again. "Hi."

"I can't stop thinking about kissing you," he whispered.

"You too?" Sunee eyes were huge.

"You keep me awake nights." One small kiss wasn't enough but it would have to do. Ashe was inside. Eventually Harris would tell Ashe he was attracted to his friend, but why invite an unnecessary confrontation? His political career had taught him to pick his battles and battlegrounds.

He and Sunee headed to the kitchen.

Ashe lounged at the counter with an open beer. "Hey, Sunee."

She moved over and gave him a hug. "How are you?"

"Going crazy." Ashe rolled his shoulders. "Can't wait to get to camp."

"I need to change." Sunee headed to the half bath.

Harris pulled the wine from the bag. Prosecco. But it was warm. He set one of the bottles in the freezer and the other in his wine fridge. "Don't let me forget I put the bottle in here."

"Sure," Ashe said.

"Does Sunee like sparkling wine?" If she did, Harris would stock up.

Ashe pulled his gaze from the television playing the news. "Is it prosecco?"

Harris nodded.

Ashe sighed. "It's what her mother drank."

"Oh." Harris found a couple of flutes and rinsed out the dust. Since sparkling wine didn't appeal to him with ribs, he popped one of Ashe's beers.

Sunee emerged from the bathroom, stuffing clothes in her large purse. She'd changed into a pink tank and khaki shorts and pulled her hair into a tail. She might be petite, but her legs looked long and were as gorgeous as the rest of her.

Ashe watched him stare at Sunee and his eyes narrowed.

"I'm chilling your wine," Harris said, trying to keep the focus off the way he gawked at Sunee. "Do you want something else to drink while it cools?"

She set her bag under the counter and headed to the cupboard. "Just water."

"When's Kat getting here?" Ashe asked.

"Soon." He wanted to talk to Sunee alone, and not about the DNA information. A week from today they would attend his parents' party. *Thank you, Kat.* Then they could really get to know each other. The idea of mingling with Sunee by his side made him smile. What an asset she would be to his campaign. Brilliant, caring and a doctor with a mission. "We can relax in the media room until Kat gets here."

"I want to see how my interview was received today," Ashe said.

"Channel 5?" Harris asked.

"Yeah." Ashe hurried down the hall.

Harris turned on the big screen in his media room and took a spot on the sofa. An ad played.

Ashe prowled the room behind him. Sunee sat next to Harris, and he reached out his hand for hers and stopped. He was smarter than that.

The anchor woman returned, talking about the upcoming Barney murder trial. There was a shot of Harris on the courthouse steps from a couple of years ago.

"Nice picture." Sunee looked at him through her eyelashes.

"Thanks." He smiled down at her.

Ashe stopped at the sofa behind them. "You don't think they will put us together?"

"I was wearing sunglasses." Harris's shoulders tightened.

"I wore a ball cap. And I haven't gotten a haircut or shaved for a week." Ashe blew a breath out between his lips. "This is getting bad. I'm as paranoid as you are."

Harris's hands formed fists. "Hopefully no one will recognize the similarities."

"We broke a story early Friday morning involving an accident on Wednesday night." The anchor shifted to a different camera. "An SUV carrying two people ran into a bridge underpass. At the time we didn't have any names. The man has since died. Now St. Luke's Hospital is asking for the public's help in identifying this Jane Doe. She's in a coma and had no identification on her. Please call this number if you know this woman."

The screen flashed to a woman's face. Bandages covered her head. Her eyes were closed.

"I was in the ER when she came in." Sunee sat forward. "She must not have regained consciousness."

Harris stared at the screen. His mouth dropped open. Was that …? "Dr. Ashland?"

"Dr. A," Ashe said at the same time.

Harris jerked his head and stared at Ashe. "You know her?"

Ashe nodded. "You too?"

The doorbell rang. Had to be Kat.

"I'll get it," Sunee said.

Harris stood. *Get the facts. Don't jump to conclusions.* But here was a connection—maybe. "How do you know her?"

"I was part of a study she ran." Ashe's fingers beat a rhythm on the back of the couch. "Ever since I can remember, my mother would bring me to meet with her. She'd run tests and talk to me. We'd meet three or four times year."

"Me too." Harris pushed on his temples.

"Hi guys." Kat burst into the room and pulled to a stop. "Whoa. What's going on? Y'all look … panicked."

"We found a connection," Harris said. But what did it mean?

"Pull up the story we just watched from their website," Ashe said.

Harris grabbed his computer and set it on the coffee table. His fingers fumbled as he logged on and found the station's website. Sunee sat next to him. Ashe and Kat leaned over the back of the sofa as he found the Jane Doe story and hit play.

"I saw that story come in," Kat said after it finished. "Wasn't lucky enough to catch it."

"She's at St. Luke's." Sunee shook her head. "I was there when her ambulance arrived."

"Why is she significant?" Kat asked.

"We know who she is." Ashe waved between his body and Harris. "We *know* her."

Kat pulled out her phone. "Let me call it in."

"Wait." Harris held up his hand. "Dr. Ashland is somehow connected to Ashe and me."

Kat's eyes flared open. "Are you kidding me?"

"She called a couple of days ago to set up a meeting," Harris said. "She never returned my call."

"I had a message from her too." Ashe's finger rattled on his beer bottle. "She congratulated me on the trade to the Texans and left a message she would be in town and wanted to meet."

"Did you talk to her?" Sunee asked.

Ashe shook his head. "I left a message but didn't hear anything."

"Could she be part of the baby snatching ring?" Kat's gaze bounced between him and Ashe.

"I ... I can't believe that," Harris said.

"She was nice," Ashe protested.

"Then what was she doing?" Kat asked.

"I was in a long-term study," Harris said.

Ashe nodded. "Me too."

"My mother would bring me to a doctor's office." Harris shut the laptop cover. "Dr. Ashland examined and talked to me. Tested me. Watched me do things."

"What kind of doctor is she?" Sunee asked.

"I don't know," Ashe said. "But she did a lot of testing and exercises."

"Do you think it has something to do with you two?" Kat waved her hand between him and Ashe.

"We don't have enough information to draw a conclusion." Harris blew out a breath. "But it's the first connection we've found."

"What was the study name?" Sunee asked. "I'll find out what was reported."

"Something about nutrition and brain development? Or IQ?" Harris looked at Ashe. "Mom would just say we were seeing Dr. Ashland."

"I thought my mother said something about a longitudinal study of nutrition and muscle development?" Ashe's thumb beat against the sofa cushion.

"I should be able to find something on the research," Sunee said. "Maybe your parents got a copy of the study report?"

"I don't know," Harris said.

"How about your father, Ashe?" Sunee asked.

"He's moved three times since mother died." Ashe grimaced. "If it wasn't about football he wouldn't save it."

"He might." Sunee stroked his back, sympathy filling her eyes.

"I can ask." Ashe caught her hand and held it.

Harris hated the way she always comforted Ashe. And she never reached for him. But he'd set the ground rules. He needed to tell Ashe about him and Sunee before he started ripping their hands apart.

"Harris?" Sunee asked.

"Hmmm?"

"Ashe asked if you had a problem with him asking his father about the study?"

Could that information hurt anyone? "That's fine. When my mother gets back from DC, I'll ask her too."

"We're losing sight of what's important here," Kat said. "Dr. Ashland's family doesn't know she's in the hospital."

"Go ahead and call it in." Harris rubbed at the headache forming behind his eyes. "But don't connect the source to either Ashe or me."

"Got it." Kat was dialing the phone. "Name?"

He hoped this wouldn't blow up in their faces. "Dr. Elaina Ashland."

CHAPTER EIGHT

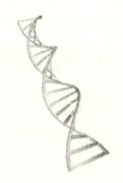

oston

Piper jerked at the sound of the doorbell. Had Mother forgotten her house key again?

She pushed away the last test runs. This newest manipulation looked promising. She hoped they'd found an enzyme that could reduce the loss of myelin in mice with multiple sclerosis. Lately their research had been one step forward and two steps back. Maybe this was a step forward.

At the door, she peeked out the sidelight.

A policewoman held up her badge.

Piper's hands shook as she unlocked the door. Police didn't come to their door—ever. "Has something happened?"

"I'm Officer Mulroney," the policewoman said. "Is this Dr. Elaina Ashland's house?"

"Yes." Piper swallowed, but the lump filled her throat.

"Are you related to Dr. Ashland?"

"I'm her daughter, Piper." She squeezed the words out through a thick throat. "Has something happened to my mother?"

Sympathy softened Officer Mulroney's face. "May I come in?"

Piper's head jerked up and down. Her fingers fumbled with the screen door latch. "It won't open."

"Take a deep breath, Ms. Ashland."

She did. Then finally pushed up the latch.

Officer Mulroney opened the door and stepped into the entry, looking around. "Why don't we sit down?"

"Did something happen to my mother?" Piper whispered.

"Let's talk. Is there anyone else here?"

Piper led her into the front parlor. "N-no. Just me."

They settled into the armchairs in front of the bay window. How many times had she and her mother sat here with cups of tea, talking. *Please let Mother be okay.*

"Ms. Ashland, your mother was in a car accident."

"My mother?" Piper shook. Cold. She was so cold. "Oh God, is she hurt? Is she dead?"

"No. She's alive," the officer said. "She's in the hospital."

Piper's breath whooshed out. "Thank goodness."

"I'm sorry. I should have said that first," the officer said. "She's alive, but she's in a coma."

Coma. "Where? Is this medically induced? Caused by trauma?"

"I don't have that level of detail." The officer looked at her phone. "But I was told she's at St. Luke's Hospital. In Houston."

"Houston. I've got to go." Piper stood. Black spots filled her vision and her legs gave out. "Oh."

The officer caught her before she collapsed and helped her back into the chair, easing Piper's head between her knees. "Is there someone I can call? Someone who can help you?"

There was only her and her mother. She ripped her hand through her hair, tugging out the band that held her ponytail. "Wait. Uncle Victor. Victor Giuseppe."

The officer called Victor and explained what had happened then grabbed a glass of water, and they waited for him to arrive.

Her mother was in a coma.

Uncle Vic rushed in and wrapped his arms around her. "Oh God, Piper. I can't believe this. Elaina."

She sobbed. Shared her pain with him.

The officer excused herself and left them in the entry.

"Grab some clothes." Uncle Vic set her away from his arms. "The plane is waiting. We'll call the hospital on our way to the airport."

"Sure." Mother had hated the corporate jet, but right now Piper was glad they had one. And why hadn't she called the hospital? She had to get her mind working again.

She ran up the stairs. Tripping on the top step, she grabbed the railing to keep from spilling down the stairs.

Mother.

She stuffed jeans, shirts and underwear in a weekend bag and threw her toothbrush and toothpaste on top of her clothes. Then she opened her makeup drawer and grabbed.

She looked around her bedroom. Sweater, in case the rooms were cold. Down in the study, she unplugged the power cord and shoved it and her computer into her briefcase.

Purse, wallet, clothes, computer. Phone.

She ran upstairs and found her phone charger.

"I'm ready," she gasped. She threw her purse and briefcase over her shoulder and grabbed her bag.

Victor held out his hand. "Give me your keys. I'll lock up."

She ran to the waiting limo. The driver took her bags and set them in the trunk. Uncle Vic came back and tucked her keys in her purse. "Let's go."

"Thank you." She swiped a tear away. She would not cry. Her mother would be fine. "Thank you."

"We have a car waiting for us in Houston."

"You're coming with me?" she sputtered through her tears.

"Absolutely." His voice cracked. "She can't leave us."

She clasped his hand. "What would Mother and I do without you?"

"I'll never forgive myself." A tear slipped down his cheeks.

"She'll be fine. She'll be fine." If she said the words enough times maybe they would come true.

HOUSTON

"The authorities have notified Dr. Ashland's family." Kat dropped her phone in her bag. "Did someone say something about dinner?"

Sunee tapped her forehead. "I ran across Elaina Ashland's name while I was scanning research articles on cloning and twins. I'll head to my lab and pull whatever she wrote."

Harris set a hand on her arm as she moved to the door. "Dinner first."

"Dinner?" This might be the puzzle piece that would solve the medical mystery that was Harris and Ashe. "I'll grab something … later."

"I'm starving." Ashe followed Kat to the kitchen. "Let's eat."

Sunee stared at the door. She wanted to find the paper she'd noticed but hadn't read. "I could get more work done."

Harris stepped close and set a finger under her chin. He whispered, "Don't go."

She stared into his eyes and got lost. Her lips were dry and she licked them.

Harris groaned. "You do that on purpose, don't you?"

"Let's eat," Ashe yelled from the kitchen.

"Do what?" she asked.

"Lick your lips. It makes me crazy thinking about what you taste like." Harris stroked his thumb over her bottom lip. "Feel like."

"It's not on purpose." But she smiled. Did she really drive him crazy? Her?

He turned her toward the hall and set a hand on her lower back, guiding her to the kitchen. "Dinner."

It didn't take long to pull the food out and be seated. Harris took the chair to her left, his foot resting next to hers.

"So, any theories on how this Dr. Ashland is connected to you?" Kat waved a rib between Ashe and Harris.

"I don't want to speculate," Harris said.

Ashe rapped the top of his beer bottle. "She wasn't the OB on either of our birth certificates."

"I've checked into the background of both the OBs for your mothers." Kat waved her rib around. "I didn't find any flags. One is deceased. One is retired."

"Maybe when I find the study report it will give us new information," Sunee said.

"I'll talk to my mother when she's back in Houston." Harris smiled at her, and under the table his foot slid against hers.

"I doubt Coach will have any information, but I'll try," Ashe said.

Did Kat and Harris catch the bitterness in Ashe's voice? Sunee heard it. Both she and Ashe had struggled with their dads' expectations of career choices. Her father was dedicated to his investment banking firm and Ashe's father to football. Both dads wanted their children to follow in their footsteps.

What if Ashe and Harris had been switched? Would Harris have become a football player and Ashe an attorney. *I wonder.*

"What do you wonder?" Harris asked.

She shook her head. "What?"

"You said 'I wonder,'" Harris said. "What are you wondering?"

"Nothing." She waved a hand.

Ashe stared at her. "Tell us."

"It's a nature versus nurture question," she admitted.

"Oh, I get it." Kat pointed between the two men. "Could Harris be a football player? Could Ashe be an attorney?"

Sunee nodded. "Yes."

Both men had identical shocked expressions on their faces.

She and Kat laughed.

"It would make a great study." Sunee gulped.

"We did take on our father's careers." Ashe peeled the label of his bottle away with his thumbnail. "I never thought about law school."

Harris tipped his head. "And I played high school soccer and ran track."

"I thought everyone in Texas played football," Ashe joked.

The conversation veered into a discussion of football and Texas. Sunee tuned it out. Was that why Harris and Ashe were studied? Nature versus nurture? What had the results shown? She couldn't wait to get her hands on the study.

Harris leaned close, his voice low in her ear. "Eat."

"Oh." She picked up a rib and bit. The barbecue sauce was sweet and tangy.

She even joined in the conversation, enjoying the fact she was with a group of people and hives weren't covering her chest and neck. Was this what it was like to have friends?

After they'd cleaned up the food and dishes, the men left the kitchen.

"There's a little prosecco left." Kat wiggled the bottle. "Let's finish this. Then I have to go home and sleep."

Sunee held up her glass. "Thank you."

"Does Ashe have a girlfriend?" Kat split the remains of the bottle between their glasses.

Kat was interested in Ashe? "I don't think so."

"No one back in Baltimore?" Kat tipped her glass to Sunee's. "Cheers."

"Not that he's told me." Sunee giggled, then covered her

mouth. "When he asked about getting a DNA test, I worried he'd gotten a groupie pregnant."

"There probably are lots of groupies." Kat shrugged. "Although I don't want him for the long-term. I'd just like to try his body on for size. Yum."

Sunee blinked. No one had ever been so—blatant about sex in front of her. Probably because she'd always been the youngest person in the room. "Wow."

Footsteps sounded in the hallway as the men returned to the kitchen. Sunee couldn't help smiling at Harris.

"I'm heading home." Kat tipped back her drink.

"I..." Sunee started.

"Do we want to meet again?" Ashe asked.

"Only if there's new information," Harris said. "And next week I'll be slammed."

Ashe nodded. "Keep me posted."

Everyone walked to the door and said goodnight.

"Are you coming?" Ashe asked Sunee.

"I forgot my bag in the kitchen."

"Okay." Ashe left, Kat close behind.

Harris closed the door. And smiled.

"I think Kat is attracted to Ashe," she murmured.

"That's an accident waiting to happen." Harris took both her hands.

"I'll go look for Dr. Ashland's papers," she said. But she let him tug her close.

"Not tonight." He took his time, brushing small kisses on the edge of her lips and circling her mouth until she clutched his head and pulled him close. Her tongue sought his.

He backed her against the door, kissing her deeply. Stealing her breath.

When he dropped his forehead to hers, their chests heaved in unison.

"Can you stay the night?" he gasped.

His words were the ice water to chill the heat he'd kindled inside her. This was too soon. Having sex was—serious. "I don't think that's a good idea."

He sighed, his chest pressing against her. "But it would be fun."

"I ... I'm not ready." But she was more tempted than she'd ever been. "I'm sorry."

"No apology needed." His gray gaze softened. "I'm attracted to you. I'd like to make love to you."

Sunee's breath caught in her chest. Now she wanted to solve Ashe and Harris's mystery. For Harris.

Her chest and neck tingled. And not the good kind. *Hives.*

She didn't want Harris to see them. Didn't want him to think less of her.

She eased away from him and opened the door. "I'd better go home."

Time to escape.

PIPER WOKE WITH A JUMP. Her heart pounded. Something horrible had happened. Something devastating.

Mother. Oh God. Mother was in a coma.

Uncle Victor sat across the aisle from her. He gave her a weak smile. "I talked to the hospital. There's no change on Elaina's condition. That's good."

Good? "Did they put her in a coma? Is there cerebral swelling?"

"They didn't say."

She'd never seen her godfather looking less than pristine. Now his wavy brown hair stood on end and his slacks looked like they'd been balled up in a corner for a week.

She'd always suspected Uncle Vic was in love with Mother, but Mom had treated him like a big brother. Her godfather brought his arm candy to family and work gatherings but rarely the same woman twice.

Another limo met them in Houston. She hurried down the steps of the plane, throwing her bags into the open trunk.

Thank goodness she wasn't required to think. All she had to do was sit and wait. And feel. She swallowed back tears. She couldn't imagine life without her mother. She couldn't imagine not hearing her calm voice in the kitchen, in the lab, or as they took a walk.

Please let her be all right.

Piper had already lost one parent, one she'd never known. She couldn't lose two. She didn't care if her pleas were selfish, she didn't want to be alone.

The limo pulled up to the hospital. She rushed to the reception desk, leaving Victor behind. "I'm looking for Elaina Ashland. I'm her daughter."

The young man barely looked. "It's three in the morning. You'll have to wait for visiting hours."

"No."

The man's head snapped up.

"I've just come from Boston. I will see my mother." Her voice cracked even though she wanted it to be strong.

Victor placed his hand on Piper's shoulder. "We got word she was in a car accident. Please let us see her."

"I'll ... get you to the nursing station, but it will be up to them whether you can see the patient." There was sympathy in his eyes when he typed in her mother's name and gave them her location. "Check in at the nursing station. Let them know your family."

The hallways were endless and the elevator slower than a glacier. They buzzed the nursing station from the locked door and waited until the lock was released.

Piper rushed to the desk. "I'm here for Elaina Ashland. I'm her daughter."

The woman nodded and checked a whiteboard behind her.

"I'll find her nurse. There's a waiting room," she pointed, "over there."

Why wouldn't anyone let her see her mother?

The woman went to a white board and jotted down "family" in a box.

She and Uncle Vic walked into the waiting room. The smell of coffee clashed with the burn of bleach. She picked up the pot and sniffed. Not too old. Uncle Vic stopped next to her. She held up the pot and he nodded.

After handing him a cup, she poured and added cream and sugar to dull the acid. Then she took her coffee and sat in an armchair.

"I've booked rooms in a nearby hotel," he said.

She nodded. She wouldn't be staying in a hotel until her mother was better.

The door pushed open and a slender woman wearing scrubs entered. "Are you Dr. Ashland's family?"

"Yes." Piper hurried to the woman's side. "Can I see her? Can I see my mom?"

"Absolutely. I'm Hannah, her nurse."

"What can you tell me?" Piper asked as they moved down the hall.

"Let me say first, I'm glad her family was found. Although I might have trouble breaking the habit of calling her Jane."

"Wait." Piper shook her head. "How long has she been here? When was the accident?"

Hannah checked her mother's information. "She came in through the ER early Wednesday morning."

"Wednesday?" Piper's knees caved in. "It's ... Saturday."

"Wednesday," Uncle Vic echoed. His hand cupped her elbow, holding her up.

"Actually honey, it's Sunday," Hannah said.

Her mother had been alone all this time. "Has she regained consciousness?"

"No." Hannah sized up Piper and then Uncle Victor. "Let's hope familiar voices help."

Piper clutched Victor's arm. Hannah held the door.

"Mom." She rushed to the bed.

Bandages covered a quarter of Mother's head and chin. At least her orbital sockets were undamaged. Her right arm and leg were immobilized. Two IVs were installed in her arm and a port was taped to her hand. A chest port drained pink fluids into a bag.

"Mom, I'm here." She took her mother's uninjured hand and gently squeezed it. "I would have been here sooner if I'd known."

Uncle Victor stepped next to the hospital bed and laid his hand on her leg. "Elaina."

Hannah carried a chair closer to the bed. "Here," she said.

Piper sat. "What happened?"

Hannah walked them through her mother's arrival in the ER and her surgery.

"She had neurosurgery and they removed her spleen?" Piper asked.

"Yes. And she has a broken arm and leg," Hannah said.

"How?" Piper whispered. "How did this happen?"

"I don't know." Hannah checked the chart. "Now that you're here, the police will want to talk to you."

"The police?" Victor swallowed, his eyes wide. "Was she alone in the car?"

The nurse shook her head. "I don't know."

"Did someone cause this accident?" Piper asked.

Hannah patted her arm. "That's another question for the police."

The cause of the accident wasn't important. Having her mother regain consciousness was.

"I'll check in at the hotel and drop our luggage off." Lines etched Victor's face. Lines that hadn't been there the last time he'd come into the lab.

"Go ahead." She wasn't leaving her mother. "I'm staying here."

Boston

"Report," Mark Dell barked out as Simon entered his office on Tuesday afternoon.

"The operative who picked up Dr. Ashland is dead." Simon's voice didn't vary at all. It was like his genetic modification had eliminated all emotions.

"What?" Mark pushed away from his desk.

"There was a car accident early Wednesday morning. Our man died without regaining consciousness. Dr. Ashland somehow dialed 9-1-1, but the recordings are incoherent."

"Damn it." Mark moved to the window but couldn't focus on the view. "Dr. Ashland?"

"Still in the hospital. She wasn't identified until last weekend." Simon kept staring at the tablet in his hand. "As far as we know, she hasn't regained consciousness."

"At least she didn't meet with Torrington or Bristol." Mark rested his fists against the windowsill. "Is there anything new on them?"

"Based on facial matching of Ashe Bristol and Harris Torrington, and Giuseppe's belief, we think Dr. Ashland used one zygote in her experiments."

"She cloned it?"

"Maybe. Or split the zygote. We suspect the modified zygotes were hers and her husband's. The men's birthdates are over a year after the death of her husband."

"If Torrington and Bristol run into each other, it might lead them to question how they came into being." Mark's jaw ached from clenching his teeth.

"We don't need anyone questioning our right to genetic editing," Simon said.

"No one can find out what we're doing," Mark said. "Ashland has put everything in jeopardy."

What would global leaders think if they discovered the Foundation had created designer children through genetic manipulation? The children, loyal to Mendel, were poised to step into key positions throughout the US. Even now, their global program participants were hitting their teenage years. His bosses wouldn't tolerate a hint of exposure.

"We have information regarding Torrington and Bristol," Simon said.

"Yes?"

"The operatives watching Torrington and Bristol haven't seen them together in public. But Bristol has been spotted driving into Torrington's development. That could be a coincidence. They haven't been able to get close enough to Torrington's house to determine if they've actually met. The surveillance team red-flagged two other possible people of interest from all the cars entering Torrington's development, a reporter and a doctor." Simon scrolled through something on his tablet. "Katrina Phillips and Dr. Sunee Miller."

Mark inhaled. "I don't like the fact there's a reporter involved."

"According to her social media accounts, she and Torrington have been friends most of their lives."

"I still don't like it." Mark frowned. "Should I worry about a doctor?"

"Dr. Miller is a pediatric oncologist *and* a geneticist. She met Bristol in college."

"A geneticist?" Mark swore. How much did they know?

"Orders, sir?" Simon asked.

"Put Miller under surveillance." Mark exhaled. "We need to know what she's uncovered."

Simon nodded.

"We need eyes on Dr. Ashland too. Who has medical training?" Mark asked.

Simon typed on his tablet. "David Lassiter. He trained at Johns Hopkins. The plan is to have him eventually at Walter Reed."

"We need him on site in Houston."

"Understood." Simon nodded.

Mark turned. "Dr. Ashland must not wake up."

CHAPTER NINE

Houston

Friday night there was a knock on Sunee's door. She took a breath and smoothed her dress. Her chest itched. At least the dress had a high collar that would cover any hives if they erupted.

When she opened the door, Harris's eyes lit up. "You're gorgeous."

"Is it too much? It's too much." The red dress covered her from her neck to her knees. It had red embroidery on it and black edging that followed the buttons down the front of the dress. "I should change."

She turned to head back to her bedroom.

"Don't!" Harris caught her hand and pulled her close. "You're beautiful."

"The dress is okay? Kat picked it out. Apparently, she knew the designer." She was babbling.

"It's perfect." Pulling her up on her toes, he kissed her.

She sighed against his lips and let him in, her tongue stroking his.

"I missed seeing you this week. Talking on the phone wasn't enough." He changed the angle, plunging deep.

"I love our calls." They were the highlight of her day and had brought them closer.

She clung to his shoulders, her heartbeat thumping in her ears.

As Harris kissed her, he stroked from her waist up to her breast. Her nipple pebbled beneath his palm.

When he rested his forehead against hers, his breath puffed out in short pants. "If we don't stop, we might not make it to my mother's party."

"I wouldn't mind." It would save her from meeting strangers and she was ready. After almost a week of phone calls, she wanted to take their relationship to the next level.

Bending, he brushed his lips against hers. "Are we on the same page? Are we … maybe you …" His eyes closed and he blew out a breath. "I want to make love to you."

Joy sparkled through her body. "We're on the same page."

He touched her cheek. "Would you come home with me after the party?"

The party. Reality hit. She panicked in groups.

"Sunee?" His eyebrows pinched together.

"No. I mean yes. I'd love to come home with you." She shook her head. "I'm nervous about this party."

"Don't be." He gave her a swift kiss. "Are you ready?"

"Let me get my shawl." She turned toward the mirror and gasped. "My hair!"

She rushed to the bathroom, pulling out the combs holding her hair back. She brushed and replaced her mother's cloisonné combs.

Back in the entry, she grabbed a light shawl and a small purse. "Keep your hands out of my hair, Mr. Torrington."

"Absolutely, Dr. Miller." He held open the door.

She headed down the hallway to the stairs, but Harris wasn't moving.

"Keys?" he asked.

"Why?"

"To lock the deadbolt."

"I forgot." She dug them out of her clutch.

"You can't forget." He took her keys and locked up. "There's no security in your apartment building."

She grimaced. "It was the first place I looked at, and it's close to the hospital."

"Remember to lock the deadbolt." He helped her into his Tahoe and then hurried around to the driver's seat. "I wouldn't want anything to happen to you."

"I will." She popped out an antihistamine.

"Are you okay?" He glanced at the pills while he started the car. "Do you have a headache?"

"No." She dry swallowed one pill. A half dose. Hopefully it would be enough tonight. "Did I tell you I'm terrible in group settings?"

He turned into the street. "Hmmm?"

"I … I'm …"

He took her hand again. "What?"

She took a deep breath. "I get anxious meeting new people. Being in social settings. Sometimes I break out in hives."

"You do?" Was that horror in his voice?

"I'll try not to embarrass you." Her face burned. "I'm hoping my antihistamine will help."

"Sunee." He squeezed her fingers. "You would never embarrass me. You'll be fine."

But his hand slid back to the steering wheel.

She had a history of embarrassing her father and grandmother. She didn't want Harris to look at her with disgust if hives broke out. "I'll try."

"Let me know if you have problems. It might give us an excuse to leave." Harris didn't say much more as they drove to his parents' house, but he linked their fingers together as they walked up the steps.

"Your parents' home is beautiful," she said.

It looked like an Italian estate including loose stone paths crisscrossing the yard. A massive light hung between giant stone arches. Huge black lacquered double doors loomed in front of them. Two-story widows bordered the doors.

She'd grown up in a New York City penthouse. She was used to wealth, but not land. To her father, wealth meant living above everyone, the higher in the air, the better. Sometimes living in Texas made her feel ungrounded. Reverse claustrophobia.

"You grew up here?" Her voice quivered a little.

"We moved here when I was seven. My mother fell in love with this house. She's pure Texan and she falls for an Italian-looking estate. Almost broke the senator's heart. He wanted to expand his family's ranch house, but Mom wanted to move into the city. Although this place has stables."

Stables? Texas was a foreign country compared to New York City.

At the door she drew in a deep breath, rolled her neck and shook out her hands.

"Hey, don't worry." Harris took her shoulders. "Be yourself. You'll be fine."

He didn't understand her anxiety. "I'll try."

"Your hands are shaking." He frowned.

She started to take a deep breath, but he kissed her. "Don't mess up my hair," she murmured as he pulled her closer.

"Harris Theodore Torrington, it is about time you arrived. Any later and we would not have any quiet time before the storm. Let that woman go and come in."

The woman in the doorway looked perfect. Blonde hair

curled around her face. Her gray dress shimmered silver and matched her awesome shoes. Harris's mother must be almost six feet tall.

The flaming blush that had started in the car re-bloomed. Harris's mother had caught them kissing. Not a great first impression.

"Mom." Harris released Sunee's shoulders and kissed his mother's cheek. "You're beautiful as always."

He laced his fingers with Sunee's and escorted her into the house. Taupe plaster molding topped the cream-colored entry walls. The crown molding was spectacular. The room opened up to a curving staircase with a stunning wrought iron railing. The space even had a loveseat. Useful if she fainted from embarrassment.

"Mom, I'd like you to meet Dr. Sunee Miller. Sunee, this is my mother, the indomitable Leah Torrington. Don't let her sweet tone fool you. She has the sharpest mind and tongue in Texas and the Beltway."

"It's a p-pleasure to meet you, Mrs. Torrington." Sunee winced at her stutter.

"Ignore this rascal and call me Leah."

Leah pulled her away from Harris and tucked her arm in hers. To Harris she said, "I thought Kat was coming with you."

"She's working tonight," Sunee said.

"You know Kat?"

Sunee nodded.

"I'm glad you're here." Leah's eyes sparkled when she smiled. "How did you meet?"

"Mom." Harris walked right behind them. "Don't scare her away."

His mother tossed over her shoulder, "Maybe we'll have lunch."

Sunee's head spun. "Oh, sure."

They entered a large room. The color scheme changed to cream, taupe, and dark random width wood floors. A stunning marble fireplace was the focal point. Windows flanked the fireplace and looked out at a lighted fountain. Beyond the fountain were a patio and pool.

Sofas and large armchairs created a conversation area at the far side of the room. Sunee's apartment could fit in this room and not fill it.

She and Harris sat on a cream colored sofa while his mother took an armchair across from them.

"You're a doctor," Leah said.

"Yes." She wanted to scratch her neck. *Please let the antihistamine kick in.* "I also do research."

"Lovely." She looked over at Harris. "Your father's in his study. Why don't you say hello."

"I'm staying to protect Sunee."

Leah narrowed her eyes. "Then make yourself useful and get us a couple of glasses of prosecco."

He headed to the bar. A cork popped. "Would you like something other than that, Sunee?"

"Prosecco is perfect." She would allow herself one drink during the party. Maybe the prosecco was a sign her mother would watch over and keep her calm.

Harris handed them flutes bubbling with golden wine, and he sat next to Sunee.

"We've hardly spoken for two weeks," Leah said to Harris.

"I've been busy." Harris leaned forward. "I have a question."

"Yes?" Leah asked.

"Do you remember that study I was in? The one with Dr. Ashland?" Harris asked.

"Of course." Leah smiled.

"Did you ever get the results or a report from it?"

"I don't think so." Leah frowned. "I haven't thought about that for years."

Sunee set her drink down on the coffee table. "Harris mentioned the study to me. I was intrigued. But I can't find a published research paper. I was hoping you might have a copy."

"I never asked. The study ended right around an election." Leah shook her head. "Participation in the study was one of many stipulations from the IVF clinic."

"IVF clinic?" Harris sat up straight. "What's that?"

"In vitro fertilization," his mother explained, smoothing out her skirt even though it was perfect.

"You went through ..." Harris looked stunned.

Leah's voice got softer. "It was our last chance. Our only chance to have you."

"In vitro," Sunee said, twirling her hair. This explained Harris and Ashe's different birthdates.

"I didn't have any idea." Harris sounded stunned. "You never said anything."

"Those were tough times." Leah shook her head. "I decided to concentrate on having you. Not on *how* you came to be."

Sunee wondered if Harris knew his hands were in fists.

"We tried everything, but I couldn't conceive." Leah's eyes closed. "Actually, they implanted a donor embryo."

"A donor?" Harris sank into the sofa.

Sunee wanted to comfort him, but his mother had already caught the kissing.

"We tried so hard." A sad smile crossed Leah's face. "I don't care if it was a donor embryo. You've always been my child. Our child."

"Do you know who the donors were?" Sunee asked.

"No, they were anonymous. I was just so thankful to finally be pregnant."

Harris went over and hugged Leah. "I'm lucky you're my mother."

Leah wrapped her arms around him. "I'm glad you're my son."

Sunee should give them a minute, but she didn't know where to go.

"I love you, Mom," Harris whispered.

Leah's eyes filled with tears as Harris squeezed her one more time and sat back on the sofa. His genetic relationship with Ashe made a little more sense, except they weren't twins and were closer than siblings.

Sunee clutched Harris's arm. "That explains some of the similarities."

"Similarities?" Leah asked.

Relief softened Harris's face. "But not all?"

Sunee shook her head. "No."

"What are you talking about?" Leah asked, her voice sharp.

"Do you know *anything* about the donors?" Harris asked.

"Only their health histories, traits and IQs." Leah's gaze bounced between her and Harris. "What's going on?"

"Has my son shown up?" a deep voice called from the hallway.

Leah grinned and turned to the archway. She lit up like a Christmas tree hearing her husband's voice.

Sunee sighed. It had been the same with her parents. Now when her father looked at pictures of her mother, a sheen of sadness swept over him.

"What's wrong?" Harris asked.

How had he noticed? People rarely read her face. "Please cherish your parents. You never know how long you'll have together."

Maybe that was why she'd never rejected her father's idea of working for his firm. She hated the concept, but how many more years would she have with her father and Po Po?

The senator perched on the arm of Leah's chair. Luckily it was large and sturdy. He must have stood six-foot two or three, shorter than Harris, but he was big-boned. Even with his shock of thick silver hair and perfectly tailored suit, the man looked like he should be wearing a cowboy hat and jeans. He reached out and a big hand engulfed hers. His light blue eyes twinkled as he smiled.

"Dad, this is Dr. Sunee Miller. Sunee, my father, Ted Torrington."

"It's a pleasure to meet you, Senator," Sunee said.

"Ted. The pleasure is all mine." She could almost hear *little lady* in her head as he talked. He even looked a little like John Wayne.

Based on the height and eye color, people wouldn't question Harris's parentage. Harris's eyes were grayer than his parents. And it was possible the black hair came from his father, but you couldn't tell when the man had silver hair. His mother was blonde, but who knew if her perfect platinum color was original.

"You said something about similarities?" Leah asked.

Sunee waited for Harris to sum up what they knew. It was his specialty.

The doorbell rang.

"Drat." Leah looked at her diamond watch. "People are actually on time."

Harris stiffened. "We can't talk about this right now."

Leah's questioning gaze skimmed Harris and then her. "After the party?"

Harris nodded.

Two couples entered the room.

"Showtime," Leah whispered.

The family stood and Sunee followed a beat later. Her breath accelerated. Her neck itched.

I can't embarrass Harris.

Harris whispered in her ear, "Don't let the fear show."

He looked as smooth and clever as a rising politician should.

She wouldn't shame him by having an anxiety attack. She straightened and held her head high. This dinner was important to Harris.

But the itch on her chest grew. Pulling another antihistamine from her purse, she took the pill with a sip of prosecco. Let that keep the hives from showing.

"Relax," Harris whispered, alarmed by Sunee's anxiety.

The terror filling her gaze eased a little. "I'm trying."

"I could kiss you," he suggested.

Her jade eyes flared open and her hand flew to her hair. "No."

"Kidding," he said and dug deep for a smile. Tonight was filled with too many surprises. He was still reeling from the news he'd been a *test-tube* baby. At least that was what he assumed. He didn't feel any less attached to his parents, but it was ... strange.

At least his parents hadn't adopted him through a black market baby ring. The worry that had kept him awake at night lifted. There was still the mystery of how he and Ashe were related, but his ancestry wasn't a barrier to running for governor.

Now if he could get Sunee to relax, everything would be great. Unfortunately, she was so stiff it was as if *she* were on trial.

From the first time she'd mistaken him for Ashe and hugged him, he'd thought she was beautiful. In her red dress with her black hair held away from her face, she took his breath away. Having her by his side for a campaign was everything he wanted.

But her reaction to this party was disturbing.

"Sunee, I'd like to introduce you to someone." Mother pulled her away and moved across the room.

Sunee glanced back at him. Should he follow?

"Harris." There was a tap on his shoulder.

He turned. Grinning, he shook the man's hand. "Gary, how are you? How's retirement?"

"Boring."

Gary Simons was a political genius. He'd run his father's many senatorial campaigns but had retired this last year.

"I'm wondering why people call them the golden years after

you retire." The ice in Gary's drink rattled as he took a sip. "Hitting sixty-five hits back. Now everything hurts."

"It's your life of debauchery catching up with you," Harris said.

"Ahhh, the memories." Gary nodded at Sunee. "She with you?"

Harris nodded and sipped his club soda.

"Much better for your image than the reporter you always bring around." Gary's voice grew serious. "Tell me about her."

"Dr. Sunee Miller." Harris hated that Gary's question wasn't casual. "She's a pediatric oncologist and geneticist and works at MD Anderson."

"Wow. Brains and beauty," Gary said. "Is she from here?"

"New York."

"New York? Miller?" Gary frowned. "Who are her parents?"

"I don't know."

Gary gave a sharp nod. "I'll find out."

Harris's nostrils flared. "Sunee doesn't need to be vetted."

Gary clapped a hand on his shoulder. "Everyone you associate with impacts your political career. Remember, *you* chose this life."

"I did." Harris had a reason. He wanted to heal the divisiveness permeating politics. Show people there was a better way to get things done.

"I had an interesting conversation with your mother last week."

Of course his mother had talked to Gary. "Yes?"

"Are you sure you want to take such a big political step?"

"Absolutely," Harris said, his voice soft but firm.

Gary nodded over at Sunee. "How serious is this?"

"I don't know."

Sunee glanced over and a hesitant smile broke over her face. Harris grinned back at her.

Gary chuckled. "I can work with that kind of chemistry."

The words sunk in. Warmth blossomed in his chest. "Are you thinking of coming out of retirement?"

"Only if you run," Gary said. "You have a sound bite grabbing murder trial to put you into the forefront of the voters' thoughts. Trial couldn't have come at a better time."

"Kind of Mrs. Barney to kill her husband and further my career."

Gary clapped him on his back. "Let me work the room. Behave like a candidate. And let people see you and your pretty little girlfriend together."

He didn't need Gary's encouragement. He nodded, stopped and said a few words to people as he moved across the room. But the conversations were short.

Finally he stood next to Sunee. He didn't put his arm around her shoulders because it might get him votes. He did it for himself. Because he wanted to touch her. And he wanted every man in the room looking at Sunee, to know she was his date.

"Harris," Sunee said. "This is Leonard Gilbert. His company has done fascinating studies on gene suppression. He's offered to let me look at his research."

"Your work is fascinating too," Leonard said.

"I'll get that confidentiality agreement back to you as soon as I can," Sunee said.

"Your interest in clinical trials would be invaluable," Leonard replied.

Her eyes were shining. Excitement shimmered off her like light off the Hope Diamond. Harris leaned down. "Are you having fun?"

She smiled up at him. "Yes."

And she didn't look nervous. Excellent.

Leonard and Sunee talked shop. Usually he understood something about the topics people chose to discuss at a cocktail party. But these two were talking about genomes, splicing and germ lines. He didn't have a clue and he didn't care. Sunee didn't look worried or nervous. She looked enthralled.

Harris should make another pass around the room. But he wasn't leaving Sunee with a man who made her eyes light up.

His mother did a little hand wave. "Dinner is ready."

He and Sunee followed everyone into the glittering dining room. Light from the chandeliers reflected off the crystal wine glasses and cut glass candelabras.

He and Sunee ended up across the table from each other. Sunee sat between a tech company owner and an oil man. The table was too wide for him to hear what her seatmates were saying, but he didn't like the way she tugged on the neck of her dress.

One of the men said something to her, but instead of answering, Sunee's skin went pale. She stared at her salad. The other man turned and talked to her. She nodded but didn't open her mouth.

What was wrong? She'd done so well talking to Leonard. Harris wanted to move around the table and change places.

His mother sat at the foot of the table. She smiled and her gaze circled the table and came to rest on Sunee staring at her plate. The men sitting on both sides of her were talking over her head.

His mother's smile slipped. She glanced at Harris and flicked her head at Sunee.

He was too far away to rescue her.

"I hear the Barney trial will start soon," Meredith Molitor said, sitting at his right hand. She was one of his mother's oldest friends, an oil heiress and a campaign supporter of his father's.

"We're prepping for pretrial motions." He smiled at Meredith but kept his eyes on Sunee.

"How long will that take?" Meredith asked.

He answered, keeping it succinct. Pleasant. But he couldn't take his eyes off Sunee. Her eyes locked with his. There was agony there. Like the stray dog he'd once found with a broken leg.

And he couldn't do a damn thing.

Sunee tugged at her collar. A welt itched right under the neckline. *When would dinner end?*

The men next to her ignored her, and with good reason. She'd been unable to answer their questions, much less carry on a conversation.

Harris stared at her. Again. Then he glanced at his mother, who was frowning.

She picked up her fork and pushed around the roast. It was probably delicious, but her throat was so tight she couldn't swallow. If she ate anything, it might come back up.

Why couldn't she be like her mother? Sunee had watched from the stairs as her mother had charmed everyone at her parents' many parties. She'd been Keesha, a model so big she'd only needed one name. If she couldn't have inherited her mother's height, she sure wished she'd inherited her mother's confidence.

A cell phone rang. Then rang again. Someone whispered, "How rude."

Sunee clapped a hand over her mouth. It was her hospital phone. She pushed away from the table, her purse in her hand. "I'm so sorry."

She moved into the hallway, turning her back on the dining room. "Hello?"

"It's Marcus."

He rarely called her. "Is everything all right?"

"The lab was broken into."

"What?"

"Earlier tonight. It's a mess." Marcus's voice cracked. There were sounds in the background, hospital sounds.

"Were you there?"

"I walked in on them."

She clutched her chest. "Are you all right?"

"They knocked me out."

Harris came up and stood next to her, his arms crossed over his chest.

"Oh Marcus. Are you still at the hospital?" she asked.

"Yeah."

"I'm on my way."

"I can handle the cops."

"No arguing. I'll be there as soon as I can." She hung up.

"Is it one of your patients?" Harris asked.

"My grad student. Someone broke into my lab." She shook her head. "Why would anyone break into my lab? There's no drugs. There's nothing worth stealing."

He took her hand. "What can I do?"

"I need to get to the hospital." Her voice quivered. "I'll…get a car."

"You're not going by yourself," he said. "I'll come with you."

"This party is for your career." She swiped her password on her phone. "You need to stay."

He took her phone out of her hand. "I'm coming with you."

"But your mother already thinks I'm a freak." She pulled in a deep breath. "She'll hate me."

"No, she won't." He stroked his hand down her arm. "You're not facing a break-in alone."

Her shoulders softened. "Thank you."

He stroked her cheek. "Wait here."

From the archway, she watched him lean down and whisper to his mother.

Leah shot a glance at Sunee, her face stern. She whispered something back, but he shook his head and rejoined Sunee.

In the dining room, Leah announced, "My son's friend is a doctor. There's an ... emergency."

Harris took Sunee's elbow and guided her out of the house, helping her into the car.

"What did your mother say?" she asked.

"It doesn't matter." Harris clenched his jaw.

Obviously, it did. She'd never seen his face so—harsh.

"Tell me what happened." Harris steered the SUV toward downtown.

"Marcus sometimes works in the evening. Tonight there was someone in the lab. They knocked him out." Sunee rubbed her forehead. "I do cancer research. What did thieves think they could steal?"

"Were other labs broken into?"

"I didn't ask." Sunee looked over at him.

He took her hand. "We'll find out soon enough."

At the medical center, she said, "Thank you for the ride. You can drop me off. I'll get a ride home. Then you can return to the party."

"No." He didn't argue. He just parked in the visitor's lot.

She blinked. "You're such a good person."

When they arrived at her lab, a security guard blocked the hallway. His nametag read James.

"Hi, James," Harris said before she could even formulate a greeting. "Have the police already been through here?"

"They're still in the lab." James set his hand on the butt of his gun.

"Who's the investigating officer?" Harris asked.

"Who are you?" James asked.

"I'm Dr. Miller. This is my lab." Sunee dug her ID from her purse. "And this is District Attorney, Harris Torrington."

James frowned. "Can I see ID, sir?"

Harris pulled out an official looking badge and handed it to the guard.

James looked and handed it back. "Has anyone told you, you look like the Texan's new quarterback?"

Harris's smile was forced. "Someone mentioned that."

James walked them to the open lab door. "Detective Lucinda Cruz's in charge."

It looked as if a mini-tornado had trashed the room. Paper covered every surface. File cases were tipped over. Broken glass glistened in the light. The massive microscope lay sprawled on its side. Black powder covered the counters and remaining equipment.

"Oh no!" Sunee clapped a hand over her mouth.

"Thank goodness you weren't here," Harris whispered.

A woman with a badge attached to the belt of her dark pants glanced over. Glass crunched under her shoes as she met them at the door. "Can I help you?"

"This is my lab," Sunee gasped.

The detective stared at Harris.

He flipped out his badge again. "DA Torrington."

"I'm Detective Cruz," the woman said.

Her lab! Sunee pushed through debris.

"Wait!" Harris grabbed her arm. "Those sandals won't protect you from the glass."

"Oh." She pushed back her hair and a comb slipped out. "I have shoes in my desk."

She pointed at the tipped over partitions. The contents of her desk and file cases were scattered on the floor.

He picked up her comb. "If it's okay with Detective Cruz, I'll find them."

"Go ahead," Cruz said. "We're almost done here."

Sunee tapped her foot as glass crunched under Harris's shoes.

He tugged a clog out from under the partition and found the other wedged behind a tipped file cabinet. On his way back to the door, he pulled a paper towel from the dispenser and cleaned them out. "Make sure I got all the glass."

She shook, then swiped with the paper towel. Holding onto Harris, she slipped off her sandals and stepped into her clogs.

The second they were on her feet, her world righted. This was her. Clogs and her lab, not heeled sandals and cocktail parties.

"Why did someone break in?" Sunee asked the detective.

Before Detective Cruz could answer, Marcus stopped in the doorway. A bandage covered the side of his head. James stood behind him.

Sunee ran to him. "How are you?"

"A couple of stitches and I've got a headache." Marcus took a shaky breath. "But the ER doc says there's no cracked skull."

"Oh Marcus." Sunee stared into his eyes. "Are you on a concussion protocol?"

"Yeah." Marcus rolled his eyes and winced again.

"Could you get a chair?" Sunee asked the officers.

A cop pulled one from the mess and wheeled it to the open doorway.

"Sit," Sunee said.

"What happened?" Harris asked.

"Are you a cop?" Marcus asked.

"This is District Attorney Torrington," Sunee said.

"Hang on." Detective Cruz introduced herself, pulled out a tape recorder and dictated the details, then said, "Go ahead. Tell me what happened."

"I came in to prep the slides you wanted for Monday. The lights were still on. I thought maybe you hadn't gone to that mucky-muck dinner party." Marcus looked at Sunee and then Harris. His mouth dropped open, then snapped shut. "Whoops."

Sunee squeezed Harris's hand.

"Don't worry," Harris assured Marcus. "I sometimes think about my parents' friends that way too."

Marcus shrugged and pain crossed his face.

Sunee asked, "Did the ER clear you to leave?"

He gave her a sheepish grin. "I told them I needed to talk to you."

"Marcus." Sunee patted his arm.

"What happened next?" Lucinda asked.

"I opened the door and ... a guy was going through the files." He waved his hands at the cases along the wall. "Someone clocked me. I came to on the floor. They were gone."

"How many people?" Harris asked.

"Two?" Marcus scratched his head. "I can't be sure. I saw a blur of black or brown."

"Face or clothes?" Cruz asked.

"I don't think I saw faces or clothes. One guy had blondish-brown hair, lighter than yours," he said.

Harris pointed to his black hair and Marcus nodded and then winced.

Sunee turned to James. "Were any other labs broken into?"

"As far as we know, only this one," James said.

"What time did everything occur?" Harris asked.

"I got here at six," Marcus said.

"Have you checked the security records?" Sunee asked James. "Access is recorded, right?"

"We're checking," James said. "But something happened with the security computer a little before six."

Sunee looked at Harris. "What?"

James nodded. "All the access codes were activated at the same time."

"Someone hacked your security system?" Harris asked.

"The manufacturer and tech specialists are trying to figure out what happened." James blew out a breath. "Our first concern was securing the narcotic cabinets. We didn't get the word on this break-in until Marcus showed up in the ER."

"Do you have video surveillance in here?" Detective Cruz glanced around the room.

"Hallways only," James said.

"Is someone reviewing the tapes?" Harris asked.

"Chatter on my radio is the cameras covering the lab hallways malfunctioned around six o'clock tonight, the same time the security system malfunctioned," James said.

"We're getting copies of the recordings," Detective Cruz said.

"Someone planned this?" Sunee squeezed Harris's hand.

"What did they get?" Harris asked.

Sunee and Marcus looked around the room.

"I'll need Dr. Miller to tell me that," Detective Cruz said. "Looks like we're done here. I'll need fingerprints of you and your assistant and anyone else who frequents this room."

"Of course," Sunee said.

An officer took their prints.

"Marcus should be resting," Sunee said to Detective Cruz.

"I want to help," Marcus said.

"You're going home." Sunee softened the order by squeezing his shoulders.

"I can help," Marcus said.

"No. You're injured," Sunee said. "Do you have someone to check on you?"

Marcus nodded. "My roommate."

"James, please have someone from security take Marcus home," Sunee said. "He can't drive right now."

James grimaced but nodded his head.

"And have someone drive Marcus's car to his apartment," Sunee said.

"Dr. Miller," James said. "We need to leave *some* security at the hospital."

"My roommate's girlfriend will pick up my car," Marcus said.

"Okay." Sunee looked at Detective Cruz. "I'd like to clean up and figure out if anything is missing."

Detective Cruz nodded.

Sunee cleared a spot on the counter for her purse.

The detective handed out business cards and a case number to Sunee, James and Marcus. "Let me know what you find."

Everyone left the room.

"You don't have to stay," she said to Harris.

He ran his thumb along her cheek. "I'm staying."

Relieved, she scanned the room. "Let's see what they took."

HARRIS STRIPPED off his suit coat. He wasn't leaving her alone to deal with this mess. Plus he liked how in charge she was. So different from earlier at the party. "What should I do?"

Sunee wrapped her hair in a bun and stuck pencils in it. She pulled a lab coat over her dress. "If you could gather the papers, I'll find cleaning supplies."

The woman who'd been out of place at his parent's dinner table was in control, and it was—exciting. Too bad she couldn't channel her in-charge behavior into small talk. Then Mom wouldn't have been so disappointed. When he'd told her he and Sunee needed to leave the party, she'd whispered, "She could damage your career."

His mother was probably right. He needed someone who could handle the pressure of the media and fundraising.

That apparently wasn't Sunee.

He gritted his teeth. The problem of Sunee and his career wouldn't be solved tonight.

He started in the corner, working around the broken glass and shoving shards into small piles.

Sunee returned with cleaning supplies.

Even though it was a bad situation, Harris enjoyed working side by side with her. "Were Ashe and my DNA results in your office?"

"The only copies of the report are at your house." She swept the section of floor he'd cleared. "The samples are at the lab. But the paperwork is in code."

"Maybe they didn't find what they were looking for," he said quietly.

Her broom clattered to the floor. "Do you think this has something to do with you and Ashe?"

"I don't know. Now that we know my mother was impregnated through an in vitro clinic, it doesn't make sense." He tipped his head. "Maybe it was drug seekers?"

"Why would anyone break into a research lab?" Sunee chewed on her lip. "And if it was drug seekers, why would they trash everything?"

"I wish I knew." He set down the stack of papers and wrapped his arms around her.

She burrowed into his chest. The tension that had tightened his body since she'd sat across from him at dinner, eased. Peace settled over him. Sunee was safe.

"Let's see what the police find," he said. "Maybe they'll get something off the videotapes."

They cleared the floor of broken beakers and slides. Finally they could walk around the lab without crunching.

If this attack on Sunee was because of the genetic testing she'd done for them, he couldn't drop her off at her apartment and leave her alone. "It's midnight. How about we call it a night?"

She looked around her lab. "You're right. I'll spend the weekend reorganizing and figuring out what equipment needs replacing. I hope the scope is okay."

The microscope was dented, but nothing looked twisted or broken. He muscled it upright.

Sunee called the security department. "I'm leaving my lab."

On the way to the parking lot Harris took her hand. "You shouldn't be alone tonight."

"I know we talked about me going home with you, but we're both tired." She slipped into the passenger seat.

"We don't know who broke into your lab." His fingers clenched into fists. No one would hurt Sunee. Not on his watch. "Until they catch whoever broke in, you shouldn't be alone."

He didn't care if she stayed in the guest room, but he wanted to wake up and eat breakfast with her. He wanted to spend the day with her and if he was lucky, he wanted to make love to her.

"Just tonight, right?" she asked. Her body language didn't give him any hint what she was thinking. Maybe she'd changed her mind about wanting to be with him. Before the party, they'd been on the same page of wanting to sleep together. Now? He couldn't read her.

"Not just for the night." He put the car in gear. "Until the cops figure out who broke into your lab, I want you to stay at my house."

CHAPTER TEN

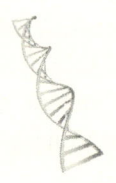

"I don't need to stay with you." Sunee set her hand on his arm.

"I'm not leaving you alone," Harris said.

"We could stay at my apartment."

"My house." Harris backed his Tahoe out of the hospital parking lot, and her hand slid off his sleeve. "I live in a gated community with a guard. Plus I have a security system."

"But …" It was tough to argue security when her apartment didn't have any.

"I have plenty of bedrooms."

"Oh." She swallowed.

He'd obviously changed his mind. She'd been an embarrassment at his mother's party, he was no longer interested in her sexually. Sure, he'd hugged her, but only after she'd launched herself into his arms.

He hadn't kissed her since before the party.

"Should we swing by your apartment and pick anything up?" he asked.

"Do you have an extra toothbrush?"

"You bet."

A twinge of jealousy curled in her belly. Did he store extra toothbrushes because he invited women to his home often? She wrapped her arms around her chest.

"Are you cold?"

"Yes." But it wasn't the temperature in the car. He was pulling away from her, and she still wanted to sleep with him.

He turned down the air conditioning. "You should have said something."

Silence settled around them. She closed her eyes, wishing she could sink into the seat and disappear. She'd humiliated herself at the party. He probably never wanted to see her again, and now he was stuck.

This was a repeat from school when everyone made fun of her. *Keep your head down. Don't let the kids know you're hurting.* But now it was, *Don't let Harris know he was hurting her.*

She waited as they moved through the security gate. Waited through the garage door opening and waited as Harris unlocked the kitchen door.

He turned on the under-counter lights, leaving the room half lit, and dropped his keys in a tray on the kitchen desk. After stripping off his jacket, he hung it over the back of a chair. Then he pushed the Play button on his answering machine.

It must be a habit.

"Harris, call me." It was his mother. Irritation threaded her voice. "You shouldn't have left tonight. It was important for you to—" He pushed the button and cut off his mother's message.

"I'm sorry." She set her clutch down on the counter and then picked it up. Then set it down again. "You should have stayed."

His hand slashed through the air. "I needed to be with you."

She jumped. "But ..." she pointed at the answering machine.

He shook his head. "When I call her tomorrow I'll explain."

"I really should go home." She flipped open her clutch and pulled out her phone. "I'll call for a car."

"Stop." He crossed from the kitchen desk to where she stood by the island. "It's my fault your lab was broken into."

His fault? "We don't know that."

One eyebrow arched up. "We don't have all the facts, but if this was random, why would vandals pick a lab so far down the hall? Why your lab?"

She shivered and wrapped her arms around her waist. "I don't know."

He rubbed his hands up and down her arms.

"Don't," she whispered.

His hands stopped. He stepped away from her.

"I ... I don't want your pity," she choked out.

"Pity? You think I pity you?"

"I embarrassed you." She swallowed. "I'm socially ... inept."

He stared at her. "I don't care."

"You're—"

He pressed a finger to her lips. "No."

"But—"

This time he cut off her words with his lips. As they kissed, his tongue stroked hers. His hands smoothed down her back and cupped her bottom, tugging her flush against his tight body.

Her head spun. She clutched his shoulders, afraid she might topple. Heat raced through her, pooling in her core.

With a gasp, he pulled away, resting his forehead against hers. "Are we good?"

"Very," she whispered.

Easing back, his fingers curved around her face. His gaze locked on hers. "We should head to bed."

She nodded and followed him up the stairs.

"Let me find a toothbrush." Harris left her standing in the hall. Bedroom doors stood open. From around the corner another door opened, then closed.

Should she trail after him?

Harris came back, holding out a box. "Here you go."

She caught her lower lip between her teeth. "Thank you."

"Pick any bedroom." He waved at the open doors. "The one on your left has a tub and shower. The one on the right has a shower."

She nodded. And took a breath. "And the master bedroom?"

"I have both a tub and a shower." Had his voice gotten a little deeper?

She swallowed, her throat as dry as cotton. "I'll ... I'll try there."

"You don't have to." Harris's nostrils flared. "Just because I don't want you to be alone, doesn't mean you have to sleep with me."

It was true. She straightened her shoulders. "I *want* to sleep with you."

He yanked her into his arms. "Thank goodness."

His thighs rubbed against hers. So did his erection. Only light layers of cloth separated them from being skin to skin, his trousers and her silk dress.

Sunee wrapped her arms around his waist. This close she could smell his sandalwood aftershave, but the rest was all warm, aroused man.

She didn't belong in his world. But she wanted this night.

Holding hands, they moved toward the double-doored room at the end of the hall. His hand brushed a switch and soft lights above the headboard lit the room.

Dark greens and blue upholstery and bedding offset the light wood floors and furniture. Anchoring the room was a massive bed on a pedestal. She stared. "It's so big."

He chuckled. "I don't like my feet hanging off the end of a bed."

"Then it's good we're here. My bed is normal." She tried to infuse confidence in her comment. Tried to tease. But her voice quaked.

"Hey." He turned her to face him, running his hands up and down her arms. "We don't have to do this."

"But I want to." She shook her head and the pencils clinked on the floor. *Pencils!* She'd forgotten she'd shoved them in her hair.

He brushed her hair back, rubbing the strands between his fingers. "I do too."

Standing on her toes, she kissed him. Her breasts swept across his hard chest, and her nipples pebbled in the lacy bra she'd slipped on with Harris in mind.

She trailed her tongue along the seam of his lips, and he allowed her to explore his mouth. He was gentle. Too gentle. He was holding back. But under her hands, his energy pulsed like a beating heart.

He was so tall. She tunneled her fingers through his hair.

For a moment she was weightless and then her bottom settled on the cool comforter. Her sandals slipped off her feet and fell with a muffled thunk.

Harris tried to step between her legs, but her tight dress stopped him. She wiggled, sliding the skirt up to accommodate him. His hands slid under her skirt, tugging her to the edge of the bed and against his heat.

He bent down.

She covered his face with kisses, and her fingers wove into the silk of his hair. She could spend hours tangling her fingers in it. She wanted to touch him and have her tongue memorize every muscle group in his body.

"Are these buttons for show or is this how you get in and out of this dress?" Harris growled.

"They work." She pulled on his tie.

"Damn." Harris's brows knit together in frustration. His fingers tried to slip the tiny buttons through the silken loops. "Why the hell do they make these buttons so tiny?"

She laughed, brushing his hands aside and sat up. "Let me."

He stepped back, his gaze glued to her fingers as she flipped open each button. Her first striptease.

His fingers skimmed her now exposed collarbones. His gray eyes locked on hers.

She wanted to tip her head back and let him run his teeth right there. But she wanted more. She wanted him to fill her.

She'd barely flipped the buttons open to her waist before he shoved the silk away. His mouth sucked in one lace-covered breast. His fingers stroked and pinched her other nipple.

She groaned. Everything arched toward him; her breasts, her pelvis and her heart. She wanted to be so intimately connected she would feel his blood pumping through his veins.

He pulled away and worked on unbuttoning his own shirt. "You make me stop thinking."

"Oh my." She felt like purring. She pushed away his hands and worked the buttons free on his shirt. Slipping it off, she found the flat disc of one nipple and clamped her teeth and lips on it. If she liked him lavishing attention to her nipples, maybe he did too.

"You're driving me mad." Harris pulled her up and kissed her, a kiss of invasion. He plundered her mouth, forcing her to cede control.

"You're beautiful." He pulled her up from the bed and pushed her dress until it was a red pool at her feet. One hand covered the red lace bra, the other stroked her butt and slid around to her aching center. He dipped a finger into her core.

Pleasure wrapped around her like a vine.

He stumbled as he toed off his shoes and pants. His clothes covered her dress. She didn't get a chance to identify boxers or briefs. Change spilled out of his pocket. His erection jutted out from a black thatch of hair.

The way he looked at her as she lay on the bed made her wish she had a garter belt and stockings on so he could rip them off with his teeth. She started to slide back.

"Wait," he growled.

As he loomed over her, his hands corralled her hips. Her legs dangled off the bed. He ran his tongue along her collar bone and then made a straight line down between her breasts. One hand rolled a nipple through the flimsy material before he shoved the cup aside and used his teeth to make it even harder. Then that wicked tongue continued south. He stopped and swirled it in her belly button, playing with her belly button ring. The one piercing she'd done when she'd turned eighteen.

"Nice," he murmured.

She wanted his mouth lower. She raised her hips.

He chuckled. "Patience."

Her hands clawed at the comforter as he rained kisses down her stomach and around her hip bones. She tried to push down her underwear and he caught her hands.

Instead of focusing on her core, he ran his hands up her legs. Then he hoisted her calves onto his shoulders.

"Ohh," she gasped.

His mouth covered her mound. His tongue forced the fabric aside and invaded her.

"Ahhh." Her breath exploded in choppy waves. His fingers kneaded her butt. He ripped the thong off, twisting and flinging it over his shoulder. Then he inhaled. His thumb worked its way to her clitorourethrovaginal complex as he fixed his mouth on her.

"Please." Savage sounds clawed their way out of her throat. "Come inside me."

His laugh vibrated against her core. His tongue and thumb pushed her over.

She crashed, exploded. Screamed. Had an eruption of dopamine, oxytocin and prolactin ever been so sweet?

Even as her body quaked, Harris gently slid her up and placed her head on the pillow. A drawer creaked and there was a crackle of paper.

She closed her eyes. Savoring the aftershocks.

"Don't fall sleep on me," he murmured as he slipped on a condom.

She wrapped her arms around his neck. "Never."

He settled between her thighs, his delicious weight pinning her to the bed. A moment of panic threatened to overwhelm her. What if she couldn't please him? What if…

Harris must have heard her small gasp. "I'm too heavy, aren't I?"

He rolled so she rode him. "Better," he murmured as she used his hips like a saddle.

His thumbs rubbed, stimulating her nipples. How could they get harder? She mated their mouths together and rocked back and forth as his erection sought her vagina.

"You're in control." He linked their fingers together. His eyes were half-closed, only a sliver of silver glimmered in the dim light.

She lifted, positioned for penetration. God, she was a doctor, this would work.

He slipped inside. She panted, worried she would hyperventilate. She felt poised on the edge of a cliff. Her life was about to change. Meeting Harris had changed her already.

His hands glided up and down her thighs, helping her rise and fall. Their bodies' rhythm echoed the pounding of her heart.

Harris breathed her name, as if in pain.

"Am I hurting you?" she gasped, sitting up a little more.

"You're killing me." His hands urged her faster. "Take all of me, damn it."

She did. He filled her. Never had she been so free. She ran her hands up her body. With her fingers in her hair, she rode him. Her pelvis rocked and twisted, clashing gloriously with his.

Another climax rolled through her. She leaned forward, prolonging the pleasure.

He pulled her face to his, conquering her mouth with his tongue as his body conquered hers. With a flip, she was under him, Harris thrusting into her. His face was a rocky continent of concentration. She hooked her ankles around his thighs and clasped his glutes, hanging on.

"Sunee!" Agony and pleasure infused his cry.

He collapsed with his head next to hers, sweeping a kiss on her cheek as he fell. His lungs worked like bellows.

She had brought him to this, brought him pleasure enough to cry her name.

She drew in huge breaths. Her every muscle was as pliable as silly putty. She'd been pulled, manipulated and snapped back into position. Wonderful. She wiggled her toes, pleased she had control of the pile of mush her body had become.

"I'm crushing you." Harris rolled them side by side. "Was I too rough?"

"Incredible." She stroked his brow, amazed her fingers responded.

"Yeah. Incredible." He stroked his thumb on her bruised lips and searched her face.

"What?"

"I'm wondering..." His voice trailed off.

"What?" she whispered.

"If this meant as much to you as it did to me," he whispered back.

Her heart threatened to burst. "I never imagined someone like you could feel that way—about me." She closed her eyes, wanting him to understand. "I don't ... I've never felt like I've belonged. I've always been a ... a freak."

"You're no freak. You're an accomplished intelligent and beautiful woman." He kissed her. "I think I've been waiting for you all my life."

He pulled her into the heat of his body. It warmed her more than a fire.

Could she fit into Harris's life?

She shivered. Tonight had only been a small dinner party, and she'd failed. She didn't belong in his world.

"I need to clean up." Leaning over, he skimmed a finger down her cheek. "I'll be right back."

"I'll be here." At least for a while.

Harris tucked Sunee's back into his chest and contentment washed over him like a dip in a hot spring. He was relaxed. Because of her.

His life was chaotic, but holding Sunee was perfect. Natural.

How could she ever feel like a freak? She was grace and intelligence personified. She put other people first. She could outgrow her shyness—right? Exposure therapy. Because if he ran for governor, he wanted her by his side.

But his mother didn't see Sunee's good traits. Maybe Mother could give her pointers. Mother had been an asset for the senator.

What if she couldn't survive the political arena? Would he give her up or politics? He hated both options, but being of service was his destiny.

She brushed her bottom against him, making him want to slip inside her warm velvet body again. If she were awake he might, but she was exhausted.

He needed to let Ashe know about the break in, probably even Kat. And they needed to find out more about the IVF clinic.

Instead he drew in a deep breath, inhaling her unique scent of flowers. Jasmine, she'd told him. His flower to protect and keep.

CHAPTER ELEVEN

Mendel Campus and Research Center
Iowa

Mark Dell stood next to his car in the parking lot of the Mendel Foundation research complex. The stone buildings tucked in the Iowa farmlands looked like they were part of an Ivy League college campus. The locals thought it was an experimental boarding school.

They had the experimental part right.

Children's voices echoed from the playground. Must be the kids from Wave six or seven. Or was it eight? He couldn't remember their specialization—engineering?

He'd become too removed from their research. That changed now. He pushed open the door. Security should have already verified his identification.

"Sir?" Marie, the receptionist, looked startled. "I didn't know you were coming in today." Panic filled her voice.

He never came to the training center unannounced. Maybe he should do this more often.

"Good morning, Marie." She was a second wave modification. The second wave showed a little more emotion.

"What can I do for you?" Her heels clacked as she tried to keep pace with him as he climbed the stairs.

"Nothing." He opened the second floor door and headed down the hall.

Simon wasn't at his desk. Mark pushed into his office. And stopped.

Simon sat behind the array of computers surrounding *his* desk. Mark's desk. Not Simon's.

"Mark." Simon's eyes widened.

He'd sent Simon to Iowa, but why was he working in his office?

Maybe he should worry about so many exceptionally bright people working in one organization. He would schedule time with the program's psychologist to ensure they were all loyal. Losing control was not an option.

"I want to review the ongoing projects statuses." Mark threw his jacket over one of the guest chairs and rolled up his shirtsleeves. He left his gun and holster on. "Didn't figure I'd throw off everyone's day."

Marie waited at the door. Simon tapped at the keyboard, stood and vacated Mark's desk. "Marie, can you bring in a carafe of coffee? I'll have water."

"Right away." She scurried out.

Mark moved behind the curved black walnut desk. The screens were blank. What had Simon been doing? He jiggled the mouse back to life and entered his password.

Simon stood in front of the desk. "Is something wrong?"

"I want to make sure we don't exacerbate this Dr. Ashland mess." Mark pursed his lips. "Damn Giuseppe. He should have known Ashland had used her own DNA in the original trial. We're risking exposure because of her."

"Exposure ruins our plans." Simon shook his head. "We'll handle it. We can't fail."

"We've already failed. Ashland's not dead."

Simon tipped his head.

Marie brought in a tray of coffee, water and fruit. She handed Mark a cup before leaving. He sipped, hoping she hadn't given him decaf. The group was almost too health conscious. Dieticians controlled every subject's menus, right down to snacks. When you were building the next dynasty, you didn't take half-measures.

Sometimes Mark longed to devour a doughnut.

"I want to review every placement we've made." He would make sure there weren't any other possible exposure risks.

Simon sat and activated the tablet in front of him. "I have two meetings today."

"Cancel them," Mark warned. "This will take a while."

Houston

"Thank you for helping." Sunee buckled her seatbelt.

She and Harris had worked Saturday and Sunday to clean up the lab. Nothing was missing that she could find. "Without you, Marcus might have tried to come in."

Harris squeezed her hand as he exited the hospital parking ramp. "I didn't do that much. I'm sorry I had to run to my office."

"You saved me so much work." She rolled her shoulder. "Is your team ready for tomorrow?"

"We're ready."

"I'm sorry you had to spend so much time with me. You have your own work."

He smiled at her. "I like spending time with you."

Sunee caught her lip between her teeth. The car hit a bump and the sharp pain brought a tear to her eye. Her grandmother's voice *Stop biting your lips, Sunee* played in her head.

Her mother had always been so calm. Even when cancer stole

her beauty, it couldn't steal her serenity. Sunee needed an infusion of her mother's tranquility. They were heading to Harris's parents' house to finish the conversation they'd started before the party.

Harris was put together in khaki shorts and a golf shirt while she wore the capris and T-shirt she'd had on while reorganizing her lab. Not what she wanted to wear the second time she saw Harris's parents, especially after the disastrous dinner party.

He glanced over and frowned. "You look like you're facing a firing squad."

She squared her shoulders and inhaled one more cleansing breath. "I keep remembering what a ... a fool I was at dinner."

He clenched his teeth. Silence blanketed the car. Finally he said, "You're just ... shy."

He was ashamed of her. "I wish it was just shyness. It's anxiety. And h-h-hives. Stuttering."

"Maybe there's medication?" He stared out the windshield. "Therapy?"

She'd tried everything. "Avoidance works the best."

"Avoidance." He drew out the word.

She didn't want to talk about her attacks. "How much should I tell your parents about the DNA results?"

"I guess everything." He rubbed his forehead. "I keep wondering if Ashe and I are the cause of your break in."

"Whoever went through the lab didn't *take* anything. And IT says our computers weren't accessed." Now it was her turn to sigh. "Maybe it *was* drug seekers."

"It doesn't feel right, not with the security cameras going off line at the same time. When I talked to Cruz today, she said there wasn't anything taken from the narcotics supply cabinets either." Harris shook his head. "This sounds premeditated."

"How could anyone know I have your DNA results? And if they're looking for them, wouldn't they break into my apartment?" She and Harris had stopped by her apartment Saturday morning to pack clothes. "Nothing was disturbed."

"If they're smart enough to shut down security cameras, maybe they got in and out of your apartment without detection."

A chill ran through her.

He parked in front of his parents' home. Leah must have been watching. Before they got to the front door, it was opening.

"Come on in." Leah hugged Harris. Then gave a cool nod. "Sunee."

Leah's warmth from Friday night was gone. She led the way. "Dinner is ready."

"I have something I want to show you," Harris said.

"We'll eat first." His mother turned to Sunee. "How is your lab?"

"Thanks to Harris's help everything is back in order. I'm waiting to see if the microscope needs repairs."

"My son is very helpful." Leah led them to the patio next to the pool. The table was set for four under a spinning fan. "I'll get Ted."

"Right here." The senator came up behind his wife and tickled her.

"Behave. We have guests." Leah's tone may have been scolding, but her kiss looked ... sweet.

Sunee wanted a relationship like Harris's parents had. And her parents had had.

She hoped the longing didn't show in her face.

Harris rubbed her shoulder as he pulled out her heavy metal chair.

"At least five people asked me Friday when you would announce your candidacy for governor." Leah passed around a beautiful salad of greens, beets and oranges and a lovely bottle of Pinot Grigio. She shot a cold glance at Sunee. "Since you left before dinner was over, everyone got a chance to talk about you."

"Woman, are you feeding me rabbit food tonight?" the senator growled.

"You got chicken last night. Tonight is fish with rice." Both of Leah's eyebrows arched over her bright blue eyes. "Until you have your physical, you'll get beef once a month."

Sunee squeezed her mouth shut so a giggle wouldn't escape. Senator Torrington was one of the most important men in Washington, but Leah was equal to his power.

"I've scheduled my damn doctor's appointment. It's not right that a man from the longhorn state can't eat his own cattle."

"Interesting you should bring up doctors." Harris looked at his parents. "I want to finish our interrupted conversation on my —genetics."

"Is something wrong?" Leah set down her fork and stared at Harris. She turned to Sunee. "He's not sick, is he?"

"I'm not treating your son," Sunee said.

"Can you tell me more about …" Harris's hands wove patterns above his plate "… my birth?"

Leah blinked. "You mean the fertility clinic I went to?"

Harris nodded.

"Your father and I tried so hard to have a baby. It wasn't in the cards." Leah sighed. "After the third failure, the clinic said we'd qualified for a clinical trial. Rather surprising, since we hadn't applied, but we jumped at the chance." She clasped Ted's hand. "We were lucky it took the very first time."

Ted and Leah exchanged a poignant look that brought tears to Sunee's eyes.

"Do you remember the trial name?" Sunee asked.

"It took me weeks to memorize the phrase—zygote intrafallopian transfer." Leah smiled at Harris. "You were part of the study too. The doctor you asked me about, Dr. Ashland, was studying the long-term effects of test-tube conception."

"I thought it was about nutrition and brain development," Harris said.

Leah frowned. "I guess the study changed over the years."

"Zygote intrafallopian transfer. Maybe that's why I couldn't find any papers on a nutrition and brain development study." Sunee twisted her hair. At least now she had a study subject. Had she seen research papers on zygote transfers?

A maid came out with a platter of fish and a bowl of rice.

"Thank you, Louisa," Leah said.

Everyone was silent until the maid left the patio.

Harris opened his phone and pulled up a picture. "This is Ashe Bristol. The Texans' new quarterback."

The senator's fork clattered to his plate. He stared at the picture. When he handed the phone to his wife, his hand shook.

Leah's hand went to her heart. "My sweet Lord in heaven."

Their shocked expressions weren't faked. They hadn't known.

Harris handed out copies of their birth certificates. His parents passed the documents between each other.

"You look like twins, but your birthdays are different," his mother said. "I would remember if I'd had twins."

"I guess it's true, everyone has a double." The senator's voice was a deep rumble.

"I wouldn't go that far," Sunee said.

Harris nodded at her to continue.

"I did DNA testing on both Harris and Ashe. They are definitely closely related. You would think identical twins except there are differences that don't make any sense to either the testing personnel or me. Ashe and Harris are too closely related to be fraternal twins, but they're not identical. It's almost as if they were clones, but then their DNA should be a match."

"I don't understand." Leah's face was pale. She pointed a manicured finger at Sunee. "Why are you involved?"

"Ashe asked for my help." Sunee swallowed, but her throat stayed tight. "It's my field of work. Genetics."

"How secure is your testing?" Ted growled. "Is this why your lab was broken into?"

"We don't know." She scratched her neck. "The police don't have any answers. But Ashe and Harris's results weren't in my lab and my results are anonymous."

"Mom, Dad, don't attack Sunee." Harris clutched the table. "This isn't her fault. She's trying to help unravel this mystery."

"What was taken in the break-in?" Ted's face was so hard it could have been carved from granite.

"N-n-nothing." Sunee wanted to run. Escape.

Leah stared at her.

Sunee itched her chest and found welts. And she was stuttering.

"Stop it!" Harris clutched her hand. "Can't you see you're upsetting her?"

His parents slid back in their chairs, their arms crossed over their chests. No one touched their food.

"This might hurt your chances of running for governor," his mother said.

"Don't you think I've thought about that?" Harris shouted.

"Don't raise your voice, young man." His father's voice was even deeper.

Was she causing all this angst? "I should leave."

"Stop it," Harris barked at her.

"But … your parents want to blame someone. Let them blame me."

"Everyone take a breath," Ted said. Everyone inhaled and exhaled with him. "What are the next steps?"

"I want to confirm you used National Reproductive Services as your fertility clinic," Harris said.

Leah nodded.

"So did Ashe's mother but in Minneapolis," Harris said.

"Don't tell me some doctor impregnated women all over the country?" the senator sputtered. "Is that why you and Bristol are related?"

"It wouldn't account for how closely related they are. Like I said, they're close enough to almost be identical twins." Sunee kept her head down, it was easier to talk that way. "There are only a few different sectors. It's as if someone tampered with the DNA."

Tampered with the DNA. Gene manipulation?

She covered her mouth. She wouldn't leap to a conclusion, but gene manipulation might be the truth. Were the techniques available thirty plus years ago? If they were, they would have been in the experimental stage. She drummed her fingers on the table. She would need to look for evidence someone had been editing genes back then.

"Sunee?" Harris asked.

She looked at him. "Yes?"

He wrapped an arm around her. "We lost you."

Leah glared at them. Sunee scooted forward so Harris's arm wasn't wrapped around her. She was not here to antagonize his parents.

"It's a possible hypothesis of why the DNA results are the way they are. I need to do more research." Sunee pushed around the fish on her plate, but her mind kept organizing searches she could perform.

"While you are doing that, make sure no one, *no one,* knows about Harris and this ... this mess." The steel was back in Leah's voice.

"Confidentiality is part of the oath I took when I became a doctor."

Leah picked up her wine glass and pointed it at her. "See that you don't break that vow."

"Dr. Ashland," a familiar voice said from the doorway.

Piper looked away from her mother's expressionless face. "Good morning, Dr. Sutton."

DISCOVERY

"Happy Monday. I asked you to call me Nathan," the resident responded.

"And I asked you to call me Piper." They'd had the same conversation every morning for the last week and a half. It was becoming something of a good luck charm. Anytime they had the same conversation, her mother's condition improved.

Now if she would regain consciousness.

"I'd like to introduce Dr. Lassiter. He's researching comas caused by trauma at Johns Hopkins. He asked if he could observe your mother's treatment." Nathan indicated the man standing slightly behind him.

Dr. Lassiter wasn't much taller than she was, shorter than six feet. His hair couldn't decide if it was blonde or brown. And his face was—blank.

"Anyone who can help my mother regain consciousness is welcome," Piper said.

Nathan handed her a form. "This will allow him access to your mother's records."

She didn't read it. She just signed.

A nurse moved into the room and signaled to Nathan. "Dr. Sutton, can you clarify the orders for room 215?"

Nathan nodded. "I'll be back. Dr. Lassiter, why don't you explain why you're interested in Dr. Ashland's case while I handle this."

"In Baltimore we have a high incident rate of comas caused by trauma. Any treatments that can help my patients recover would be beneficial."

"You heard about my mother's case in Baltimore?" That didn't make sense.

"No." Dr. Lassiter moved next to the hospital bed and stared at her mother. His brown eyes barely blinked as he watched the monitor. "I'm visiting Texas on vacation. I saw the news report when she was a 'Jane Doe.' I contacted a medical school classmate who works at the hospital to see if I could observe your mother's care."

There was something creepy about the lack of expression on Lassiter's face. "What's the name of your friend? Doesn't he know he can't talk about a patient?"

"Gordon Rowlings." Dr. Lassiter blinked. "He didn't violate HIPAA. I didn't know her name...until I met Dr. Sutton."

Piper knew the name of every nurse, doctor and aide caring for her mother. There wasn't a Gordon in the mix, and she was good with names. Very good.

"When did he see my mother?" she asked.

"He's a contract ER doctor." Again those brown eyes blinked. "He wasn't involved in her care."

"Oh." No wonder she hadn't heard of his classmate.

"I'm sorry," she said. "I'm a little paranoid. No one knows why my mother was with the man who died. And her purse, cell phone and suitcase are missing."

He nodded. "May I do a neurological exam? A simple exam for responses?"

She didn't know why she hesitated. But maybe he could make helpful suggestions. "Sure."

"If you want to get a cup of coffee or take a walk, feel free," he said.

"No." Not that his credentials, if he practiced at Johns Hopkins, wouldn't be stellar, but she wasn't leaving her mother alone. The one time she'd gone to the hotel to shower and change, a pediatric oncologist had been asking questions. Why would an oncologist be asking about her mother?

She moved to her mother's bedside.

Dr. Lassiter frowned. He performed all the steps Nathan had done, trying to assess where her mother fell on the Glasgow scale. She'd actually responded to noxious odor, when at her initial ER examination she had not. But recent improvements were slow.

Piper bit her lip, wanting to hear her mother's voice.

Dr. Lassiter manipulated her head and then stuck a pin into her mother's nail bed. *She was going to have nail damage.*

She was not letting him fill her ear with water. "You could look at last night's test results." Her tone was as dry as a desert.

"I wanted to perform an initial assessment."

Nathan pushed open the door and jerked to a stop. "Dr. Lassiter, our discussion was observation, not examination. I'll share the patient's records and my course of treatment, but you're not allowed to touch my patient. The administrator would have my head."

Piper stepped between Lassiter and her mother. This doctor had the skin crawling up the back of her neck.

"I'm sorry." He backed away, his hands in the air. "Habit."

Nathan seemed appeased.

"I'd still like a chance to … observe." Lassiter didn't take his eyes off her mother's monitors.

"Fine," Dr. Sutton said. "Come with me and we'll look at her scans."

Piper was relieved to see the two doctors leave. Nathan wouldn't show Lassiter anything she hadn't already seen because she saw all results as he received them.

"Mom, time to wake up." She laid her head on her mother's pillow. She should smell of Amber Rose, her favorite perfume. Even when Piper had tried to get her to change, her mother wouldn't. It was the perfume her father had always bought for her.

Now her mother smelled of chemicals and antiseptics. Piper pulled out her mother's perfume and rubbed it on her mother's wrists and collarbones. A tear slipped down her cheek. "Come back to me."

"Any change?" Uncle Victor strode into the room looking fresh and rested.

She swiped at her face. No negative thoughts. "Not since yesterday."

"I know you're staying, honey, but I've got to get back. I've got a negotiation I can't cancel." He brushed her mother's hair back with one finger and grimaced. "She wouldn't like looking this way. Can't you get someone to wash her hair?"

At that moment she hated her godfather. Hated that he only cared about the company and how things looked. Hated he could be so blasé about her mother's life hanging by tenuous threads that could be snipped by fate too early. Her father's life had been too short. She couldn't lose her mother too.

She rubbed her face. It wasn't fair, but her mother always said life wasn't fair.

"Keep me posted," Victor said. "Is there anything that needs to be handled at the office?"

Her lips formed a straight line. It was as if he'd decided her mother wouldn't recover. The woman he'd pursued all her life no longer mattered.

"If there's anything that needs to be completed, I'll call." To hell with the experiments they'd been running. It didn't matter. Being at her mother's bedside was the only thing on her mind.

"Do you want me to wait with your mother while you go to the hotel and clean up?" Victor grimaced.

With a smile as false as her godfather's hair color, she said, "No, you don't have to wait. And don't let me hold up your return flight to Boston. Heaven forbid you don't license mother's work fast enough."

MENDEL CAMPUS *and Research Facility*
   Iowa

"Sir, I'm not able to get close to Dr. Ashland." David Lassiter's face didn't show a flicker of emotion on Mark's screen as he sat in his Iowa office.

The lack of facial expression wasn't the computer camera's fault. For some reason the first wave of most of their modifications lacked emotions.

"What have you tried?" Mark asked.

"I attempted to give her a physical exam, but the daughter refused to leave the room." David's image shimmered. "She's suspicious. Wanted to know exactly how I found out about her mother's case. Then the supervising physician interrupted."

"Did you set the daughter's mind at ease?" Mark's fingers drummed his desk.

"I'm not entirely confident I did. I'll stay close and monitor any tests they are performing. Dr. Sutton is letting me observe, but he won't allow me to wander the hospital at will."

Great. David had one task, eliminate Dr. Ashland. Maybe Mendel's modifications weren't as successful as everyone assumed. The other operative had also failed and died.

Mark didn't want attention being brought to Dr. Ashland and her work. If anyone connected Torrington, Bristol and Dr. Ashland, what was to stop them from digging up the fact the zygote implantation funding had come from the Mendel Foundation? There was a money trail linking The Legacy Group and the Foundation. If they discovered the link, would they dig into what the Foundation was doing now?

Secrecy was critical. Mark had spent thirty plus years ensuring no one knew about the Foundation and their plans. Common men and women had screwed up the world, it was up to smarter and stronger people to take over. Mendel's people were poised to make that happen.

They'd placed key operatives in major corporations, the military, and arms of government. Only last week an operative had been promoted to national news reporter faster than anyone anticipated.

"Have you at least located Dr. Miller?" Mark asked. Displeasure filled his voice.

David's expression didn't change. "The cameras the team placed at her apartment showed her entering with Torrington. She packed a bag and left. We don't know what was said since there wasn't any audio."

And this was the best they had to offer? How successful could they be if they couldn't even plant effective surveillance? Mark ran a hand through his hair.

"Orders, sir?" A tick beat under David's right eye.

"Stay put. See if you can warm up young Dr. Ashland. If you can't get Dr. Elaina Ashland alone, kill them both."

Mark disconnected. He stared at the moonlit field of corn surrounding the campus. For the first time the entire plan could be exposed. Pulling a bottle from the bottom drawer of his desk, he poured a shot of whiskey and slammed it back. It burned a path to his gut.

He turned back to the desk and activated his computer. Scanning the files of over two hundred possible candidates, he searched for the perfect personnel to handle this problem. Electronics, weapons, planning and observation. Maybe he'd leave David as backup for the group if he hadn't dealt with Dr. Ashland.

He sent messages through the Foundation's secured messaging system. The NSA would love to have their capabilities, but the Foundation had grown beyond federal government support. The fools hadn't even known what they'd financed. The Foundation was now self-sustaining, receiving licensing revenues from their own discoveries. As the modified groups matured, the research facilities were making even greater strides.

But they'd never released information on the embryonic genetic modification protocols. That was their best kept secret. And it must remain secret.

The only weak link was Ashland, Torrington, Bristol and

now, Dr. Miller, the geneticist. And Giuseppe. Mark had no clue what Torrington and Bristol's DNA results might show, but he wasn't taking any chances. They were expendable pawns in a much bigger game.

To save what he'd created, he would lie, cheat or kill.

Survival of the fittest? Hell no. This was survival of the best designed.

CHAPTER TWELVE

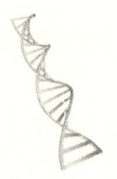

Houston

On Wednesday morning, Sunee made a cup of tea while Harris's coffee brewed. She was living with a man she'd only known for a few weeks. Being with Harris was the highlight of her day. The highlight of her *life*.

Her hand covered her mouth. She was falling in love with him.

She couldn't. It was too soon.

But her parents had fallen in love almost on their first date. At least that was what they had told her. Maybe this was genetic. She shook her head. She hadn't identified any genes that controlled emotions.

Unfortunately for her, Harris was destined for political office. She had anxiety attacks thinking about crowds and speeches.

Her hand shook as she mixed granola with yogurt. Since he wouldn't let her go anywhere but the hospital alone, they'd gone grocery shopping together. She bit her lip. Even though there hadn't been anything other than her lab broken into, he didn't think she was safe.

She flipped on the remote.

"Please take my Tahoe today," Harris said.

"We talked about this last night." She dug her spoon into the yogurt, refusing to look him in those steel gray eyes. "I'd rather drive my own car."

Harris snapped down bread in the toaster and poured a bowl of cereal. "You stalled on the freeway yesterday."

"AAA fixed it." And when Harris had heard she'd broken down, he'd freaked out.

He sat next to her, and his shoulder bumped hers.

She wanted to lean into him, but she had to be ready for this to end. As soon as they figured out who'd broken into her lab, she wouldn't need his protection. She didn't belong in Harris's world. She belonged behind her microscope.

"I don't want to worry about you." He tipped her face up and kissed her.

The taste of coffee met her tongue. Her arms wrapped around his neck as he deepened the kiss.

"Please take my Tahoe." He dropped his forehead to hers.

Sighing, she said, "For today."

She finished her yogurt and tea and placed her bowl, spoon and mug in the dishwasher. "I'm sorry I haven't been able to look for Dr. Ashland's research."

He set his dishes in the dishwasher too. It was so—domestic. "I understand your patients come first. Do you think you'll be home earlier than last night?"

"Oh, I hope so." She'd been at the hospital until late the last two nights. But she and Harris had found the energy to make love. Her face heated at the lovely memories.

"Are you all right?" He touched her cheek.

"Just remembering last night," she whispered.

He yanked her into a kiss that would have curled her hair if she'd had that genetic disposition.

He pulled away and just held her. His heart pounded under her ear. "I wish we could both stay home."

"But your trial."

"And your patients."

"Maybe I'll find the clinical trial you and Ashe were part of by tonight."

"Maybe this will be over soon."

Over. She would move back to her apartment. Back to her quiet life. She rolled her shoulders, but it didn't release her tension. It was what she wanted—right? It was where she fit.

Rounding on her patients that morning helped Sunee push aside her worries. After looking over the last labs for Adam, she said, "How's your nausea?"

He shrugged. "Okay."

She squeezed his leg. "I'm glad."

Cards and balloons now losing their helium and floating halfway above the ground filled Adam's room. The flowers had wilted, but the massive gorilla looked like he'd been loved during the hospital stay.

It was time for Adam to go home and heal.

Adam focused on the video game he was playing. His mother sat next to the bed, looking more rested than she had two weeks ago.

"I'm discharging you," Sunee said. "From now on you'll get your treatments in the clinic."

Adam's mother heaved a big sigh, her face brightening with a smile. "What a relief."

"Do I have to go back to school?" Adam paused his game.

"You'll need to have a chemo treatment every twenty-eight days. We'll work out the schedule so you miss the least amount of school possible."

A glum look covered Adam's face. Sunee almost laughed. His mother's smile made up for his sadness.

This was where she belonged. Where she was comfortable. Her patients grounded her. She needed to heal children and find solutions to medical mysteries. Trying to survive a relationship with Harris, a politician, wasn't a battle she could fight.

She rubbed her chest. When she thought about never seeing him again, it hurt. But she'd been alone before. She would endure.

Sunee discharged Adam. Since he was her last patient for the morning, she headed to the lab. Marcus was already there.

"Hey, Sunee. We've got the marker reports back on your patient's family."

"Any genetic disposition in the family history?" she asked.

"Nothing." Marcus used a pipette to add solution to the slide he prepped. "I left the printouts on your desk."

"Thanks." She sipped her tea, booted up her computer and settled into her chair. Studying the family's DNA results, she agreed with Marcus's assessment. Adam's abnormal genes were not repeated in his parents' or siblings' chromosomes. Good news for the family, but they weren't eligible for her study.

After she documented their findings, she decided to concentrate on Harris and Ashe's problem. She hadn't had a chance in the last three days.

What kind of long-term study had Dr. Ashland been running? Was it the zygote intrafallopian transfer or nutrition and brain development, or was it Ashe's recollection of nutrition and muscle development?

She opened up the Public Library of Science website. She would only be able to find papers available to open access, but it was a start. She searched for papers authored by Elaina Ashland. When the website returned over one hundred hits, she sat up. She organized the articles in date order. *My goodness, they started almost forty years ago.* She checked the link after her name, Department of Medicine, Harvard University. Sunee searched Dr. Ashland's name to see if she could determine when she'd been in med school. Dr. Ashland even had a Wikipedia page.

Elaina Harrison Ashland

Harris—Harrison. Ashe—Ashland.

Harvard University—MD, PhD in Molecular Engineering

Another connection.

Married to Andrew Gregory Ashland.

Founding principal of The Legacy Group. She clicked on The Legacy Group link.

The Legacy Group, a genetic research company based in Boston, Massachusetts, was co-founded by Elaina Harrison Ashland, MD, PhD, Andrew Ashland MD, PhD (deceased) and Victor Giuseppe MD, PhD. All Harvard Medical School graduates, they each brought different skills to the startup company. Dr. Elaina Ashland is a molecular engineer, Dr. Andrew Ashland was a cytogenetic diagnostician and Dr. Giuseppe a biochemist.

She clicked on each founders' links.

She created a timeline noting births, graduation dates and the one death. Then added the papers Elaina Ashland had authored. The genetic modification papers had stopped about thirty years ago.

"Hey." Marcus stuck his head in her office. "I'm heading to the cafeteria. Want anything for lunch?"

She glanced up. Almost one? She pulled out some cash. "Thanks. Soup and salad would be great."

Her hand hit the mouse and it rolled to a picture of the three co-founders. Sunee's heart bumped, once, twice and then stuttered. No one could mistake the black hair and those cheekbones. When she found Elaina's picture there were Harris's gray eyes.

She'd found Harris and Ashe's biological parents. They had to be. Her fingers shook as she printed the pictures.

Marcus arrived with her lunch and she tucked the pictures and her timeline into her briefcase.

"Soup choices were chicken noodle or split pea. I brought you chicken."

"Thanks." They talked about the upcoming two o'clock team meeting. Luckily she wasn't presenting today. All she could think about was the timeline and her discovery of Ashe and Harris's possible parents.

In the meeting, Sunee announced, "We couldn't identify any markers for Adam's family, so we can't enroll him."

When the meeting concluded, she said to Marcus, "I have another patient to see."

"Okay. I'm heading out." Marcus waved as he caught the elevator.

She rolled her shoulders, hating that she'd lied to Marcus. If Dr. Ashland was still in the hospital in critical care she wanted to ask her some questions. Last week she'd been turned away.

At the nursing station, she asked for Elaina Ashland's room.

The nurse smiled at her. "Are you family?"

"No. I'm Dr. Miller." She made sure her hospital ID was visible. "I was hoping I could ask Dr. Ashland about her research."

A man turned and stared at her. She glanced at his visitor's badge but only caught the beginning of his name. *Las.*

"I wish you could." The nurse shook her head. "She's in a coma."

"Oh." Sunee's shoulders slumped. "Is there any chance you could contact me when she's conscious?"

"What is it you need?" the nurse asked.

"About thirty years ago she published a paper on gene therapy. It's applicable to my … research." Sunee's neck crawled like someone was staring at her. Or maybe it was the white lie she was telling. "I was in the ER when she came through. I'm hoping I can talk to her."

"I'll take down your name." The nurse didn't promise to contact her.

"Thank you."

When she walked away, her neck itched. She glanced behind her. The visitor sitting at a nursing station computer was still staring.

NAN DIXON

She rolled her shoulders but the itch wouldn't stop. She scratched her neck. Damn it. Hives.

"Mom, what's up?" Harris put his phone on speaker, pushed away from his desk and rocked back in his chair. Wednesday night. It would be a late one tonight.

"I'm glad I caught you," his mother said. "Can you stop at the house?"

"I'm at the office and I'll be here late." He smiled. Sunee was picking up Denver sandwiches and they would have dinner together.

"Gary and I need to talk to you."

His chair squeaked as he leaned forward. "Something about the campaign?"

"No. It's about that woman you're dating."

He sat straight up. "Her name is Sunee."

"And her father is Michael Miller, a prominent fundraiser for the opposition party." Her voice was clipped. "They call him the kingmaker."

"Michael Miller?" His gut bucked like a bronco.

"You cannot associate with her."

"Mom." He swallowed. "He's in New York. People in Texas won't know who he is."

"The party leaders will know." His mother's sigh echoed through his office. "You need to cut off whatever is going on between you. Now."

Cut off his relationship with Sunee? His mother was cutting out his heart. "But …"

"You want to run for governor?" she asked.

"Yes." But to stop the best relationship he'd ever been in because of Sunee's father was wrong. His fingers flexed, then formed fists.

"You saw how she behaved at dinner," his mother continued. "Gary and I think she would be a liability to your campaign. You need to stop seeing her."

Stop seeing Sunee? "I'll ... I'll think about this."

"Have I ever steered you wrong?"

He gritted his teeth. "I said I would think about this."

"Think about the future. Think about the difference you can make," his mother said before hanging up.

He could make a difference. He could bring compromise and collegial dialogue back into politics.

But giving up Sunee? She calmed him. Kept him sane. He wanted her by his side. Always.

Always?

Was he falling in love with her?

He'd never been in love. He loved people. His parents. Grandparents. Probably even Kat as a friend.

But he'd never fallen in love.

His office phone rang, the readout indicating it was lobby security.

"Torrington," he said.

"There's a Sunee Miller here."

"I'm on my way down." He pushed away from his desk and stared out the window into the night.

Why did her father have to be Michael Miller? And why hadn't she told him?

The elevator carried him to the lobby. When it opened, there she was. Smiling.

"I'm glad you had time for dinner." Her voice washed over him. Soothed him.

He couldn't give her up.

She stepped into the elevator. As the door closed, she stood on her toes and kissed him.

"Are you okay?" She stroked a finger between his eyebrows.

"Fine. Just ... working through case documents." Not quite the truth.

"I can leave dinner with you." She held up a bag as the elevator reached his floor and opened.

"No." He led her to his office. "This might be the only chance I can spend time with you tonight."

She sighed. "You'll be home late?"

"I'm not sure." He helped her pull out the food. "Thank you for dinner."

"This is nothing." She shook her head. "You've done so much for me."

"Helping you is not a hardship." At least that statement was the truth.

They ate and talked about their days. Again her concern for her patients, for him, came through.

"I wish we could spend more time together," he blurted out.

"Your trial takes priority." She touched his hand. "Maybe when the trial is over?"

Not if his mother and Gary had their way. "Sure."

"I can't believe this started with you and Ashe wondering why you looked alike." She laced her fingers with his. "Without that, I might never have met you."

He pulled their joined hands up to his lips and kissed her hand. "And that would be bad?"

"I ..." she stared at her half-eaten sandwich. "I've never felt this way. About anyone."

His heart twisted. What they had was special. Important. But what he could do for the state, and maybe the country, was too.

His stomach churned, and he pushed away his plate unable to eat.

He needed to get back to work, but he didn't want tonight to end. He didn't want *them* to end.

"I'll let you get back to work." She picked up the garbage. "Oh. I stopped up at critical care to see if I could talk to Dr. Ashland."

"How is she?"

"She hasn't regained consciousness." Sunee sighed, drawing his eyes to her chest. Damn he wanted to make love with her. "I wasn't allowed to see her."

"Why did you try?"

"I wanted to find out why she stopped publishing papers on her genetic modification research. And I can't find anything published on the studies you and Ashe were involved with either. And nothing on a zygote transfer study. It's ... frustrating."

"At least she's still alive," he said.

"I forgot about what I brought you." She dug in her briefcase and pulled out two pictures. "I was hoping to show this to both you and Ashe."

He shook his head. "I can't have Ashe coming to my office."

"I know." She pushed the pictures across the table.

He stared at them, and then back at her. "I know Dr. Ashland, but who is this?"

"Andrew Ashland. Elaina Ashland's husband."

"Ashland?" Another person with his face. He was almost getting used to the experience.

"Elaina and her husband, Andrew, founded a company called The Legacy Group based in Boston." She squeezed his fingers. "Elaina's full name is Elaina Harrison Ashland."

What the hell? "Our names."

"That's what I thought too."

"Nothing makes sense." He rubbed his temples. "Guess I need to ask my mother where my name came from."

"It's one of the reasons I wanted to talk to Dr. Ashland."

He picked up the picture. "You think this is my biological father?"

"I suspect so. I thought you would want the photo." Sympathy painted her lovely face. She smoothed out another document. "I've made a timeline."

He traced the information. "He's dead?"

She rubbed her neck where it was pink. "He died more than a year before you and Ashe were born."

A year. "What do you think?"

She paused, her fingers covering her mouth.

He wanted to touch her lips.

"I don't want to make assumptions," she said. "I would like to perform DNA tests or find out what Dr. Ashland knows."

"Who is she to me?" he said under his breath.

"I think she's your biological mother. You have her eyes."

There was a rap on his door.

He flipped over the photos and papers. "Come in."

"Can you come back to the conference room?" Marta asked. "The team has some questions."

"I'll be right there," he answered.

"I'll leave." Sunee swept up the papers and tucked them into her briefcase.

"I'll walk you out," he said.

"You have work to do." She headed for the door.

"Sorry, I need to escort you downstairs. Marta, I'll join you in the meeting room."

"Thanks." Marta nodded.

He wanted to hold her hand but didn't. His mother's phone call weighed on him.

While waiting for the elevator, Sunee kissed him. "Wake me if I'm asleep when you come home."

"I will."

He walked with her to the security desk and as she handed her badge back to a guard, he asked, "Would one of you walk Dr. Miller to her car?"

"Harris—" she started to say.

"—non-negotiable," he interrupted.

"Sure, Mr. Torrington," a guard said.

He waved as she headed to the parking ramp.

Back in the elevator, he shook his head. He and Ashe were

spitting images of Andrew Ashland and he guessed he shared Elaina's eyes. The Ashlands might be his biological parents, but the man had died over a year before he and Ashe had been born.

Back on his floor he entered the Barney prosecution team conference room. The scent of pizza sat heavy in the air. It was what he would have had for dinner if Sunee hadn't called.

"Harris," Marta said, "we have some thoughts on the order of witnesses."

He needed to focus. "Yes?"

For the first time in his life, a pending trial didn't hold one hundred percent of his attention. Some of it had walked out with Sunee.

His relationship with Sunee wasn't casual. Not to him. His mother and Gary wanted him to end their relationship.

He wanted more.

But until he was assured she wasn't in danger, he refused to make any changes.

CHAPTER THIRTEEN

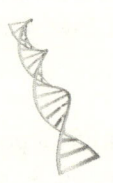

Friday afternoon, Piper brushed her mother's light brown hair. She and Suzie, her mother's nurse, had just washed it. Even when engrossed in a problem, her mother's hair was always tidy.

The remnants of her anger at Uncle Victor faded a little more. It was nice to see her mother with clean hair. She almost looked normal, as if she were only sleeping.

She dotted perfume on her mother's wrists. But it didn't block the hospital's scent or the tang of sickness oozing from her mother's skin.

"Wake up, Mom." She'd been in the coma for almost two weeks.

The waiting ate holes in Piper's heart. She couldn't reach her mother. Couldn't ask what had happened. Or even find out why she was in Houston.

The scientist inside of Piper needed the facts, the data. The little girl huddled inside needed her mother.

"Eat, honey." Suzie, one of her mother's nurses, re-entered the room. "You're fading away. A good old Texas wind will pick you up and blow you clear to Louisiana."

"I don't think I could eat." Everything tasted like sawdust. And she was afraid if she left, something might happen.

Suzie took her mother's vitals. "At least let me get you something. How about tomato or chicken noodle soup?"

"Thanks. Tomato would be nice," Piper agreed, even though she knew she wouldn't eat more than a spoonful or two.

The respirator's steady whisper lulled her to sleep. Time had no meaning. Her days were defined by the change of the hospital staff tending her mother. There were no interruptions from her cell phone because she'd shut it off.

Piper jerked awake. Suzie had her hand on her shoulder.

"Here's your soup," Suzie said. "We're taking your mother for another EEG. She'll be in the neuro lab for over an hour. Why don't you run to the hotel and take a shower? I'm off in an hour, I'll sit with her until you get back."

"Thanks, Suzie." She squeezed her mother's hand.

The Houston heat slapped at her as she crossed the street.

In her hotel room, she turned the shower as hot as she could stand and let the spray pound her shoulders. She scrubbed her hair, and then sank against the wall.

Hadn't they done an EEG the last time she'd taken a shower? When had that been? A couple of days ago?

Her breath came quicker. Were they testing for brain activity? She couldn't remember the neuro tests they'd run today or whether Mother had responded. When Nathan had made his rounds Suzie suggested she get coffee. With Nathan, Suzie and creepy Dr. Lassiter there, Piper had been glad to stretch her legs and grab breakfast.

No one had said anything about the test results. She'd assumed everything was status quo. What if that wasn't the case? What if they hadn't gotten a response?

She shut off the shower. Wrapping her hair in one towel and her body in another, she rushed out of the bathroom and tore through her suitcase. She threw on her last clean pair of underwear and jeans. Then added a T-shirt.

Piper whipped the towel off her head and swiped at her hair with her comb. After pushing on a headband, she was back at the nursing station within five minutes. "Where's Dr. Sutton?" She gritted her teeth, afraid she would scream at the woman manning the desk.

"He said he'd return around six," the nurse said.

Piper needed her mother's chart. Boy she wished she had a password to the hospital records. "Is anyone from his practice in the hospital?"

The nurse shook her head. Was there sympathy in her eyes? Oh God, don't let her pity her. Please, no.

Piper swallowed. "I want to talk to Dr. Sutton when he gets here."

"I'll make sure he knows."

She dragged herself back to her mother's room, dreading the smell and view of the cafeteria roof. Fear sat like an anvil on her chest. Each breath ached. Her shoulders could barely move. This was the first time Nathan hadn't shared test results and tried to give her encouraging words.

Someone had made the bed with clean sheets. Piper added water to the flowers, afraid to sit down. Afraid of what Nathan would tell her.

Please God, let her EEG show something. Don't take her from me.

Suzie pushed her mother back into the room, not looking Piper in the eye. "You're back."

An orderly helped Suzie transfer her mother to the bed. The sheets were so harsh Piper should check for bedsores.

"Anything new?" Piper asked, hoping to force Suzie to look her in the eyes.

Suzie tucked the sheets around her mother, keeping her gaze on the bed. "Dr. Sutton will let you know."

Piper stroked her mother's hair back. Where was her mother's vitality? This brilliant woman couldn't be gone. She had too much to live for. "Can I see the EEG results, Suzie?"

"Dr. Sutton will be by tonight, hon." She double-checked the IV. "Why don't I shut the blinds and turn off the lights?"

"Yes, thanks." She would try to rest.

Piper slid her chair next to the hospital bed and pulled her mother's hand out from under the covers. Tears spotted the white sheet. She longed to feel her mother's fingers squeeze her hand. Some sign she was in there.

She closed her eyes and whispered, "I love you, Mom."

ALARMS CLANGED. Piper jerked awake. *What?*

The hospital room was dark. Another false IV alarm? Her gaze scanned the monitors. *Cardiac arrest.*

A man in a white coat stood next to the IV bag, pushing a syringe into the port.

Another alarm wailed. The man jumped over and silenced the monitor and light caught his face.

"Dr. Lassiter?" Piper pushed out of her chair. "What are you doing?"

He jerked and dropped the syringe.

Her mother's heartbeat grew slower, more erratic.

"What have you done?" She ran around the bed and shoved him, yanking the IV out of her mother's arm. Blood spurted from the site. "Get away from her."

Lassiter backhanded her.

Pain rocketed through her face. Piper slammed into the IV tree. It clattered. Her feet tangled in tubing and metal as she fell.

Stars filled her vision, but she scrambled to her feet and grabbed the call button. "Help! Help!"

Lassiter stared at the monitor. Her mother's pressure and heart rate plummeted. Feet thundered in the hall. He shoved

Piper and rushed out the door, plowing through incoming hospital personnel.

Piper flailed and fell again, her hip screaming in pain. "Help!"

"Piper!" Nathan pulled her off the floor.

"My mother!" Piper pointed at the syringe on the floor. "Lassiter injected something into her IV."

A nurse picked it up. "Unmarked."

Why? She scuttled out of the way.

"Call security. Find him." Swearing, Nathan checked her mother's pulse. "Crash cart!"

A nurse made the call. "Code blue," echoed in the hallways.

Nathan pounded on her mother's chest and began compressions. Piper counted with him. Another nurse bagged her mother.

No!

The cart arrived along with more people. The room filled with words she knew. Words she'd spoken. *One milligram epi. Paddles. Clear!*

Her mother's body jumped.

Come on, Mom. Piper stared at the monitor, willing the pulse to change. Anything.

"Again!" Nathan jabbed another dose of epi in her mother. "Clear!"

Her mother's body jumped again.

Please, please, please.

There was a beep. A long pause. Then another. And another. The beeping and lines settled into normal sinus rhythm.

"She's back," a nurse called.

Piper slumped to the floor.

Nathan glanced at her as he listened to her mother's heart. "You okay?"

She shook her head. How could she be okay? "Lassiter tried to kill her."

Nathan prescribed medication, one that would stabilize her

mother's heartbeat. Then he pointed at the syringe. "Get that to the lab and find out what was in there."

Why had Lassiter done this?

Nathan held out his hand and pulled her off the floor. "Come sit."

"My mother ..."

Nathan held up a finger. "Is stable."

"For now," Piper whispered. "Why would he do this?"

"I don't know." Nathan's jaw clenched. He tipped her chin. "Let me check out this cut."

"Cut?"

"The side of your chin."

She touched it and her fingers came away bloody.

A nurse handed Nathan supplies. He snapped on a pair of gloves and then took a bottle and gauze from the nurse. "Let's see if you need stitches."

Piper winced as he cleaned out the cut, but she never looked away from her mother's monitor. Mom's heartbeat was steady. Strong.

"I think butterflies will close this," Nathan said.

The nurse brought over the bandages.

"Why do you think—" Piper started.

"—don't talk." He applied the bandages. "There."

"Why?" she whispered.

A hospital security team member pushed open the door.

"Did you catch him?" Nathan asked.

"He had a car waiting near the ER." The guard shook his head. "The police have been notified. They'll want to talk to you."

"Anything I can do to help find that murderer, I will," Piper said. "But none of this makes sense."

Nathan shook his head. "I don't understand either. I'm sorry I let him observe."

"What if he comes back?" she asked.

"Until the police arrive, I'll guard the door." The security guard headed to the door.

"Thank you." She pushed the words out. The adrenaline must have dissipated. She could barely move her body and talking was a strain.

Nathan pulled off his gloves and stroked a finger on her cheekbones. "You should get some sleep. You're exhausted."

"I have to make sure my mother is safe."

Her phone buzzed. *Uncle Victor.* He may not be an uncle by blood, but he was almost family. "I should take this."

"I'll see you tomorrow. Try to rest." Nathan closed the door.

She fumbled with her phone. "Uncle V-V-Victor?"

"Piper, what's wrong? What happened?"

"Someone tried to kill her," she sputtered through her tears. "Tried to kill Mother."

"What? No! No!" Victor swore. "Are you sure?"

"I woke up to him injecting something into her IV."

Victor gasped. "I'm sorry. This is ... I'm so sorry."

"You don't have anything to be sorry for." She sniffed. "Can you ... can you come back?"

"I'll be there as soon as I can."

She sobbed. At least she would have someone who loved mother by her side. "Hurry."

Monday morning as Sunee headed to her lab, her phone buzzed. Her body perked up, maybe Harris was calling. She'd hardly seen him over the weekend.

It was the receptionist from the admin floor.

"Hey Sharon," she said. "What's up?"

"There's a Mrs. Torrington here. She's wondering if you have a few minutes to meet with her."

Sunee blinked. What could Harris's mother want? "Where is she?"

"The administration waiting area."

In the elevator that would take her to the administrative office suites, Sunee checked her lab coat. Clean. Her navy blue slacks? Slightly rumpled. And black clogs. Not a fashion statement, but with the miles she walked in the hospital and the hours she stood in the lab, they were a necessity.

She entered the administrative waiting room and spotted Dr. Goodman, head of surgery, chatting with Harris's mother.

Mrs. Torrington glanced up. "There she is."

"Mrs. Torrington." Sunee twisted her fingers together. Then stuck them in her lab coat pockets.

"Hello." Leah stood. "William, do you know Sunee Miller?"

An uncertain smile filled Dr. Goodman's face. "I don't think I've had the pleasure."

Of course not. Sunee didn't breathe the same air as the head of surgery. And she lost a few more points with Harris's mother.

"I work in pediatric oncology, and I'm on the team researching family genetic traits for cancer patients."

"Ah, Ben Sussaman's team."

"Yes."

"Great to see you, Leah," Dr. Goodman said. "Give my regards to the senator."

"I surely will." Leah waved him off. "I'll see you at next weekend's barbecue."

"Mrs. Torrington," Sunee said, then corrected. "Leah. What are you doing here?"

"Is there someplace we can chat?" Leah looked around. "Maybe get something to drink?"

Sunee's office was tiny. "Sure. The cafeteria?"

They wound their way through the hospital corridors. Sunee made painful, stuttering small talk in the elevator and the cafeteria as she purchased two cups of tea.

Leah pointed to an isolated table in the far corner. "Why don't we sit there?"

"Sure." Sunee's cheeks were hot. Was *Sure* the only word she knew? She'd been called a genius. Why couldn't she talk to people?

"Thank you for seeing me." Leah looked wrong drinking tea out of a recycled paper cup. She should be using a china teacup with a saucer. "I hope I didn't take you away from your patients."

"I'd finished my rounds and was heading to my lab." Researching her son's possible biological parents, but she couldn't blurt out that information.

"Don't you have clinic hours?" Leah's sharp eyes examined her over the edge of her cup.

"Tuesday and Thursday afternoons."

Leah nodded.

Sunee scratched her neck. *No*. Welts were beginning to form. She snatched her fingers away, hoping Leah wouldn't notice.

"I understand your father is Richard Miller at Miller Investments," Leah said.

Sunee couldn't stop her eyes from widening. "Yes."

"He does a lot of fundraising for liberal candidates in New York." Leah's brown eyes captured hers like a tractor beam.

How did Leah know that? "He's very active."

"There was a picture of you in the New York Times last month attending a fundraiser."

That was the command performance she'd made for her father. Because of the hives, it was not a fond memory. "I didn't realize there were photographers there."

Leah set her cup down and placed her palms on the table. Diamond rings flashed on both hands. The friendliness washed out of her face. "My son is conservative."

Sunee looked up and swallowed. "I ... I didn't know the DA position was political."

"It's an elected position."

"Oh." She and Harris hadn't discussed political ideologies.

"What happened at the dinner party last Friday?" Leah asked.

"T-t-here was a break-in at my lab." Sunee squirmed in her chair.

"No. After I introduced you to Leonard Gilbert, you were totally engaged." Leah waved her hand. "But at dinner, you didn't talk to the men next to you. Didn't say a word."

"I ... I ... I ..." Her face was hot. Her words tangled in her mouth.

"Yes?"

"I ... get anxietyattacksinsocialsettings." Sunee spewed out the words in one big bite.

"What?"

She took a breath. "Anxiety. Attacks."

Leah set one of her diamond heavy hands on Sunee's. "Oh bless your heart. That's terrible."

Sunee nodded.

"How would you ever be an asset to Harris? You couldn't even converse at a small dinner party." Leah held up her hand. "My son needs someone who can *help* his career, not damage it. He plans to go all the way—maybe even president. Would you stand in his way?"

"No," Sunee croaked, her throat so thick with pain she had to force the words out. "I want Harris to achieve his dreams. He's such a good man."

"Yes, he is." Leah pointed at Sunee's neck. "Are you okay?"

Sunee covered her neck with her hands. "Hives."

Leah shook her head. "Do you think *you* can help him?"

Pain lanced through her chest. Harris needed someone sophisticated and comfortable in social settings. That wasn't her.

"I'm sure you agree that anyone who detracts from his ability to achieve greatness needs to step aside for the good of the country."

Sunee's pulse pounded in her ear. Her diaphragm whipped

breaths in and out of her lungs. There was a scrape of a chair and the rattle of silverware from other diners. The only thing she couldn't hear was her heart breaking.

Mrs. Torrington made sense. She *would* hurt Harris's campaign.

"If we date, voters won't vote for him?" The words scratched a path through her throat, ripping holes and riddling her with a familiar emptiness.

"Your family is too prominent." Leah folded her napkin. "I've already talked to Harris, but I needed to talk to you."

Harris knew? "What did he say?"

"My son is too honorable." Leah set her hands on the table and leaned closer. "*You* need to break this off."

The words were like ice cold water. Sunee jerked. "Me?"

"You need to be the selfless one. If you don't break this off, eventually he'll hate you for ruining his career." Leah pushed her chair back and stood. "I trust you'll do the right thing—for Harris. For the country."

Mrs. Torrington didn't look back. Her heels clipped against the tile floor.

Sunee froze in her chair. She had to break up with Harris.

She could wait until he came to the same conclusion as his mother, or she could be the one to finish their affair.

A tear burned down her cheek. Now that she needed to let him go, she knew.

She loved Harris Torrington.

Mendel Campus and Research Facility
   Iowa

"Lassiter," Mark barked. "You haven't answered your phone in three days."

"I destroyed it," Lassiter said. "I couldn't call in until I was secure."

"What happened?" Mark's fingers tightened around the edge of his desk.

"It's possible Dr. Ashland is still alive." Lassiter's expression never changed.

"Explain," Mark ordered.

"I made several attempts to be alone with Dr. Ashland, but the daughter never left her side. On Friday I finally took a chance while she slept, but I failed to silence one alarm and the daughter woke and ripped out the IV."

"The IV?"

"During the evening shift change, I injected Dr. Ashland with a lethal dose of morphine. I thought I had silenced all the alarms, but one went off. The younger Dr. Ashland woke and pulled the IV before the drug fully dispersed."

"You idiot. You should have killed the daughter first!" Did he have to direct every agent's actions? Lassiter's line was supposed to be the brightest of all the modified lines.

They should have programmed in common sense.

"There were indications Dr. Ashland was starting to regain consciousness. I needed to make my move."

"Now they know you were there to kill her." Mark's body tightened. "And it took until Monday to report in?"

"When I ran, she was flat-lining. I spent the weekend evading capture. I abandoned the car. Got cash to rent another." Lassiter blinked. "I can't return to Johns Hopkins."

"No. That is not advisable." Mark's hands clenched into balls of fury. "Where are you now?"

"Oklahoma. What should I do next?"

"Give me a minute." They could use Lassiter's intelligence in their research lab. Maybe he could tweak the line *he'd* evolved from. But results took so damn long.

What a waste.

They could alter his appearance through plastic surgery and possibly get him back into a hospital setting. Mendel wanted an agent at Walter Reed. It would take a lot of record altering, but the tech line was more innovative than the science groups.

"Sir?" Lassiter asked.

"What?" Mark snapped. Thirty years they'd stayed hidden. Now as the pieces were dropping in place, they were risking exposure.

"A Dr. Miller from the facility wanted to talk to Dr. Ashland about her early genetic research."

"Miller." Why did he know that name? He pressed a button. "Simon, come here."

"Yes." Simon opened his office door.

"Who is Dr. Miller? In Houston."

"She's a female doctor of Asian and Irish descent. Specialization—pediatric oncology. She also has a doctorate in molecular genetics." Simon tapped on his ever-present iPad. "Sunee Miller has been seen with Harris Torrington. It was her lab we … explored."

"Molecular genetics?" Mark worried his head would explode. "Lassiter, drive to the Iowa facility. And don't get caught."

He slammed off the feed and turned to Simon. "Find out what happened to Dr. Ashland."

"Yes."

Mark drummed his fingers on his desk. What had Dr. Miller discovered?

He'd been promoted beyond handling dirty work, but to keep their secrets, he would head to Houston. No one would jeopardize their plans.

CHAPTER FOURTEEN

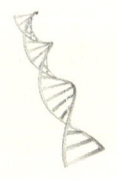

Houston

At the end of the day as Sunee drove back to Harris's house, she tried out conversations.

"We're too different."

"I have to concentrate on my research."

"I'm not attracted to you."

All lies. The truth? She loved him. But she had to break up with him. Tonight.

Unfortunately when she pulled up to the house, Ashe's and Kat's cars were in the driveway. She would have to wait until they left.

She entered the house through the garage. In the kitchen, Harris was bent over the beverage fridge. His presence filled the room, overwhelmed her. His voice, body, brain, scent. There had to be a medical explanation for this, but she didn't know it.

"Welcome home." Harris hurried over and kissed her. "You weren't as late as you thought you would be."

"Ashe and Kat are here?" she asked. Everything ached inside.

"They're in the media room."

His next kiss took her deeper, his tongue stroking hers. Her bag slipped off her arm and crashed to the floor.

She pulled away and knelt, shoving her phone, keys, pens and lip gloss back in.

"I'll take these beers back to Kat and Ashe. Do you want me to grab anything for you?"

"I'll get it."

"Did you eat? I made a plate for you. It's in the fridge."

"Thank you." His consideration hollowed out her stomach.

He softly stroked her cheek. "Why don't you warm it up and join us?"

"I will."

"Are you all right?" He frowned. "You look tired."

"I ... guess I am." Her heartbreak must be etched on her face.

"Let's get this meeting over with and get some sleep." He stroked her cheek once more before leaving the room.

She squeezed her eyes shut, trying to force back her tears. They wouldn't be sleeping together tonight. Not after she broke up with him.

Leah's words echoed in her head. *"My son needs someone who can help his career, not damage it. He plans to go all the way—maybe even president. Would you stand in his way?"*

If Harris and his mother had discussed her—unsuitability, why was he being so kind and loving?

It was time to put some distance between them.

She would get through this ... this discussion with Ashe and Kat. She would fulfill her promise to help Ashe and Harris figure out how they were related. But tonight she would leave this house. Leave Harris.

She warmed up the enchiladas Harris had saved for her and then added the leftover salad she'd made earlier this week. On the way to the media room, she tucked the file she'd put together on Dr. Ashland under her arm.

Ashe and Kat sat in the armchairs. The only spot remaining

was on the sofa next to Harris. She couldn't sit there and keep inhaling his mouth-watering combination of sandalwood cologne and the maleness that was all Harris. Instead she sat on the floor near the coffee table.

He patted the sofa next to him, but she ignored his non-verbal communication.

"Hi Ashe. Kat." Sunee forced her shoulders to relax. She had to learn to be in the same room with Harris without wanting to curl into his lap.

Sunee slid the file to Harris. He flipped it open and pulled out the photos of Elaina and Andrew Ashland.

Ashe leaned forward. "Who are they?"

"Elaina Harrison and Andrew Gregory Ashland," Harris said.

Kat snatched the copy. "Oh. My. God. He looks just like you. The hair, the jaw line. And you both have her eyes."

Kat jotted notes in the notebook she left at Harris's place.

"Harrison–Harris. Ashland—Ashe." Harris grimaced. "And we look like them."

Ashe's foot beat a rhythm on the floor. "So is the husband in Boston?"

"He died thirty-two years ago." Sunee swallowed a mouthful of salad. "Hang on, I've made a timeline."

She spread it across the table and everyone scooted closer. "They both attended Harvard Medical School. After graduation, they formed a research and development corporation. The Legacy Group. There were three co-founders, all out of Harvard. The two doctors Ashland and a Victor Giuseppe. Their education is heavily geared to genetic research, and that is what they were working on. Legacy is still around, still doing R&D and doing well."

Harris pointed at her notations. "What are these?"

"The published papers on genetic editing. I started with Elaina first, then added papers authored or co-authored by Andrew and Victor."

"You can access the papers?" Kat covered her pad with shorthand Sunee couldn't interpret.

"There are a number of public websites. PLoS, PubMed." She shrugged. "I couldn't spend much time today, but I'll keep checking."

"Why do the papers stop?" Harris pulled it closer. "About a year after we were born?"

"It could be they were still writing papers, but they aren't posted to public websites. Maybe the research is private." Sunee gnawed on her bottom lip. "I think Elaina Ashland stopped doing the editing research. From what I can piece together, the company began looking at corrective genetic research. Corrections that take place *after* a child is born."

Harris looked over at Kat. "Can you dig up intel on Legacy?"

She nodded, taking notes.

"Anyone think we should call the remaining partner?" Harris looked around the group.

"Dr. Victor Giuseppe." Sunee twirled a hank of hair around her finger.

Kat bounced her pencil on the timeline. "Why don't I research the corporation."

"If they're in the biotech space, my father would have information on them," Sunee said quietly.

Harris's head snapped up at the mention of her father.

Leah hadn't lied. Harris knew who her father was. Her dinner threatened to come back up.

"If anyone knows, it's your dad." Ashe looked at Harris and Kat. "Her father's a bigwig in biotech financing."

Sunee nodded, hating the way Harris's face closed up.

Wouldn't that top the night? Breaking off what was happening between her and Harris and then needing to talk to her father.

"You don't have to talk to him." Ashe patted her hand. "If there's another way to get the information, Kat will find it."

"He knows more about biotech companies than the FDA. I'll … talk to him tomorrow." Sunee hoped the information cost from her father wouldn't be too steep.

"I need to head home." Kat folded up her notebook and tucked it into her bag. "I have to be at the station early."

Harris held out his hand. "Notebook stays here."

"Right." Kat slapped it into his hand. "No notes."

"I'll head out too." Ashe kissed Sunee's cheek.

She and Harris walked them to the door. Now she would tell him. Then she'd pack and leave.

Harris shut the door. "Thank goodness."

He backed her against the door, the wood cooling her back, the heat of his large body searing her chest and stomach. "I missed this last night. Missed you."

She couldn't say a word. Couldn't stop him. Didn't want to stop him. His mouth took hers and arousal shot through her like a laser beam. She sealed their lips together, not wanting to let him go.

"Bedroom," he gasped. Then he grabbed her hand and ran up the stairs.

She tripped.

"I can't wait." He swung her into his arms and kissed her. He tasted of Harris and beer and desperation.

One last time. So she would remember. She would make love to him and then let him go.

In the bedroom they stripped each other. She pushed away his clothes and memorized the taste of his skin and the softness of his hair. When she straddled his hips, he shivered, and power surged through her body.

"I love it when you take control." Harris's voice was rough. Dark.

She whispered, "I love making love to you."

One. Last. Time.

When Harris entered the Justice Center the next morning, Gary waited in the lobby. "What are you doing here?"

"We need to talk," Gary said.

"I can give you ten minutes," Harris said. This morning they were presenting pretrial motions.

He was late because he and Sunee had made love twice last night. Last night, she'd been wild. And taken him to heaven. He knew he was falling in love with her. He hadn't wanted to leave her this morning.

"I only need five," Gary said, but getting a security badge and taking the elevator to Harris's office took that long.

Harris set his briefcase next to his desk. "What's up?"

Gary closed the office door. "I've been putting out feelers on your candidacy. There's a very positive reaction. The age thing isn't much of an issue." Gary nodded like a bobblehead doll. "The fact that you're a bachelor hurts."

Harris's thoughts zipped back to Sunee. Maybe he wouldn't stay a bachelor much longer. "I can't get married next weekend, but I'll get there."

He expected Gary to grin.

Instead Gary's face was as solemn as a funeral. He pulled out a chair. "Let's talk about that, Torrington."

"Not on your life." He gathered the files he needed, not sitting down. "My private life stays private."

"Don't be an idiot. You don't have a private life." Gary's lips formed stiff lines. "If you want to be governor, I suggest you stop consorting with the daughter of New York's biggest Democratic fundraiser."

"What her father does has nothing to do with Sunee." Harris shook his head.

"It has *everything* to do with your image."

"I don't even know Sunee's political views." Harris spit the words out. They'd never had that discussion. She knew he was thinking about running for governor but hadn't voiced an opinion. "Just because her father's a fundraiser, doesn't mean that's who she supports."

Gary dug in his briefcase and handed Harris a printout of a New York Times article. There was Sunee in a dark blue gown, standing next to Senator Aversa from New York and Governor Rice, both Democrats. She looked ill.

Gary pointed at the only male Harris didn't recognize. "Her father raised two million for the New York Democratic Party at this shindig."

"This doesn't mean anything." Harris checked the date. "This was five years ago."

"And she was at a fundraiser five *weeks* ago." Gary shook his head. "This woman would be poison for your campaign."

"She's a doctor."

"One the press thinks is a lush." Gary pulled out another article. This one from a tabloid. He read the paragraph highlighted in yellow. *This reporter found the Kingmaker's daughter throwing up in the bathroom. Hopefully she sobered up before heading back to the hospital where she works.*

He tossed the article back to Gary. "This doesn't mean she was drinking. She could have been sick. Or ... it was her anxiety."

"Anxiety?"

"She has anxiety attacks in group settings." His stomach churned.

"You can't associate with someone like her." Gary threw up his hands. "The press calls her the Mute Doctor."

"No!" His body jerked. He couldn't break up with her.

"Just so we're clear, Torrington," Gary looked at his watch, "you need to stop seeing her."

Harris forced his lips into the smile he used when he met a witness for the prosecution, one he wanted to trust him. He couldn't stop seeing Sunee. She was an island of calm in his crazy world. "Let *me* make something clear. My personal life is just that —personal."

"You're making a mistake." Gary left the articles on Harris's desk. "If you want me to work on your campaign, you have to trust me."

There was a knock and Deb stuck her head in. "Harris, you need to get to the courtroom."

"Thanks, Deb."

Harris walked Gary to the door. "I'll think about what you've said."

That was all he would commit. He wouldn't stop seeing Sunee.

He swallowed back the bile burning the back of his throat. He and Sunee needed to talk. Soon. They should talk about her political affiliations. Talk about what was happening between them. He should man up and admit he might be falling in love with her.

But what if being with Sunee, the only woman he'd ever loved, derailed his career?

He wanted both. Was that even possible?

AFTER HER LAST PATIENT, Sunee sank into her office chair. The morning and early afternoon had flown by. Now exhaustion settled on her shoulders as heavy as her newly repaired microscope.

She and Harris had stayed up late, but it had been wonderful. And awful. Endings were awful. But she hadn't ended their relationship. Not yet.

Time to call her father and find out everything he knew about The Legacy Group. She picked up her personal phone, took a breath and then took two more before pushing dial.

"Sunee, you finally called." Her father's deep voice rumbled in her ear. "Did you get my message?"

"Message?"

"From last night."

She put her phone on speaker, checked her voice mail and winced. "I'm sorry. I missed your call."

"I'm in Houston. I'd like to have dinner."

"Oh." She'd planned to pack the things she'd brought to Harris's place and then tell him she was moving home.

"Let's meet at Ruth's Chris," he said.

"Dad, you can't keep eating like that. Your heart."

"Scold me at the restaurant." He laughed. "I'll … let you order my dinner."

"Salad it is," she joked.

He groaned. "I'll be there at seven."

"Yes. I have …"

"Sorry. Gotta go."

"Okay." But he'd already hung up.

She texted Harris, letting him know she was having dinner with her father. With a seven o'clock reservation, she couldn't talk to Harris. Relief streamed through her like irrigation on a wound. Harris deserved a conversation, but knowing her father, she wouldn't get home until late.

The rest of her afternoon sped by. She checked on the medical status of Dr. Ashland. No change. If Dr. Ashland would wake up, they might solve this genetic mystery. Then maybe this would be over.

Her alarm buzzed. She shook her head, but it was filled with the research studies she'd been reading. Time to head to the restaurant.

Even though Harris had made her promise not to go to her apartment alone, she wished she'd had enough time to change her clothes. Her slacks and blouse weren't NYC dinner worthy, but they would have to do. For once she left her lab coat hanging on her chair. Progress, right?

She valet parked and tucked the ticket into her purse. Straightening her shoulders, she headed inside. *Time to face the dragon.*

"Good evening," the host said. "Do you have a reservation?"

"Michael Miller?"

"He hasn't arrived, but I can seat you," the young man said.

"Thank you." She followed him through the restaurant. He pulled out the massive chair and handed her a menu.

When the server stopped by, she ordered a ginger ale. Her stomach hadn't been right since Leah had stopped to *chat*.

"Sunee!" Her father pulled her to her feet and hugged her.

His bright green eyes held a smile. His cedar cologne was as comforting as his hug. "I've missed you. It's time to kick the Texas dust off and come back to New York."

Love filled his gruff voice. Then the meaning of his words, the pure assurance she would return to New York and live out *his* dream for her, snapped her heart like it was a rubber band.

Instead of helping cure cancer, he wanted Sunee to use her knowledge to analyze *other people's* research. She would be the medical expert helping him understand the efficacy and science of possible drug targets. With that knowledge, he'd decide whether investing in the company would be advantageous. He eventually wanted her to run his firm.

"Believe it or not, I'm doing important things here." Sunee kept her voice low, her tone respectful. "I have patients that need me. Research that thrills me."

"They pay you chicken feed." Her father liked to use expressions from his Ohio farming background. He thought it hid his fierce intelligence. "I'd pay you more. A lot more."

"I'm happy." Her voice cracked. She sank into her chair. "What are you doing in Houston?"

"There's a company ready to begin clinical trials who needs

capital. Their second round of financing." Her father sat. "My team and I pitched handling their business."

"Is the drug a good target?" she asked, slipping into the lingo she'd heard all her life.

"Very. I'd love you to look at their data, but the confidentiality agreements are in place." He grinned. "When you're on my team, that won't be a problem. With your knowledge we'll increase our chances of making the right call on research drugs."

Before she could protest, the server arrived and took her father's drink order. Manhattan. Some things never changed. Her father ordered a cabernet for dinner.

"Have you heard of The Legacy Group out of Boston?" she asked once the server left. Maybe her question would keep her father from harping on her working for his firm.

"Legacy." He nodded. "They're still privately held."

"What do you know about them?"

"There were three founders. I tried to woo them when they were ready to do an equity deal, but they pulled out." He shook his head. "I don't know where they got their funding. No one in the banking world admitted they'd invested."

He recalled what he could about their research, and it matched the papers she'd found. Although her father's background was finance, he had one of the sharpest minds in biotech.

When the server brought her father's drink, she ordered salads, fresh vegetables and petit fillets for both of them.

"How about a ribeye?" he whispered. "And a baked potato."

"This is leaner meat," she said. "And you promised to let me order for you."

The server waited.

Her father rolled his eyes. "Fine."

"I'll get this right in," the server said.

"You're so much like your mother." Father rubbed the top of his head, messing up his hair, now shot with more silver than red.

"Stop trying to change a meat and potato Irishman into a vegetarian."

"You're getting a steak."

"A woman's steak." He sighed. "Why are you interested in Legacy?"

"I ran across some interesting research on germline therapies and genetic manipulation from thirty years ago. But nothing since then."

"Their initial research was all in vitro." Her father sipped his cocktail, frowning. "Now they've switched to designing genetic disorder tests."

"Do you know why they moved from pre- to post-birth?" she asked.

"No. I met with a founder, a Victor something, a few times. He wanted to take the company public. The other partners disagreed." He snapped his finger. "One founder died. He was married to the other partner. It's possible the surviving partner controls two-thirds of the company."

Interesting. But what did it have to do with Harris and Ashe? "Did you meet the other partner?"

"I tried. She apparently left the financing discussions to Victor."

Their server dropped off their salads, and a sommelier brought their wine to the table. He made a production of opening and letting her dad taste.

"Excellent," her father said.

"It's one of our best." The man poured her glass and topped off her father's glass and quietly left their table.

She swirled, sniffed and sipped. Let the wine roll in her mouth. "This is fantastic."

"At least I taught you to appreciate fine wines," he said.

"Yes, you did. How is Po Po?" She hadn't called her grandmother in over a week.

"Wondering when you will be home."

"I ... I'll look at my schedule." She tried to swallow her salad, but a lump blocked her throat. She didn't want to go to New York. "Maybe both of you could visit over Labor Day?"

"I'm not talking about for a holiday or weekend." His face took on the stern look reminiscent of her childhood. "I want you back permanently. I didn't pay all that money for your multiple doctorates to have it wasted on patients."

His words were like fists pummeling her diaphragm. "I can't do what you do," she choked out.

"Yes, you can. You're my daughter," he said. "You just need to learn the business."

"I ... I ..." Working with patients and doing cancer research was her calling. Harris understood this. "That's not what I want. I never took ... finance classes."

"You'll get your MBA while you learn the business." He waggled his fork at her. "With your brains you'll graduate in half the time."

She shook her head. "I'm good at what I do. I'm making a difference."

He frowned. "You can make a bigger difference by bringing the right drugs to market."

She clawed at her neck. "I love what I do."

Disgust crossed her father's face. "You're breaking out in hives. Take something."

A busboy cleared her father's salad plate.

Sunee pushed her half-eaten salad away, dug through her purse for an antihistamine and came up empty. She took a deep breath and another.

The server dropped off their entrees, took one look at her and asked, "Are you okay? Are you allergic to something?"

"I'm fine," she lied. Her embarrassment made her neck itch more.

The server nodded and backed away.

"I don't want to join your firm." Her words barely carried over the table.

"It's always been our plan." He didn't even look at her. Just cut into his steak.

And she'd never been brave enough to say no. She hated confrontation. "I can't."

"You can." He still focused on his dinner.

"Look at me," she choked out.

His head snapped up. "What?"

She grabbed her neck. "This isn't going to change. I'm … having an anxiety attack talking with *my own father*."

"There are drugs."

Her hands shook as she folded her napkin. "I have to go."

"Sunee," her father barked. "We're not done here."

"I am." She snatched her purse on the back of her chair. "I can't be what you want."

He half-stood, hovering over the table. "You're my only child. You will succeed me."

"Why would you want to make me miserable?" She sniffed back tears but had to make him understand. "I won't join your firm."

"Won't?" he whispered, his mouth dropped open.

She straightened her shoulders and looked him in the eyes. "No."

Her father snapped his mouth closed. "We'll talk about this later."

"I love you, but I can't do this." She walked out of the restaurant, her spine erect. She had finally said *no* to her father.

And it hurt.

CHAPTER FIFTEEN

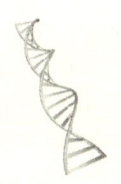

Harris pulled his truck onto the interstate, trying to shake off his exhaustion long enough to drive home. His courtroom adrenaline had evaporated hours ago.

Tonight he and the team had nailed down the prosecution witnesses order. And every minute they'd worked, he'd resented the team keeping him from returning home, returning to Sunee. But she was having dinner with her dad.

If his mother or Gary knew Sunee and her father were together, they'd go ballistic. He hated the pressure they were exerting to break him and Sunee up. He wanted both, Sunee and the governorship. But how did he protect her from anxiety *and* separate his campaign from her father's reputation?

When he pulled into the driveway, the house was dark. Was she home?

The garage opened and the Tahoe he'd lent her was inside, parked next to her unreliable Volvo.

His shoulders relaxed and a smile crossed his face. He couldn't wait to see her, to absorb some of her tranquility. Even if she was sleeping, he wanted to wrap his arms around her and get lost in her jasmine scent. Maybe even whisper he loved her.

No. Telling her he loved her was something to say when they were awake.

As he entered the dimly kitchen and headed to drop his keys on the desk, he stumbled over a suitcase. "What the …?"

"I'm sorry." Sunee turned from the island. "I … I shouldn't have left that in your path. I'm sorry."

He focused on her suitcase. Took in her purse and laptop bag sitting on the table. Ice ran down his spine. "What's going on?"

She slipped off the stool and wrapped her arms around her waist, staring at the floor.

Dread churned through him like a twister.

He hurried to her, needing to touch her. "What's wrong?"

"This isn't what I signed up for." When she looked at him, her face was blank. "I was only supposed to test whether you and Ashe were related."

His heart pounded in his chest. "I thought we were a team."

"I'm a doctor, a researcher." She shook her head. When her hair shifted, red welts dotted her chest and neck. "I want out of this mess."

"Sunee." Her words were like punches to his chest. Were her hives because of him?

"I … I can't handle this anymore. I want to get back to my patients. My research." She took a deep breath. "I'm done."

This wasn't Sunee. This wasn't the calm woman he loved. "Was it your father? Did he tell you we couldn't be together?"

"My father?" Her gaze snapped up to meet his. Finally.

"Did he tell you to stay away from me?" He wanted to punch something. Anything.

"You?" Her brows crunched together. "Why would you ask that?"

"I know he raises money for political campaigns for the opposition. Is this because of him?"

She didn't look him in the eye. "My father doesn't have anything to do with this decision."

His head ached. For once he couldn't ferret out the paths of logic, alternatives and possibilities. Nothing in his life added up anymore. But being with Sunee made his life—better. He tried to hug her. "Then why?"

"It's your ambitions." She backed away and his hand fell to his side. "I can't ... live in the limelight. I can't handle the stress. I can't. I ... won't."

"Sunee." Even though the room was cool, sweat dripped down his back. Her leaving was exactly what his mother and Gary wanted, but he couldn't let her go. "Don't do this. Please. We have something special. I've never felt this way about anyone."

She grabbed her belongings. "I can't change who I am for you."

"I don't want you to change." He caught her arm. This couldn't be happening. Before she'd come to live with him, this had just been a house. Now it was *their* home. "Where are you going? You won't be safe."

"The police haven't found any evidence the lab break-in was aimed at me. I'll be fine." She shook him off. "You're not responsible for my safety."

"Yes, I am." Responsibility had been drilled into him since he was young. He was here to make the world a better place. That included keeping Sunee safe.

"No." She shook her head.

Sunee walked out of his kitchen. Out of his life.

SUNEE STARED one more time at Harris's house. *I love you.* Then she put her Volvo in gear and left him.

This was the right thing to do. Harris deserved someone who could help his career, not hurt it. When he married the perfect political wife, she'd feel sorry for the woman stuck living in the spotlight.

She couldn't change who she was. Not for Harris. Not for her father.

Even though she'd done the right thing, her chest throbbed in pain. He'd find another woman who would touch him. A tear slid down her cheek. Another woman would love him.

Tonight, she'd taken control of her life. She'd told her father she wouldn't join his company. She'd left Harris. And every muscle ached in her body.

Somehow she drove to her apartment. Swallowing the lump in her throat, she parked the car and took deep breaths. Obviously she needed to get used to being alone again.

She shivered even though her Volvo's air conditioning wasn't working very well. She was better being alone.

Wrestling her suitcase from the backseat, she entered the building. Her suitcase bumped as she tugged it up the stairs. Ridiculous. She was stronger than this. She adjusted her purse and laptop case and picked up the case. She could carry it up three floors.

"Let me help you." A man dashed up the stairs. Silver hair flashed from under a ball cap.

"I'm fine." She tried to pull the handle from the man's hand.

"I insist." He hauled the case up the stairs.

She stared at his hands. Not hands. Gloves. In this heat?

"I can help you, Dr. Miller."

Her head jerked up. "How do you know my name?"

"I know a lot about you." In his other hand was a gun. And he wore a mask.

She stumbled.

"Dr. Miller." He pointed the gun up the stairs. "Move."

She staggered up the steps. Was this the man who'd broken into her lab? "What do you want?"

He shook his head, the mask scraping against his collar. "In your apartment. Now."

If she screamed would anyone help her? What if this man hurt them? She couldn't allow that to happen. Her hands shook, the keys banging on the wood as she unlocked the door. "I don't have much to steal."

He pushed her into the room.

"Oh God!" Paper crunched beneath her shoes. Broken glass shimmered in the hall. Crooked pictures hung from her wall as though she was in a carnival fun house. A putrid smell emanated from the kitchen.

He shoved her into the living room and waved his gun. "Sit."

She moved around the overturned coffee table and tipped lamps. The sofa cushions covered the floor.

Her phone rang in her purse.

"Don't," he growled.

"What do you want?" This could be anything. Drugs. A robbery.

But she knew it wasn't. This was about Harris and Ashe.

"Sunee, answer your damn phone," Harris yelled after her phone rolled to voicemail. "Talk to me."

He punched in redial. No answer.

He slammed his fist on the truck console. He should have stopped her. Nothing she'd said had rung true. It had taken him a few minutes to put it together. Unfortunately by the time he'd started his truck, she was gone.

If she'd been a witness in a trial, he would have guessed she was lying. Her repeated insistence they were through. Her hand covering her mouth. Her inability to look him in the eye.

She'd lied.

Why? He breathed his first clear breath since she'd driven away. The muscles in his chest released. His fists relaxed. He would find out the real reason she'd left him.

At least her car was in her apartment parking lot. If she'd gone somewhere else he wouldn't know how to find her.

He scowled as he jerked open the apartment building's unlocked door. This wasn't protection. She should never have left his house.

He dashed up the three flights of stairs to her floor. He wanted to scream—*Sunee*—but that was too reminiscent of a Tennessee Williams play.

At her door, he stopped and took a couple of deep breaths. He couldn't go in there guns blazing. He wanted to know what had changed. Especially after the way they'd made love last night. Why had she left him? Why had she broken his heart?

He raised his hand to knock. A deep voice on the other side of the door stopped him. *She'd run to another man?*

No. This was Sunee. He put his ear to the door, trying to understand the man's muffled words and the door moved. The lock wasn't latched.

Should he knock? Hell no. If he had to apologize to Sunee later, he would.

He eased the door open, relieved it didn't squeak. He opened it enough to glide inside.

Shit. The hall table was upended. Pictures hung twisted on the wall. The stench of rotting food had his head rearing back.

He fought the urge to rush to Sunee. Instead he slipped out the door and called 9-1-1.

"There's been a break-in." He kept his voice calm and low.

The operator took the specifics. "Please wait for the officers to arrive."

"My friend is in there with the perp."

"Sir—"

"I'm going in." He hung up and slipped back inside Sunee's apartment.

"I don't know what you're talking about." Sunee's voice quivered. "Who are these men?"

"Don't be stupid, Dr. Miller. What do you know about Bristol and Torrington?"

Crap.

Harris slid along the wall, sidestepping glass on the floor and trying to recall the living room layout. If he was at six o'clock, the sofa was at noon with armchairs at eleven and one. The TV was on the wall left of where he stood, at seven o'clock.

"I don't understand your question," Sunee said.

Harris paused near the archway and risked a glance into the dimly-lit room. Sunee was perched on the edge of the bare sofa. The cushions lay on the floor.

Her eyes were huge. Her hands clenched.

The coffee table was on its side. Magazines and broken glass covered the floor.

A man faced Sunee with his back to him. The guy was shorter than Harris by five or six inches. Was he wearing a mask under his ball cap?

"What do you know about Bristol and Torrington?" The man waved his hand, and metal flashed in the light shining through the windows.

Damn it. Gun.

Harris ground his teeth. As district attorney he was licensed to carry, but his gun was locked in his safe.

"Bristol is a football player. Torrington is an attorney." Sunee caught sight of Harris and her eyes opened wide. She clutched at the sofa's edge.

Harris held a finger to his lips.

"I know you've visited Torrington in his office. Tell me what you know," the man growled. "I'll kill you if you don't."

Her mouth dropped open. "I ... I ..." Tears streamed down her face. "Who are you?"

Harris crept into the room. He had one chance.

The guy waved the gun again. "What have you discovered?"

"I—" Sunee started.

Harris leapt and grabbed the gun, yanking it toward the window. "Sunee, run!"

A shot exploded. Glass shattered. Harris ripped harder at the gun.

Another shot. The barrel burned his fingers, but he refused to let go. He and the man crashed to the floor.

The guy twisted. Rolled. Kicked. Caught Harris in the knee.

Pain rifled through his leg. Harris held on, twisting the man's hand. Sunee's safety was all that mattered. He slammed the man's hand on the floor. Again. And again. His hand stung with each smack.

The gun skittered away.

The man punched him in his chest, then in the side of his head.

Harris rolled with the blows. His ears rang. Grabbing the man's shoulders, he forced him on his back and straddled him.

The guy twisted out of reach, bucking and rolling. Harris slid with him.

"Freeze!" Sunee shouted. "Freeze!"

He and the man froze.

Why hadn't she run?

Sunee held the gun in both hands. Shaking.

Harris started to slide away.

The man kicked. Harris flew backwards and smacked his head on the wall under the TV.

The intruder scrambled to his feet and tore out of the apartment.

Harris shook his head, but it still rang. No. Sirens.

"Harris!" Sunee dropped to her knees next to him. "Oh my God. Are you okay?"

"Fine." He inhaled. Sharp aches filled his chest. Did he have a broken rib? "I wish you'd shot the bastard."

"You were hurt." She pushed back his hair and stared into his eyes. "Did you lose consciousness?"

"No."

"How many fingers?" she asked.

"Two." Or maybe three?

His shoulder and knee screamed in agony. He took a minute, and then clutching his aching abdomen, he slid up to rest against the wall. "Is he gone?"

"I think so."

"Hand me the gun."

She picked it up and handed it to him.

"You're hurt." She ran her hands on his ribs.

He groaned.

She turned his arm and blood ran down to his palm. "I'll be back."

He frowned at the blood. Had he broken the guy's nose?

Sunee returned with a tray of first aid stuff and a flashlight. "Look at me."

She flashed the light in his eyes.

"Hey." He blinked.

"Pupils are equal and reactive," she announced.

"Police!" a woman shouted from the hall.

"In here," Sunee called out. "The intruder's gone."

"Don't say anything about Ashe and me," he whispered. He needed to think through any consequences, and his brain wasn't working right now. He slid the gun out of reach.

"But..." she said.

"No." He held up a finger as footsteps moved down the hallway.

She blinked, then nodded.

The police woman came around the corner, her weapon leading the way. "Hands up."

They complied. The cop stepped over to the gun and kicked it away from them. "Whose apartment?"

"Mine. Can I clean his wound?"

The cop nodded.

Sunee swabbed hydrogen peroxide on Harris's hand.

He winced. "That's the intruder's gun. We've both touched it."

The policewoman pulled out gloves and an evidence bag. Then she bagged the gun. "We'll look around."

"How's your chest?" Sunee asked.

"I'm f—"

"Don't say that," she hissed. "You're in pain."

He exhaled. Mistake. "Yeah. Feels like I was kicked by a mule."

"You need X-rays." She didn't look him in the eyes.

As Sunee tended his cuts, the police woman and her partner checked every room.

Then the officer flipped out a notebook. "Tell me what happened."

Sunee walked through the events. Harris added his perspective.

"Someone tossed your apartment before you walked in?" the female officer asked.

Sunee nodded.

"Did you recognize the intruder?"

Sunee plucked a piece of glass from Harris's arm. "He wore a mask and a ball cap. And he had gloves on. Oh, he had silver hair."

"Dr. Miller's lab was broken into a week ago." Harris grasped for the detective's name, his brain fuzzy and slow. "There's a Detective … Cruz working that case."

"Lucinda Cruz," Sunee added, frowning at Harris.

The cop nodded to her partner. "Why don't you give Cruz a call?"

Harris took Sunee's hand. "Are you all right?"

"Fine." She tugged her hand out of his. "Can you stand?"

Her rejection was as sharp as the glass she'd pulled out of his arm. "Yes."

He used the wall to take the pressure off his ribs.

This time it was Sunee giving him a hand. Apparently Dr.

Miller was fine putting her hands on him, but Sunee, the woman he'd made love to, fallen in love with, hated his touch.

What went wrong?

She tugged up the sofa cushions and helped him sit down.

"Can we open the windows?" she asked the police. "The smell is awful."

A cop dusting the window sash for fingerprints cranked one open.

Footsteps echoed in the hall.

"Dr. Miller. DA Torrington." Detective Cruz worked her way through the mess and into the living room. "Sorry to see you again. Another break-in?"

Sunee nodded, her arms wrapped around her stomach.

They walked her through the events, leaving out their suspicions that this was related to him and Ashe.

"Did you recognize the man?" the detective asked.

"No. He wore a mask," Harris said. "Silver hair. Brown eyes. Under six feet tall."

"I need to take Mr. Torrington to the ER," Sunee said. "He might have broken ribs."

Detective Cruz nodded. "We'll canvass the building and see if anyone saw anything. Too bad there aren't security cameras in the building."

The detective handed Sunee a form and a packet. "Ms. Miller, please detail your losses. This is your case number." She pointed to the top of the page. "The fax number is on the form."

"I will. Thank you."

A uniformed officer called the detective over. "Ma'am, there's a camera in the entry."

"A camera?" Sunee asked.

"Tucked on top of the mirror. And another in the kitchen."

Sunee's gaze shot to Harris, her face pale.

"Any chance you can trace who was monitoring the camera?" Harris asked.

"We'll try." Detective Cruz looked between them. "Anything you want to tell me?"

They both shook their heads.

Cruz didn't look convinced. "You can get him to the ER. We'll lock up."

"You can't stay here, Sunee," Harris said once they were in the hallway. "Not alone. You understand that, right?"

Her shoulders sank. She sighed. "I know."

"You're coming home with me after the ER." He would use his injury to keep her safe.

She stopped on the second floor landing and faced him. "Don't tell me what to do."

He exhaled. "Where can you go that's safer?"

"I ... I could stay with Ashe. Or in the hotel where my father is staying."

"Are they safer than my home?" He took her hand.

She pulled away and sighed. "No."

"Please." He wanted to hug her, but didn't. "Stay with me."

"I ... I don't want to, but I will." Her gaze locked on his. "I'll sleep in a guest bedroom."

Another crack split his heart. At least she was coming home with him. Now he had to find out why she'd left in the first place.

CHAPTER SIXTEEN

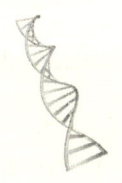

Piper brushed her mother's hair. "You're looking good today, Mom."

She always talked to her mother, hoping her mother could hear her and pull away from wherever she'd escaped to heal.

"Dr. Sutton says you're improving." The chair squealed as she pulled it closer to the bed. "Nathan. He wants me to call him Nathan. He's cute."

Loud voices echoed outside the door. Piper stood and blocked the path between the door and her mother. No one would hurt her mother again.

"I'm family!" a man said.

"Uncle Victor!" She ripped opened the door.

"See," Victor said to the guard. "I'm allowed in her room."

Piper wrapped her arms around Victor. "I'm so glad you're here."

To the guard she said, "He's allowed as a visitor."

The man nodded and took up a clipboard. "Name."

"Victor Giuseppe." He patted Piper on the back.

"That's what I needed." The guard wrote it down.

"Why the security?" Victor growled as they walked into her mother's room.

"That doctor from Johns Hopkins tried to kill her. I thought I told you." The night was a blur, but she had told him, right? She'd barely slept since that day. Uncle Victor had promised to come right away. That had been Friday. It was now Wednesday. What had taken him so long?

"Didn't they arrest him?" Victor asked.

"They never found him." She swallowed. "That's why her room is guarded."

Victor huffed out a small breath. "I assumed they'd caught the man."

"No," Piper said. "Can *you* think of any reason why someone would want to kill her?"

After the police had asked her that question, she'd wracked her brain but hadn't come up with anything.

"Why would I know?" His answer was abrupt. His voice too loud.

"I'd hoped you could think of something, someone …" She held up her hands.

"I can't." He stalked to the bedside. "How is she?"

"Her neurologist thinks she's improving." She squeezed her mother's hand.

They stared at the monitor.

No change.

"How long can she stay in the hospital?" He crossed to the window, picking up the cards and flower arrangements and setting them down without looking.

"I don't know." And she hadn't asked. If they wanted to transfer her mother to long-term care, what would she do?

Victor moved back to the bed and held Elaina's hand. He let it drop and grabbed the lotion off the tray and rubbed some on her hand. "Is she stable enough to move back to Boston?"

"We haven't talked about moving her." Piper's stomach

clenched into a ball. What was wrong with Uncle Victor? Why was he acting so—weird?

"We'll have to talk about it soon." Victor sighed. "I remember when your mother had to make the decision to take your father off life support."

"Don't talk about that," Piper whispered.

"Honey, you have to think about these things."

"She's improving," Piper insisted.

"The attorney is looking through the partnership agreements." Victor's hand rested on the bed. "We need to decide what will happen with the company."

"Not right now." She glared at him, but Uncle Victor was staring at her mother.

"Soon. There's a board meeting next month." Uncle Victor straightened the sheets. He looked over at her and his nose wrinkled. "Go clean up. It looks like you've been living here."

She had. Ever since Dr. Lassiter had injected her mother with morphine. "I ..."

"I'll watch her." Uncle Victor waved his hand at her mother.

"Okay." She could use a shower. "Talk to her. Let her know you're here."

"Sure, sure." He settled into the chair and took her mother's hand.

To the guard, she said, "I'm running to the hotel to clean up. Please keep an eye on Mother."

As she walked to the elevators, unease crawled up her neck. She shouldn't be worried. This was her godfather, her honorary uncle. She should trust him.

But something was—off.

Sunee grabbed her mug from her desk and took another gulp of tea, hoping for a jolt of energy. After last night's dinner with her father, the break up with Harris, and her apartment break-in at gunpoint, she was out of reserves.

Sleeping in Harris's guest bedroom hadn't helped. She'd wanted Harris to hold her.

Instead she was continuing her review of Dr. Ashland's genetic research work while one of her tests ran. She'd been at it since after lunch. The more she discovered, the quicker they could figure out why someone was after *her*. Was it something she already knew? Other than the genetic similarities with Ashe and Harris that couldn't be explained, what did she know?

She pulled out the timeline and added in the additional papers both Dr. Ashlands had published. There were interesting papers on chromosomes, inheritable diseases and cell structure. Tapping her pen against the timeline, she stared. What had this couple been doing? Before her husband's death, the doctors had published prolifically. That all stopped at his death. Or was it around the time Harris and Ashe had been conceived?

There was a knock at the door.

She tensed. They rarely had visitors.

"I'll get it," Marcus called. He was reviewing the DNA results of her latest family to see if there was a genetic explanation that the young boy had gotten sarcoma.

"I'm looking for Sunee."

"Dad?" Sunee moved out from her desk.

She introduced Marcus and then said, "I thought you were leaving this morning."

"I changed my flight." Her father glanced around the lab. "Can we talk somewhere private?"

"I guess the cafeteria." Although her last private conversation there with Harris's mom had been awful.

She scratched her neck and then grabbed her ID and wallet.

As she drew close to her father, he hugged her.

Inside she melted. This was her dad. Her arms tightened before they both let go.

"Follow me," she said, love choking her words.

"So that's your office?" he asked. Contempt filled his voice.

"That's my lab. My office is upstairs." But she rarely used it.

"You don't even have windows."

"I don't need windows. Neither does my research." She forced her voice to stay calm. "In fact sunlight and changes in temperature could be deleterious to my experiments."

"Deleterious." He smiled. "You used that word when you were five. Correctly too. You were such a bright little thing."

Was that a compliment?

He frowned as they stood in the elevator. "You look like you didn't sleep last night."

She hadn't. But she refused to tell her father someone had broken into her apartment. He would use that information as a lever to get her to leave Houston. "I had a late night."

"You shouldn't have to be on call. You should be beyond that."

She let him think that was why she was tired. But she hadn't been on call. If she had, she wouldn't have been drinking at dinner.

In the cafeteria, she poured hot water into a cup and selected a tea bag. Her father did the same but with coffee. And he insisted on paying.

"You know, I'm not a broke student anymore," she said.

He snorted. "You were *never* a broke student. I saw to that."

His financial support was one of the things he'd used to control her actions. Her father had even bought her a condo next to campus so she didn't have to worry about rent or roommates. "You're right, and I thank you for my education."

She'd been lucky. Most of her fellow students had come out of med school with backbreaking debt.

She and her father sat in armchairs near the windows. Normally she enjoyed the view. Not today.

He took a deep breath. "I'm sorry we argued last night."

"I am too." She sipped her tea, too emotionally exhausted to say more.

He looked at her. Did he expect her to apologize?

"I wish you would move back to New York," he finally said.

"My work is here."

He shook his head. "You can work anywhere. But I want you to work for my firm."

"This has to stop." She set her tea down and sat up straight. She had to make her father understand. "I'm not ever working in the investment banking industry. It's not for me."

"You're my daughter—"

"—stop." She held up her hand and ignored her twisting stomach. "I can't do what you do. I'd be miserable."

"Miserable?" He shook his head.

"How much of your day is spent with clients and strangers?" she asked.

He sipped his coffee. "Fifty percent. Maybe more."

The tea she'd sipped threatened to come back up at the thought of interacting with strangers for so much time. "I couldn't do that."

"Once you're exposed, you'll get over your," he waved his hand at her neck, "anxiety."

She scratched at a couple of welts. "You're my father and I'm breaking out in hives. This isn't going away."

"In the beginning you wouldn't spend much time with clients." He leaned forward and said, "You used to take medication."

"I was always groggy." She tucked her shaking hands under her thigh. If she could give up Harris for his career, surely she could stand up to her father. "I'm not joining your firm."

His face went blank. His green eyes dimmed.

"I'm sorry." She took a deep breath. "I have to do what is right for me."

"Right for you?" His voice cracked. "Is it wrong that I want you to be successful?"

"I am succeeding."

"But you could make more money." He held out a hand. "I want you to succeed."

"You don't think I am?" Her father's words were as sharp as a scalpel slashing into her self-image. She was a doctor.

He sat back and crossed his arms. "You can do better."

She would never be the person her father expected, no matter how hard she tried. She had to do what was right for her.

She exhaled. A weight lifted off her shoulders. "I love you."

"I love you too." He took her hand and grinned. "Sounds like you finally got the message."

Message? No. But she'd seen the light. "I love you, but I'm never changing fields or working for you. This is where I belong."

"Slaving in a dingy basement?"

"If that's what it takes." She squeezed his hand. "You're great at what you do, but so am I. And trying to stop cancer is what I do. Treating children with cancer is what I do. You hammering away at me will not change my mind."

He sank back in the chair and pushed a hand through his carrot and silver hair. "I always thought ... is this what you really want?"

"Yes." She squeezed his hand. "I hope your love isn't contingent on my working for you. I hope we can still have a relationship."

His mouth dropped open. "You're my daughter."

"Then don't tell me I have to quit doing what I love."

"I ... I won't mention it again." He stared, shaking his head. "I never realized you were so much like your mother."

How she wished she were. Her mother had been successful, married and a wonderful mother.

That wasn't in the cards for her. Sunee had pushed away the only man she'd ever loved.

She would savor this moment. Her dad finally understood. Soon she'd get back to the life she'd led before Harris had made her see there could be more. She swallowed the lump in her throat. She would focus on her work.

For once her patients and research didn't sound like enough.

HARRIS FLIPPED through the messages stacked on his desk, hoping there was one from Sunee. Nothing. There was one marked urgent. The mayor wanted to meet for breakfast. He scribbled *Yes* on the message. He might not work for the mayor, but he wanted to keep his constituents informed and happy.

Deb stuck her head in his office. "Do you need anything else?"

"No. It's after six. Go home."

"Thanks. I will."

"See you in the morning." He and the Barney trial team had worked through the judge's rulings on their pretrial motions and reworked the evidence and witness lineups.

"I added a meeting to your calendar, tomorrow at eight," Deb said.

"What would I do without you?"

"When you run for governor, remember me. I wouldn't mind moving to the capital."

"I'll keep that in mind." He waved goodnight and sank into his chair. The rumor was making the rounds. Gary needed to be more circumspect.

He should head home, but he didn't want to face Sunee. He didn't want to sleep in his bed alone. She'd gone from loving to cold in less than twelve hours. At least she was staying at his house. The police hadn't figured out who the guy was, so she couldn't leave him yet.

It was wrong, but he was glad there'd been a break in. Even though his heart had stopped as the guy had waved a gun at her.

Was it because of his career, or because she didn't want to be involved with a politician? Had Gary talked to her?

He didn't care. He'd won her once. He would do it again.

Energized, he grabbed his cell phone and headed out the door, punching in her speed dial.

"Dr. Miller." Hearing her voice made him smile.

"Hey, it's me." He waited through the silence.

"Hi." There was traffic in the background. She must be in the car.

He entered his truck and punched the starter. Amidst the chaos, she was the one thing right in his world. "Are you on your way home?"

"Don't make this harder," she pleaded. Her voice filled his car as the hand's free system came on.

"I need to know you're safe." He scanned his card and exited the parking ramp. "I needed to hear your voice. I miss you."

His life was better with Sunee in it.

"Don't say things like that," she said.

"I'll always tell you the truth." He let her digest that for a few seconds. "How long till you're home?"

"I'm pulling into the grocery store by your house right now. I thought I would get something for dinner."

"Don't go in without me." What if the guy who'd held her at gunpoint was following her? "The police haven't figured out who that guy was last night."

"I'll run in and run out. There are lots of people around."

"You promised you'd go straight to work and come straight back to my place." His fingers clenched the steering wheel.

"It's a public place." Her turn signal chimed. "Here's a parking spot. I'll see you at your house."

"Sunee—"

She hung up.

His stomach twisted into knots. She shouldn't be alone. Not when they didn't know who or what they were up against.

He wanted to call her back. Wanted to keep her from going anywhere by herself.

For some reason he and Ashe finding each other was causing Sunee problems. It didn't make sense. It hadn't been about a black market baby ring. Who was damaged by him and Ashe finding each other?

Every stop light had a vendetta against him. If he missed one signal, he missed ten. By the time he was at the store, what was normally a ten-minute drive had taken fifteen.

At least Sunee's car was still in the lot. He parked next to it and ran inside.

Where was she? He moved through the store, searching each aisle. Maybe she'd left her lab coat on?

No white jacket.

In the wine aisle, he spotted dark hair pulled into a ponytail and rushed toward the woman, setting a hand on her shoulder.

She jumped. Squealed. Not Sunee.

"Sorry, I thought you ..." He backed away, his hands in the air. Rounding one more display case, he found her pulling two bottles from the bottom shelf.

"Sunee!"

Her head jerked up and she juggled the bottles, luckily not dropping them. "What are you doing here?"

"You shouldn't be alone."

Darkness swept through her eyes, turning them a deep jade color. "I'm fine."

"But what if that guy is following you?" He should have hired security for her.

"I've barely been alone today. Marcus even walked me to my car." She pushed off the floor and set the wine in her cart. "No one followed me from the hospital. No one followed me into the store."

He cupped her elbows. "How can you be sure?"

"I can't. But I won't live my life in fear." She pulled away from him. "I have to live my life on my own terms."

"I don't understand."

"I know." Sadness filled her voice. "Someone like you couldn't possibly understand."

He wanted to pull her into his arms and shelter her. "Talk to me. Help me understand."

"Not here." She put the cart between them and pushed it toward the checkout lines.

He scanned the store as they waited in line. No one stared at them.

They loaded her bags into his Tahoe, at least she'd agreed to drive that. He pointed to his truck. "I'll follow you home. Don't lose me."

"No one is following me."

"Then you don't have to worry." But he would.

This might be her first rodeo, but it wasn't his. He'd been in danger before. It came with his job description. He wasn't letting Sunee be hurt. Not if it was because of him.

He placed calls to Ashe and Kat. It was time to rethink this problem.

"Tell me why we can't be together?" Harris asked Sunee, tucking the last dish from their dinner into the dishwasher. "Talk to me."

She swallowed. If Kat or Ashe would get here, she wouldn't have to be alone with Harris. Alone and hurting. "We just—can't."

He dried his hands and then caught hers. His gray eyes locked on hers. "We have something special. Don't give up on us."

She closed her eyes, unable to look at him, to lie to him. "If you keep pushing, I'll leave."

He frowned. "Did Gary talk to you?"

She didn't know anyone with that name. "Who?"

The doorbell rescued her from further interrogation.

Harris cradled her cheek and then headed down the hall.

She sank against the counter, curling around her aching stomach. This was too hard.

Ashe came into the kitchen. "Hey, what's wrong?"

She glanced at Harris. "Nothing."

"Are you sure?" Ashe rubbed her shoulders, then pulled her into a hug.

"I'm tired," she mumbled into his T-shirt.

When he let her go, she topped off her wine and left the men in the kitchen. The doorbell rang as she was in the hallway so she opened the door. "Hi, Kat."

"I'm glad we're getting together." Kat gave her a quick hug.

"The guys are in the kitchen, but I think we'll be more comfortable in the media room."

"I'll get something to drink and herd them in," Kat said.

Sunee hurried into the room ahead of everyone. She wanted to claim an armchair so she wasn't sitting next to Harris.

Kat carried in a glass of wine, the men trailing behind her. She pulled the notebook from its place on the shelf. "I've got more information."

"Hang on." Harris held up a finger. "We need to tell you what happened last night."

He walked everyone through yesterday's events. The non-personal stuff.

"Did you recognize the guy?" Ashe asked.

"He wore a mask," Sunee said.

Harris added, "He had silver hair and brown eyes."

"And the guy found you at your apartment?" Ashe bounced to his feet and paced the room. "You can't stay there anymore."

"She's staying here," Harris said.

Ashe turned to Sunee. "You're staying here?"

"Yes," she said.

"Have you seen her apartment building?" Harris asked. "No security. No cameras. At least this is a secured location."

"Here?" Ashe growled. "Like you're sleeping with Sunee?"

"Stop," Sunee said. "We were sleeping together. We aren't anymore."

Ashe scrambled to his feet. "I told him to stay away from you."

Harris stood too. "You're not her guardian."

Kat's gaze bounced between the two men. "Guys."

"Both of you stop." Sunee put her hands up. "We have bigger problems."

Ashe poked a finger into Harris's chest. "How could you?"

"How could I?" Harris shot back. "I'm in love with her!"

Sunee gasped. Ashe collapsed on the sofa. Kat coughed.

Harris closed his eyes, shaking his head and whispered, "Sunee, I…"

No. Every muscle in her body shook.

"If you're in love with her," Ashe shouted, "then why the hell did you break up with her?"

Sunee turned to Ashe. "I broke up with him."

The room went silent. Kat sent her a sympathetic look.

Harris touched her shoulder, but she shrugged him off and escaped to the armchair. *He was in love with her?* Her chest ached like she'd been cracked open for heart surgery without anesthesia.

For Harris's own good, she would never tell him she loved him too.

HARRIS LET Sunee shake off his hand. Let her sit back in the armchair. He hated the distance between them. It was as wide as the Rio Grande and as dangerous as the river after a storm.

He had to get through to her. He loved her.

Sunee wouldn't look him in the eye. Hives covered her neck and chest.

"You can stay with me," Ashe said to her.

Harris jerked his gaze over to Ashe. "In a hotel? That's not secure."

Ashe moved to stand behind Sunee, setting his hand on her shoulder. "She doesn't want to be around you."

Harris stood in front of Sunee's chair. Ashe behind it.

"Sunee, where do you want to stay?" Ashe asked.

"My house is safer than a hotel," Harris said before she could answer. And if she stayed here, maybe she would tell him what had gone wrong and he could fix it. "The development is secure, and my security system is state of the art."

"I'd keep her safe," Ashe insisted.

Sunee's quiet voice interrupted the argument. "Both of you stop."

"But—" Ashe started.

"No," Sunee said. "We'll talk about this later."

Kat pushed Harris toward the sofa and grabbed Ashe's hand and tugged him to the other chair. She sat on the coffee table halfway between Harris and Ashe. Did Kat think she could stop them from throwing punches? He didn't believe in violence as a solution, but Ashe might make him change his mind.

"So." Kat made a wiping motion in the air, like she was clearing a chalkboard. "Dr. Ashland had a child, Piper, on October 15th. The same year as you were born."

"Another child?" Sunee scooted forward.

"And the daughter works at Legacy." Kat blew out a breath. "But I can't find out a lot on the company."

"My dad promised to send me any information he could," Sunee said.

Harris took a deep breath. "How long after Andrew died was Piper born?" He couldn't think of Andrew as his father. He had a father.

"Hang on." Sunee scooted from the room and came back with her laptop bag. Kneeling at the coffee table, she spread out the timeline.

There were more notations than the first time she'd shown the timeline to everyone. Sunee noted Piper's birthdate, then sat back on her heels. "Almost twelve months after Andrew died."

Twelve months. "How does that happen?" he asked.

"Probably in vitro," Sunee murmured, staring at the timeline.

"So we're not triplets?" Ashe asked.

"I need to test her DNA." Sunee rubbed her chin.

"What's the status of Dr. Ashland?" Kat asked. "Is she conscious yet?"

"I haven't heard anything since I stopped on Friday." Sunee chewed her lip.

"I'll bet her daughter is at her bedside," Harris said.

He, Ashe and Kat looked at Sunee.

"I couldn't get close to Dr. Ashland's room last time." Sunee scratched her neck.

"I'll go," Harris said. He didn't want Sunee having an anxiety attack. "I can ask her about her mother's long-term study."

Sunee shook her head. "It makes more sense for me to go."

"You can probably get closer to her than the rest of us." Kat checked the time. "Is there something else I can dig into?"

"Find out everything you can about this daughter," Harris said.

Kat nodded.

"There is something I wanted to talk through." Harris took Kat's tablet and flipped to a new page. He wrote down WHO WHAT WHEN WHERE HOW WHY.

"We've answered some of these questions." He wrote Elaina and Andrew Ashland next to *Who*. "Sunee suspects there was ... genetic manipulation."

Sunee nodded. "That would be the *What* and maybe *How*."

"*Where* seems to have happened in both Minneapolis and

Texas," Ashe added, "assuming we're talking about the fertility clinics."

"The *When* can be tracked using Sunee's timeline."

Harris looked at them. "That leaves *Why*."

"Why did Dr. Ashland do this?" Kat asked. "Because her husband died?"

"*Why* did someone break into Sunee's lab and apartment and specifically ask about us." Harris waved his hand between him and Ashe.

"*Why* doesn't anyone want us to discover we're related?" Ashe's leg bounced up and down.

Why? Sunee rolled her neck. "Because embryo editing experimentation wasn't ethical back then?"

"Is it legal now?" Kat asked, pulling back her notebook.

"There was an FDA ban, but I think that involved research funding. Some states have prohibited embryo editing research," Sunee said. "We would need to verify where this occurred."

"Would that be enough to want to keep Ashe and my origins secret?" Harris asked. "Who do we hurt if we're discovered?"

Everyone sat back.

"Illegal or unethical research." Harris shook his head. "If they were doing the research, maybe their grants would be put in jeopardy."

"My father said he couldn't figure out where their funding came from," Sunee said.

"That was so long ago." Ashe tapped his foot. "Would someone take the money back from thirty plus years ago?"

There was silence.

"Why now?" Sunee asked. "Why hack into the hospital's security system and break into my lab?"

"Who's that powerful?" Kat asked. "Who has that kind of capabilities?"

Harris sighed. "I don't think we'll solve this tonight, but let's keep tugging on this thread."

"I'll research the laws and regulations," Kat volunteered.

"I can check from my end," Sunee volunteered. She stood, not looking at Harris. "I'm exhausted. I hope you don't mind if I go to bed."

"Get some sleep." Ashe gave Sunee a hug, glaring at Harris over the top of her head. "The offer's still open to stay in my hotel suite."

"I'm too tired to do anything tonight." Sunee backed away. "Night."

Harris wanted to be the one to comfort Sunee, hold her. Instead he played host and escorted Ashe and Kat to the door. Then he locked down the house.

In the library, he opened the safe and pulled out his gun. He checked and rechecked for ammunition and then snapped the safety back on. He wasn't taking Sunee's safety for granted anymore.

He stopped at her bedroom door and set his hand on the wood. They would never work things out if she was avoiding him.

CHAPTER SEVENTEEN

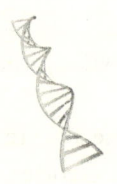

Sunee snuck out of Harris's house before dawn, too exhausted to face him.

I'm in love with her! Harris's words had echoed in her head all night. They should have filled her with joy. Instead she'd barely slept.

When he'd shouted those words, he hadn't looked happy either.

She wasn't good for him or his ambitions. The press would eviscerate her. The New York papers had questioned her role at her father's fundraising efforts. One reporter had found her throwing up in the bathroom. Another reporter had asked questions she hadn't answered.

Harris shouldn't have to deal with her anxiety. It was torture being around him. Wanting to be with him and knowing it couldn't be.

Maybe she *should* stay with Ashe. Maybe no one was after her. Maybe whoever had targeted her would leave her alone now. As long as she was dreaming, maybe she would cure cancer today.

She sighed and glanced both ways, searching for cars as she passed through the security gate.

If she could talk to Dr. Ashland's daughter, she might get more answers. But the *why* haunted her. *Why* did Harris and Ashe finding each other cause problems?

As she pulled onto the freeway, a dark SUV pulled in behind her. The back of her neck crawled. There weren't many cars around. The SUV was too far away to read the license plate.

Grabbing her phone, she booted up the phone screen. Should she call 9-1-1? Harris?

No, she was being paranoid. She focused on getting to the hospital but kept glancing back at the SUV. It might be a coincidence. It was probably just another person heading to work.

As she took her exit, the SUV closed in. Her fingers clenched the steering wheel. She took the exit fast, not wanting the vehicle to catch her. Merging onto the city street, she shifted lanes and ended up behind a police car. Thank goodness!

The SUV dropped back, never changing lanes as she turned into the hospital campus and her parking ramp.

The sweat breaking out over her body had nothing to do with Houston's heat and humidity and everything to do with her memories of the man who'd waved a gun at her in her apartment.

She ran into the safety of the hospital. Where she belonged.

MARK DROVE straight past the hospital entrance, letting a few more cars pull in-between him and the cop car. He'd tried to get near Torrington's house this morning, but the guard station was manned 24/7. As he'd driven past the development for the third time, Dr. Miller had exited the gated community.

He'd wasted an opportunity. When they'd been the only two cars on the freeway, he should have forced her car off the road.

But he couldn't kill her right away. He needed to know what they'd dug up before she was silenced. He needed to know why Bristol and Torrington were associating with a molecular geneticist. Of the three, he'd deemed Dr. Miller the easiest to get close to and the one who would understand the possible genetic ramifications. He shouldn't have trashed her apartment, he hadn't been able to control his anger. Now Dr. Miller would be more cautious.

God forbid she uncovered the trail between Legacy and the Foundation. Dr. Ashland had left them vulnerable. It was up to Mark to clean up these loose ends.

He circled the sprawling hospital and pulled into the parking ramp Dr. Miller had entered. He parked a floor above the SUV she was driving. Then he trotted down the ramp to her vehicle.

Another car with staff stickers pulled in. He pretended to look at his phone. The woman hurried out of her car, pulling on a lab coat.

He waited. Listened. When there wasn't any more traffic, he hurried between Dr. Miller's Tahoe and the car next to hers, knelt next to the wheel well and attached a tracker. He checked his phone to make sure the signal worked.

"Dr. Miller," he murmured. "You can't run from me now."

SUNEE FINISHED her rounds long before normal. Each time she headed down a hall, she looked around, trying to see if anyone was waiting for her. Watching her.

Her phone buzzed. **Harris**. An ache filled her chest. She let his call go to voice mail.

He texted. **Pls let me know you're okay**

She swallowed as she typed. **At the hospital**

Thank you came his reply. Then **I miss you**

Her stomach churned.

Leaving before he woke had been cowardly. She'd made her choice. Harris was better off without her just like his mother had said. But the thought of not seeing Harris every day made her almost as uncomfortable as the thought of working in her father's firm.

Since it was early, she chose not to head to her lab. Not enough people would be walking those halls. Time to see if she could get to Dr. Ashland.

At least she wasn't too early. The hall lights in the critical care wing were already on. The daughter might not be here, but she could leave a message.

At the nursing station, she asked, "Is Dr. Ashland still here?"

"I can't give out that information," the nurse said.

Sunee could have checked the computer system, but since she wasn't involved in Dr. Ashland's care, it wasn't ethical. "I'm hoping I could talk to a family member."

A doctor moved to the counter. "Why?"

The nurse moved away as if she were glad not to have to deal with Sunee.

She checked the man's name tag. "Dr. Sutton, I'd like to talk to either Dr. Ashland or her family."

"What about?" Hostility filled his voice.

"Some research Dr. Ashland did about thirty years ago."

He frowned. "You're out of luck."

She clasped her chest. "Did she die?"

"No." But the doctor wasn't giving anything away.

"I think her family will want to talk to me." At least she hoped it was true.

Dr. Sutton looked at her hospital ID. Then her face. "Let me check."

Sunee nodded, but her head spun. Why was everything cloaked in mystery?

Dr. Sutton moved down one of the hallways to a room. A uniformed man sat outside the door he entered. A guard? Another puzzle piece that didn't fit.

Dr. Sutton reemerged from the hospital room along with a tall woman. She had Harris and Ashe's black hair and their athletic build. As she drew closer, Sunee swallowed. The woman had piercing gray eyes—Harris and Ashe's eyes.

Their sister.

"Nathan says you want to speak to my mother?" Her arms were crossed. Dark circles underscored her eyes.

Dr. Sutton hovered next to the woman's shoulder.

"I'm Sunee Miller. I work here. I'm a pediatric oncologist and geneticist." She inhaled. "Can we talk someplace private?"

"You can't *really* want to talk about my mother's research."

"Miss Ashland," Sunee tried again. "I'd like to talk privately."

"It's Dr. Ashland." She glanced back to the room.

"Piper." Dr. Sutton put a hand on Dr. Ashland's shoulder. "I'll stay with your mother. Why don't you find out what Dr. Miller wants?"

"Fine." Distrust filled her voice. "We can use the waiting room."

Sunee followed her in and waited as Piper Ashland poured a cup of coffee. They sat in adjoining chairs.

"I'm sorry about your mother's accident," Sunee started.

"Do you know something about it?" Dr. Ashland asked. "About the accident?"

"No, but I was in the ER when they brought her in."

Piper's eyes narrowed. "Then why do you want to talk to my mother?"

Sunee opened her phone and scrolled to a picture she'd taken of Harris and Ashe. "There isn't an easy way to do this."

Sunee tipped the phone so Dr. Ashland could see it.

"What? Who are they?" Piper's face went pale. "They look like ... like my father."

"I think they're genetically related to you."

"No." Dr. Ashland wrapped her arms around her stomach. "I don't have anyone *but* my mother. It's only been the two of us. My father died before I was born."

Sunee nodded. "And these two men didn't know about each

other until June. Their mothers both had donor zygotes implanted."

"What's going on?" Piper swallowed. "Why are you showing me this?"

"Did your mother ever talk about her early research on genetic modification and editing?"

"No." Piper blinked. Harris's eyes. Ashe's eyes. "Editing?"

"I've found her papers from thirty-five years ago, but her publications stopped the year you and these two men were born. They were born in different states. On different days."

"I don't understand."

"Dr. Ashland—"

"—Call me Piper, please." She shook her head. "Does this have something to do with my mother's accident?"

"I don't know. I would love to talk with your mother and ask her that question."

Piper shook her head. "She's still in a coma."

Sunee took Piper's hand. "I'm sorry."

Piper leaned closer. "What is going on?"

"I've studied the DNA of the two men in the picture. They're too closely related to be fraternal twins and too different to be identical." Sunee straightened. "Your mother visited them. Said they were in a long-term study from birth through when they turned twenty-one. There's ... confusion on what the study actually encompassed. And I haven't found any papers on that study."

"She was visiting *them?*" Piper pushed on her temples. "She would leave for a week, maybe four or five times a year. But I don't know what she was researching."

Sunee asked, "Would you be willing to let me test your DNA?"

"I ... I can get my results." Piper shook her head. "But I don't understand."

"Neither do we." Sunee pulled out a pad of paper and wrote down her personal email and her cell phone number and gave it to Piper. "Would you be willing to meet with these two men?"

"I..."

"They're trying to understand why they're related." Sunee wanted to do this for Harris. And Ashe. "They want the facts."

"I... I need to think. My mother..." Piper's voice trailed off.

"Be careful," Sunee said. "My lab and my apartment were broken into."

Piper clutched Sunee's hand. "Someone tried to kill my mother."

Sunee gasped. "Is that why there's a guard on your mother's room?"

"Yes." Piper straightened her shoulders. "I think I need to meet these men. I'll let you know when that can happen."

Sunee nodded. Mission accomplished. She didn't have any new answers, just more questions. But the links between her and Harris were weakening. Soon she would break them and go back to her own life.

HARRIS RESTED against the elevator wall, waiting for the descent to the Justice Center's sixth floor. He should be happy. The judge had ruled in their favor on key motions. But his problems with Sunee were tainting his outlook.

"Are you okay with losing the two pharmacists' testimonies?" Becky, an associate, asked.

Harris waited as she exited the elevator and then followed her to their offices.

"Our case is solid." He would never show the staff any doubts for this or any other case. His father had taught him that. In the Barney case, he had no doubt the wife was guilty, but juries sometimes surprised him. "Go home, Becky. You've earned an evening off."

"Thanks, boss. My husband hasn't seen too much of me lately."

How nice to be able to rely on someone being home.

He wanted that with Sunee.

He turned on his phone and messages and texts dinged.

In his office, he dropped the files and legal pads on his desk and rubbed his neck.

Sunee. Her name jumped out at him. A text. He opened the message, easing into his chair.

Harris, Ashe and Kat. Piper will meet with us. 6 PM. She has a hotel room next to hospital.

Sunee left the hotel name and room number.

Harris checked the time. Damn. He had to leave now. He rushed to the parking lot and jumped in his truck. As he backed out of his spot, his phone rang.

"Sunee?" he asked, not looking at the display.

"No, your mother."

He grimaced. "Mom."

"You're not still seeing Sunee, are you?" she asked.

"What?"

"She's not good for you. For your career," his mother said. "We talked about this. We agreed."

"Who is we?"

"You. Gary, me ... she ..." her voice trailed off.

"She?" Clarity struck like lightning. "When's the last time you talked to Sunee?"

"Oh ... yes ... w-well." The eloquent Leah Torrington stuttered. "I was at the hospital earlier this week and stopped to see her. We had tea."

Gary hadn't talked to Sunee. His own *mother* had warned her away from him. Pain slashed through his chest. Mother was more worried about his career than his happiness.

"What did you talk about?" His words were clipped.

"You. Her father." His mother exhaled. "I simply suggested that for the good of the state and country, she wasn't the right person for you."

"It worked. She broke up with me." His own mother. The pain drilled into his belly. "And because she was alone, Sunee was attacked and held at gunpoint."

"What? No!"

"Because of you." Let his mother think about that.

"I wanted her to leave you alone," his mother said. "I didn't want her hurt."

"Neither did I." He hesitated. "I love her."

He shouldn't be telling his mother. He should be telling Sunee.

"Harris, you can't. Your career. She's not the woman you need for your future. She can't carry on a conversation without breaking into hives." His mother's voice was hysterical. "Her father is Richard Miller."

"I don't care. I'll survive." If his constituents couldn't understand, he would figure out another career path. One that still served the public but not in an elected capacity. "I don't need a wife campaigning for me. I need Sunee in my life."

"You need to think long term." His mother's voice cracked.

"I am." He switched lanes, moving around a slow van. "She makes me happy."

"Oh." Only the sound of tires on the pavement broke the silence. His mother was rarely out of words, but apparently he'd silenced her.

"Stay away from Sunee." He had to undo the damage his mother had caused.

"Are you sure you want to stake your career on her?"

"Yes." He'd always thought his career was the most important part of his life. But Sunee had changed him. *She* was his top priority. He wanted her in his life to share the good and the bad. He loved her.

"I'm sorry," his mother said. "I thought I was doing what was best for you."

"You weren't."

After hanging up, he focused on getting to the hotel, to Sunee. He would convince her they were perfect for each other. He couldn't picture his life without her island of calm, her smile.

He'd always imagined choosing his career over a relationship. But this was not a choice. Sunee was the woman for him.

Now he had to convince her.

As he approached the hotel, he spotted his Tahoe and his shoulders relaxed. Sunee was here.

He headed into the hotel and up to the correct floor and room number and knocked.

Sunee opened the door but didn't look him in the eye. "You got my message."

Instead of walking in the room, he took her hand and pulled her into the hallway, his foot keeping the door from latching. "After this we need to talk."

She tugged on her hand, and her green gaze homed in on his. "We've said everything."

"No. I found out my mother talked to you. She's wrong." He hugged her. "Sunee, I don't want to lose you. I love you."

"Harris." Her lips trembled.

He pulled away, his hands on her shoulders. "I love you."

"You shouldn't." Tears swam in her eyes. "I'm not good for you."

"Yes, you are." He pulled her back into a hug, right where she belonged.

She hesitated before wrapping her arms around his waist.

He closed his eyes, laid his cheek on her silky hair and absorbed her quietness. A quiet that filled his soul. His heartbeat slowed, and a sense of well-being seeped into him. Whatever the world might bring, if he could be with Sunee, he could face any problems.

Except she hadn't said how she felt about him.

Down the hall, the elevator dinged. Sunee stepped out of his arms.

Ashe jogged toward them. "Are we meeting in the hall?"

"No." Harris pushed open the door, and Sunee and Ashe preceded him. He took a breath, preparing for the shock of meeting another biological relation.

"Damn," Ashe said under his breath.

Harris moved into the room and stared at the woman standing between the two beds.

Piper Ashland. The hair, the eyes, the height. Even the body shape. It was so similar. Not quite like looking in a mirror, but they were related. He exhaled. Even trying to prep for the shock hadn't softened the blow.

"I don't believe this." Piper clapped a hand to her mouth.

Sunee made introductions.

Piper shook Ashe's hand and then his. Harris moved back and stood next to Sunee's chair. He set his hand on her shoulder, but she shifted out from under his fingers.

"It's weird," Kat said.

He hadn't noticed Kat was here.

"I ... I can't wrap my head around it." Piper gazed first at Ashe and then at him and then sank onto the bed. "How—why?"

"Piper will send me her DNA results," Sunee said.

"It's obvious you're related," Kat said.

He, Ashe and Piper nodded.

"You don't think my father ... your mothers ...?" Piper took a deep breath.

"No. no." Harris shook his head. "My mother confirmed I was an implanted donor embryo."

"My mom's gone," said Ashe. "But my dad also said I was a donor embryo."

"The timing doesn't work," Sunee said.

"This is unreal." Piper's gaze bounced between Harris and Ashe.

"Your mother never said anything to you?" Kat asked.

"I was a twin, but my mother lost the other fetus at around

eight weeks." Piper shook her head. "She never said anything about donating embryos."

"Both Harris and I were part of a long-term study." Ashe sat on the desk, his foot bouncing up and down. "Your mother would visit every quarter."

Piper's eyes went wide. "You were the people she visited? Minneapolis, Houston and San Francisco?"

"San Francisco?" Harris and Ashe said at the same time.

Piper frowned. "She always visited those three cities. She would be gone almost a week."

"There might be one more kid," Kat muttered, making a note.

"How is your mother?" Harris asked.

"Still unconscious." Piper twisted her hands together.

"A doctor tried to kill Dr. Ashland last week," Sunee added.

"What?" Harris spit out.

"You're kidding." Kat shook her head.

"What the hell?" Ashe asked. "How?"

Piper walked them through waking up and finding the doctor injecting her mother and the subsequent cardiac arrest.

Too many people were getting hurt.

Harris asked, "Can you think of any reason someone would want to harm your mother?"

"No." Piper waved her hand between Ashe and Harris. "But I never knew about you. I'm not sure I know *anything* about my mother."

"What was the doctor's name?" Kat asked, writing fast.

"Lassiter. He was from Johns Hopkins," Piper said. "The police say he hasn't returned to Baltimore, and they haven't found him."

"And someone broke into Sunee's lab and her apartment," Harris said.

Sunee took a deep breath. "I think someone followed me to the hospital this morning."

"Sunee!" Harris's fingers clutched the back of her chair. "Why didn't you tell me?"

"I wasn't sure." She itched her neck. "The car followed me to the hospital but didn't pull onto the campus."

"What kind of car?" Ashe asked.

"Dark. An SUV I think." Sunee shook her head.

"Damn it! Why?" Harris paced the crowded room. "We need to either talk to Dr. Ashland or catch whoever is doing this and interrogate them."

"I'm sorry." Piper checked her phone. "I wish I could help, but I don't have a clue."

"Do you know why your mother stopped doing the genetic editing research?" Sunee asked.

"She never talked about it." Piper ripped at her hair. "Maybe my Uncle Victor knows."

"Victor Giuseppe?" Kat asked.

Piper nodded.

"I've left messages with his secretary," Kat said, "but he hasn't returned my calls."

"He headed back to Boston. I'll find out what he knows as soon as he lands." Piper checked her phone again. "I need to get back to my mother. I don't trust leaving her alone for long."

Everyone exchanged phone numbers before leaving the room.

"I'm starved. Anyone want to eat in the hotel?" Kat asked.

Ashe pulled on a ball cap. "Is this enough of a disguise?"

Everyone nodded.

They headed down to the restaurant and chose a table in the back. Sunee sat next to Ashe. And avoided Harris's gaze.

"How can we keep Sunee safe," Ashe grumbled, wrapping an arm around her shoulders, "if we don't know who or why they're after her?"

The memory of the man threatening Sunee with a gun was as lethal as an electric shock. Harris set his hand on the gun on his hip. "I'll keep her safe."

CHAPTER EIGHTEEN

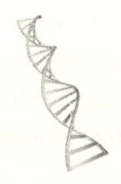

Mark Dell flung his cell phone onto his hotel bed. It bounced and dropped to the floor.

He paced the room. Nothing was going right. This morning he'd missed an opportunity to take out Miller. This afternoon he'd tried to get to Dr. Ashland, but a security guard had blocked the door.

And now? Apparently Torrington and Bristol had met at Piper Ashland's hotel. The operatives shadowing the two men weren't sure what room they'd gone to. But the two men, Dr. Miller and Katrina Phillips had eaten in the restaurant.

How had they found each other? Was it through Dr. Miller? Lassiter had said Miller had asked questions about Elaina Ashland's early genetic editing research.

If the men knew they were connected to Ashland, it wasn't a great leap to think they would keep digging into their origins. What kind of trail had Ashland left? If Dr. Miller dug too deep, the Ashland and Mendel collaboration might be exposed. Years of work would be destroyed.

His heart pounded in his chest. That couldn't happen.

After recovering his phone from the floor, he pulled up the tracking program. Time to silence Dr. Miller.

"I'm not leaving your car in the parking lot," Sunee told Harris after they waved goodbye to Ashe and Kat.

"Then let's move it to the hospital parking ramp and I'll take you home." Harris reached for her hand. "I don't want anything to happen to you. What if you're followed again?"

She tucked her hand into the pocket of her slacks. "I'll be careful."

She couldn't be this close to him. He would convince her they should still be together. His scent filling the vehicle would hurt too much. For his own good she had to keep her distance. "You'll be right behind me."

"I don't like it," Harris said, walking her to his Tahoe.

She clicked the locks open, but he stopped her before she slipped into the car.

Harris stepped close, too close. He cupped her chin and his eyes turned dark gray. "I love you. Please be careful."

Pain lanced through her like a scalpel to her chest.

She'd stood up to her father, she could do this. She could sacrifice her love for Harris and his career. But pushing Harris away was hard. "I'll be safe."

He leaned down.

A kiss would eviscerate her. Each time he said he loved her, each time he touched her ripped her in two.

But she froze.

His lips brushed hers. Tender. Sweet. One last time. He pulled her tight and deepened the kiss. And she threw her arms around his neck. One last time.

He pulled away and smiled. "I'll see you at home."

She sank into the driver's seat and stared out the windshield.

In her mind flashed a movie of her awkwardness at the Torringtons' dinner party, her hives and her constant anxiety at her father's fundraisers.

She wasn't meant for political life. For Harris.

Tomorrow she would move to Ashe's hotel. If that didn't work, she would sleep at the hospital.

Harris followed Sunee as she drove back to his house.

He'd made some progress. They'd kissed and she hadn't pushed him away. Damn his mother for interfering.

He would make Sunee see they were better together than apart. This attraction couldn't be one-sided. Not the way she'd kissed him. But he had to keep her safe.

Harris scanned the cars on the freeway, looking for a dark sedan. There was a dark gray Toyota ahead of Sunee. And a navy Ford behind him. A black extended cab pulled up next to them with a woman at the wheel.

He couldn't assume it would be a man. The guy who'd held Sunee at gunpoint might have accomplices. His heart rate picked up. Maybe he was being paranoid, but he tugged the gun from his holster and set it on the seat next to him.

Sunee drove as meticulously as she did everything else, indicating her lane changes and turns well before necessary. If someone were following her, they would know exactly where she was going.

And she could go a couple of miles over the speed limit. No cop would pick on her.

They were too exposed. Even with other vehicles on the freeway, Sunee was alone. His fingers drummed the steering wheel. He finally punched the speed dial on his phone.

"Yes?" she asked.

Hearing her voice was enough to calm him.

"Do you see the car from this morning?"

"No. But all cars look alike to me. I didn't learn to drive until I was in college."

As a Texan, that was hard to fathom. "It must be why you don't exceed the speed limit."

"It's the law," she sputtered.

He chuckled. "And everyone is passing you."

"Oh." There was a long pause. "You know, two wrongs don't make a right."

He laughed. "I'd like to get home before it's too dark."

"But the sunset is gorgeous," she said.

"Another night I'll watch the sunset with you." He was hoping they had a future. "But I'm not gazing at the sky when a crazy man is gunning for you."

There was a choked sound from Sunee. "I ... I still don't see anyone."

He followed her onto the off ramp. They'd be home in ten minutes. Fifteen tops.

He checked the rearview mirror for any vehicles taking their exit. A red truck. A silver sedan. But they turned left. He and Sunee turned right.

Maybe they were safe. For tonight. But he would drive Sunee to and from the hospital from now on. His body couldn't handle the stress of worrying about her safety.

As they neared his development, there were fewer and fewer vehicles. The sun had set and darkness closed around them.

"Watch the next intersection." The street to his right had an unruly clump of bamboo blocking the sightlines to the street. "I've almost been hit a few times."

"Okay." Her brake lights flashed on. "I'm hanging up now."

Maybe she wouldn't sleep in the damn guest bedroom. He wanted her face to be the last thing he saw at night and the first thing he saw at dawn.

He glanced at the rearview mirror. Clear. Then checked the road ahead of them. Clear.

As Sunee entered the blind intersection, an SUV raced out from the side street and rammed the front of the Tahoe.

"No!" He jammed his foot on the accelerator, closing the distance between him and the two vehicles.

Metal screeched. The SUV reversed and smashed into the Tahoe again. Harris's heart bashed against his chest.

"Sunee!"

Crash!

Sunee's seatbelt dug into her shoulders and belly. White filled her vision. She was slammed backwards into the seat. Pain seared her legs and arms. Smoke and powder filled the car. She tried inhaling and couldn't breathe.

Metal screeched. There was a flash of blue from the right, and the SUV rammed the front of her vehicle again. The Tahoe rocked, spinning sideways.

Wheels squealed. The smell of burning rubber filled her nose.

A dark shape covered the driver's side window. The door handle rattled.

She jerked.

"Sunee!" Harris pounded on the window. "Open the door."

She coughed, punching any button she could find.

"He's backing up again," Harris shouted. "Hurry!"

The locks clicked. The door whined as Harris pulled it open. He pushed back the deflating airbag.

She punched at her seat belt, trying to get free.

Harris grabbed her arm.

Pain ratcheted up to her shoulder. She whimpered. "Wait."

One more fumble and her seatbelt released.

He helped her scramble out of the car, clutching the burns on her arm. The blinding pain had tears streaking down her cheeks.

Bang! Metal smashed metal again. The car turned counter-clockwise, herding them like cattle in a chute.

Harris took most of her weight, forcing her to shift with the slowly turning car. "We need to run."

She blinked the tears away and searched for a spot to hide. "Where?"

A car door slammed.

Harris swore. "Too late."

A man rounded the front of the car, a gun in his hand.

"Stop!" Harris held a gun. He pushed her flat on the driver's seat. She gasped, pulling in the choking powder floating in the car.

A shot rang out. Harris grunted and ducked below the car door. He leaned around the edge and fired. *Bam! Bam!*

Harris swore.

"Harris!" Sunee dragged him into the car and crawled across the console. She kicked the mangled passenger door open. "This way."

He scrambled behind her. "Stay down."

Another shot rang out.

Sunee gasped. "You're bleeding."

Dear lord, there were two wounds, one in his upper chest and one in his abdomen.

He nodded, fumbling the gun to his left hand.

She wanted to stop his bleeding, but priority one was staying alive.

Sunee grabbed his gun. "I've got it."

"Sunee." He reached for the gun. "I've …"

She ignored him and crouched on the ground by the passenger door.

She'd shot a gun once. With Ashe. Didn't like it. But she would do anything to survive. To keep Harris safe.

Harris slumped against the passenger seat. Blood darkened the shoulder and stomach area of his shirt.

Fear pumped through her body. Her heart pounded in her ears.

There was a shuffle at the front of the car. Their attacker. Would he expect her to pop to the side or up from behind the open door?

She ducked underneath.

The streetlight was strong enough to show the man's shadow as he squatted in front of the car. "Dr. Miller, I just want to talk."

He was lying. He'd shot Harris.

Releasing a breath, she took aim and waited for the man to move. Rocks crunched as the man leapt up.

She pulled the trigger, the gun jumping in her hand.

More shots rang out. The windshield exploded. The passenger door window shattered, raining glass on her.

"Stop!" She fired.

The man stumbled. Another shot and a ping on the hood.

She pulled the trigger again.

He fell. Moaned. And stopped moving.

Her hand covered her mouth. She'd shot a man.

She glanced at Harris and checked his respirations. Still breathing, but the bloodstains were growing.

She crab-walked around the back of the SUV and approached the man from the driver's side. He was sprawled on the ground, the gun just out of his reach. Based on the pool of blood on the street, the bullet must have exited through his back.

Was he playing dead? If she picked up the gun, would he grab her?

She made a wide circle and kicked his gun, sending it toward the open passenger door.

The man didn't move. She was a doctor and had shot a man. Lightheaded, she swayed.

But he'd shot Harris. Tried to shoot her.

She would not faint.

Scuttling around him, she headed back to Harris, snatching the attacker's gun and setting it on the car floor.

She flipped the safety on Harris's gun and stuffed it in her waistband. "Harris!"

He moaned.

She checked his pulse. Thready.

Easing off his tie, she unbuttoned his shirt, wishing she had trauma shears to cut away the fabric. She tugged the cloth away from his wound.

One bullet had entered under his right clavicle and exited through his shoulder. The second had entered his right abdomen. Damn it. No exit wound.

"So much blood." Blood usually didn't bother her. But this was Harris's. The man she loved. "Hang on."

She snatched her lab coat from the back and shook off the airbag powder. Then she folded it into a pad and pressed down on the abdomen wound.

He groaned.

"I'm sorry." She dug under him with her free hand. Pulling her phone out of the console, she punched 9-1-1. "I need an ambulance and police. Now! Two men. Two GSWs. Both unconscious. I'm a doctor."

"Where are you, Doctor?"

She peered at the street sign and rattled off their location. "Hurry."

"Don't you die on me." She'd given him up, but the idea of him dying hollowed out her heart. "I love you. Stay with me."

A car pulled up and a woman called, "Do you need help?"

"Yes!" She didn't want to, but she needed to assess the injuries on the man she'd shot.

She checked under her lab coat. Harris was still bleeding.

The woman came around to the passenger door. "What can I do?"

"Keep pressure on this," Sunee said, easing backwards.

"Sure." The woman glanced at the gun and jumped. "There's a-a-a—"

"—gun on the floor," Sunee finished for her. "The man on the ground shot him."

The woman gulped.

"You're safe," Sunee assured her. "This is Harris Torrington. He's the district attorney. A good guy. I need to check on the … the bad guy."

"Okay." The woman bit her lip but set her hand next to Sunee's on the folded coat.

"Press hard."

Sunee watched her. Once satisfied she was applying enough pressure, Sunee wiggled out of the car and headed to their assailant.

She gritted her teeth and knelt next to the man. She'd shot his left chest and arm. Amazing. She'd been aiming for his right hand holding the gun.

She ripped off his mask and found a stranger with silver hair. "Who are you?"

Sirens wailed in the distance.

She'd also shot him in the belly. God. She tugged on the man's shirt, not as gentle as she'd been with Harris.

The man groaned, his legs flailed and he tried to push her away.

"Why do you want to hurt us?" she asked.

"You don't know?" The man groaned. "You don't know?"

"Know what?"

He didn't respond. His body melted into the pavement.

The sirens grew closer. She checked his pulse. Faint. Slow.

She couldn't worry about this monster. She rushed back to Harris. The woman let her take over.

Blue and red lights slashed through the night. The siren cut off.

A policeman moved around the front of the car. "Ma'am, please exit the car."

"Once a paramedic takes over." Harris would not bleed out.

A female paramedic tugged the driver's door open. "I've got him."

"GSW. Two. The right side abdomen is still bleeding."

"Thanks." Scissors sliced through Harris's shirt.

"Ma'am, back out of the car," the cop insisted.

She slid out the passenger door.

"Hands in the air. Lace them on your head."

She complied. "The man on the ground hit my car. Three times and then shot at us. He wounded Harris, District Attorney Torrington." She wasn't above using Harris's influence to get things moving. "After Harris was shot, I had to protect him. I picked up Harris's gun. I … I shot the man on the ground."

Another cop came up behind her and pulled the gun out of her skirt's waistband. "Spread your legs."

She didn't have time for this. She had to monitor Harris.

"Any needles? Anything sharp?"

"No. Hurry." The words spit out. "I need to check on Harris."

"The paramedics are working on him," the cop said.

"I'm a doctor."

A paramedic working on their attacker looked up. "Dr. Miller?"

"Yes." She recognized the woman.

"Officer, I can vouch for her."

The cop finished patting her down. "You're fine."

She rushed back to Harris. He was strapped to a gurney with an IV of lactated ringers running. "Was there an exit wound on the bullet in his abdomen?"

A paramedic answered, "No."

"I'll ride with you," Sunee said.

The paramedic looked at her partner, who nodded. "Sure, Dr. Miller. Let's move."

Sunee grabbed her purse, ran back and shut off Harris's truck and found his phone. When she stumbled back to the ambulance, her head swam.

"You can sit there." The paramedic pointed at a small bench. "What's his name?"

"Harris Torrington."

"The district attorney?"

"Yes." She wanted to check Harris's vitals, but the adrenaline from the accident was fading. "Did you stabilize his blood pressure?"

"Working on it," the paramedic said.

The small space spun, closing in on her. Nausea crept up her esophagus. The rocking ambulance didn't help.

"Let me look at your arms," the paramedic said.

"I'm fine. Take care of Harris."

"I've got a pressure bandage on the wound. You're not fine." The woman stared in Sunee's eyes. "You're in shock."

"Probably."

The paramedic pulled out a blanket. "Lie down."

Sunee complied, afraid she would fall over. She propped her feet above her heart.

The paramedic cleaned and wrapped the burns on her arms. "The airbag did a number on you."

"Please stay with Harris."

"Let me check your knee," the paramedic said.

"My knee doesn't matter." But it was swollen and bruised.

The paramedic handed her a cold pack. "Use this."

"How's his blood pressure?" Sunee applied the bag to her knee. *Ow.* When had she hurt her knee?

"Low," the paramedic said. "Fluids are running."

He had to be okay. She loved him.

Sunee's stomach did a churn and a flip. "I'm going to throw up."

The paramedic pulled her to a sitting position and thrust an emesis bag in her face. Just in time. Vomiting. Dizziness. Probably unreactive pupils. She didn't have time to be in shock.

Once she finished vomiting, the paramedic took the bag and handed her a bottle of water. "You know not to drink much."

Sunee nodded.

The woman monitored Harris. Sunee wished she could do more than lie here. Finally they pulled up in the ambulance bay.

"What hospital are we at?" she asked.

"Ben Taub."

It was an excellent trauma center. Exactly what Harris needed. He was too good a man to die.

The second ambulance carrying their shooter pulled in. She followed Harris into the ER.

"Ma'am, you can't go back there," a woman called.

"I'm a doctor." She tried to bluster her way into his room.

The paramedic called to the nurse, "She needs to be looked at too."

The nurse stopped her from entering Harris's room. "We'll need his information."

She was led away from Harris, limping. At the desk she relayed what little she knew. Then gave them her insurance information.

"Let me see Harris," she said.

Instead she was wheeled into a room on the opposite side of the ER.

"Please tell me how Harris is?" Sunee stared at his room.

A team of doctors and nurses burst out of Harris's room pushing a gurney and began to run.

Someone yelled, "Notify the OR we're on our way."

The nurse swung Sunee's door closed.

"No!" Tears streamed down Sunee's face. "Save him!"

CHAPTER NINETEEN

"I don't know why that man tried to kill us," Sunee repeated for the fourth time.

She'd been hydrated, warmed, bandaged and released to a small room next to the OR waiting room. Detective Cruz and another officer were questioning her.

All she wanted to know was how Harris was.

She stared at the wall, wishing for X-ray vision to see into Harris's operating room. He'd been in there an hour.

"This could be a different person than the men who broke into her lab," Detective Cruz said to the other officer. "But the silver hair and mask match the description both Dr. Miller and Mr. Torrington gave of the man who broke into her apartment and held her at gunpoint. Too bad he died. I'd like answers on what's going on."

Sunee closed her eyes and rested her head on the back of the chair. At least she hadn't had to regurgitate the previous break-ins.

A chill raced through her body. She'd killed a man.

"His fingerprints aren't in the system," another detective said.

"And his ID and the rental car agreement are for a man who's been dead twenty-five years."

Her whole body shook. Who wanted her dead?

Detective Cruz handed her a blanket. "Did he say anything to you?"

"I don't think … wait." Sunee wrapped up but couldn't get warm. "He said, 'You don't know?'"

"You don't know?" a cop asked.

She nodded, discovering new aches in her neck and shoulders.

"I think we're done for now," Detective Cruz said.

Sunee headed into the waiting room.

"Where's my son!" Leah Torrington swept into the room. Her gaze locked on Sunee's. "What happened?"

"There was an accident." Sunee's chest itched. "The man who rammed the SUV tried to kill us."

"Kill you?" Leah sank down on an empty chair. "I asked you to leave him alone."

"We need to focus on Harris surviving." Sunee tugged the blanket around her shoulders.

Leah gasped and turned to the nurse standing in the doorway. "I want to see my son."

"He's in surgery, but I'll get an update." The nurse hustled away.

The police filed out of the room. At least they wouldn't be asking questions she couldn't answer. Silence settled over her and Leah like a New York City ice storm.

"I want you to leave," Leah said.

Sunee shook her head. "I'm not leaving. He was shot protecting me."

Leah's breath whooshed out. "I wish he'd never met you."

"I don't." Sunee straightened her shoulders. "I love him."

"Love means nothing." Leah's hand slashed the air between them. "You're poison to his career."

"That isn't for you to say." She was done having other people tell her what to do. This was her life. Her relationship. "That is up to Harris. I won't leave until I know he's all right and *he* asks me to leave."

"He told me you broke up with him," Leah snapped.

"I did." She moved over to the coffee pot and poured a cup, just to have something to do with her hands. "But that's not what he wants."

"Oh." Leah sank back into the chair.

"Would you like something to drink?" Sunee asked, trying to breach the divide between them.

"Tea." Leah's voice cracked.

Sunee brought her a cup and handed her packets of sugar and cream.

They sat. Waited. Kat arrived. Senator Torrington arrived. They all waited.

And she never broke out in hives.

DARKNESS. It called to Harris, urged him to let go. In the darkness his pain disappeared.

He let go. Then jerked. *Sunee!* He had to find her.

He flailed and pain ripped through his shoulder, stomach.

"Stop." Hands held him down. "Don't move."

He pried his eyes open.

A small woman wearing scrubs held him down. "There you are."

A nurse? He was in the hospital?

"I'm Carla," she said.

"Where's ... Sunee?"

"Your mother?" Carla asked.

"No, my ..." He didn't have a description. "Dr. Miller. I need to see her."

"Your parents stepped out. I'll get them."

His heart pounded and the electronic echo of his heartbeat filled the room. "I need Sunee."

But Carla was gone.

He tried to lift his right arm, but it was casted. What had happened?

The only thought cutting through the fog was Sunee. He loved her. He had to find her. She was what was important in his life. Not a career. Without her, life would be empty.

"Harris!" His mother rushed into the room. "Are you really awake this time?"

"This time?"

She kissed his cheek. "You've been in and out for twenty-four hours."

A day. "Where's Sunee? What happened to her?"

His mother's smile grew brittle. "She ... left."

"Left?" Sunee wouldn't leave him. "When did she leave?"

His mother's hand waved, usually a sign she wasn't sure what to say. "I don't know."

Some of the fog lifted. His mother had chased Sunee away before. "What did you say to her?"

She pulled a chair closer to the side of his bed. "As little as possible."

"Mom." He found the controls for the bed and raised the head. "I want to see her."

She sank into the chair. "Sunee is not good for you."

"I don't care." He glanced around the room. "Where's my phone?"

His father pushed through the door. "Harris. Thank goodness."

Harris waited through his father's gentle hug. "I need to see Sunee."

His dad looked at his mother.

"Is she okay?" His hand shook. It couldn't be. No. "Is she dead?"

"She's in the waiting room." His dad hurried to the door. "I'll get her."

"The waiting room?" He glared at his mother.

"I ..." she sputtered.

"Get out."

His mother held out her hands. "I only want what's best for you."

"She's what's best for me."

The door creaked. There was a flash of Sunee's dark hair as she peeked in.

Warmth filled his chest. "Sunee."

His dad pulled his mother out of the door. "We'll leave you two alone."

Sunee stopped at the foot of the bed. "Harris."

He held out a hand, urging her closer. "I thought ... I was afraid you'd been hurt."

She stepped next to the bed and took his good hand. "You were the one shot. Twice. You needed surgery."

"I can't remember." He tugged on her hand until she sat on the bed next to his hip. "I woke up so afraid for you."

"I'm okay." She stroked his cheek.

He pointed at the bandages on her arms. "You are?"

"Burns from the airbag." She gazed into his eyes. "I'm glad you're all right."

He pulled her until her head rested on the uninjured side of his chest. Peace washed over him. "What happened?"

"Do you remember the SUV running into your Tahoe?"

The sight, the panic of those moments smacked into him like a semi. "I couldn't run fast enough."

"The silver-haired man shot you. In your shoulder and side." She looked up and tears streaked her cheeks.

Why couldn't he remember? "What happened?"

"You passed out. He kept shooting and I … I shot him," she whispered.

"Is he dead?"

"Yes. I might need your help with that. I don't have a gun license."

"It was self-defense." He held her close as her tears soaked his gown. "I'm sorry you had to do that."

"I'm not." Her head shot up. "I couldn't let anything happen to you. I … I …" Her hand covered her mouth.

Joy filled him. She loved him.

"I love you," he said.

"That's not smart." Her shaking hair swished against his shoulder.

"Oh, but it is." He placed a finger on her mouth. "You make me happy, keep me calm. Make my day mean something. I love you."

Tears swam in her green eyes. "Because of you, I'm learning to stand up for myself."

"I'm glad." He placed a kiss on her forehead. "Do you love me?"

"What?"

"It's a simple question. Yes or no." He tipped her face up again. "Do. You. Love. Me?"

"You're the best man I've ever known." Her fingers twisted in his gown. "You understand me."

Hope blazed in his heart. "Do I have to ask you again?"

Tears flowed like a river down her cheeks. "No. I love you."

He grinned. "I love you."

She bent and kissed him. "I'll try to conquer my anxiety. For you."

"We'll work on that together." He traced her lips with his finger. "And if you can't handle it, then we'll keep you out of the limelight."

They held each other. It didn't matter that his body ached. Sunee was here.

"I never want to hurt you or your career."

"If I don't have you in my life, I'll be empty." He tugged her close. "If we're together, we'll figure everything out. Together we can handle anything."

EPILOGUE

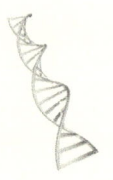

A week later Harris shuffled his way down the stairs. Each step caused sharp jabs of pain as if teeth gnawed on his incisions. It was good to be home, but until he healed he might have to sleep on the main level.

But last night he'd slept with Sunee. And lying side-by-side while holding hands had been perfect.

Following the scent of bacon, he hobbled into the kitchen.

"Harris!" Sunee wiped her hands and rushed over to help him to the table. "I was bringing brunch up to you."

"I can't lie in bed anymore." He collapsed into the chair and pulled her close. "Unless you want to stay there with me all day."

Sunee cleared her throat, a blush coloring her skin. "Harris, love, Ashe will be here soon."

He grinned. She'd called him *love*. "You did agree to move in with me last night?"

"Yes." She brushed back his hair. "Ashe and Kat will help me pack."

"I was worried that was a dream." He rested his head on her stomach. "And it's not because of the break-ins?"

"It's because I love you." Sunee wrapped her arms around him. "I want to be with you."

"Always."

He inhaled her floral scent and forgot his pain. She was what he needed.

There was a knock at the door. Sunee took a step away from him. "I'll get that."

He smiled and waited.

Ashe came in and took the seat next to him. He started to slap Harris's shoulder. Stopped. And patted his hand. "Glad to see you're out of the hospital. Sorry I didn't come see you there."

"No problem," Harris said.

Sunee brought over the coffee pot and filled cups for Harris and Ashe. Then she set out a plate of toasted English muffins, bacon, cheesy scrambled eggs and a bowl of cut fruit. "Eat. Kat called and said she would be a little late."

"I've heard what happened from Sunee," Ashe said. "But we still don't know why."

"The guy told Sunee there's something we don't know." Harris shook his head. "We have to keep digging."

He and Sunee held hands as they ate. And Ashe didn't shoot him nasty looks.

The doorbell rang, and Sunee brought Kat back to the kitchen.

"It smells good in here." Kat gave Harris a gingerly hug and kissed the top of his head. "Don't scare us again."

"I don't plan to." He laughed and winced from the twinges in his stomach and chest.

Sunee caught his grimace. "Did you take your medication?"

"Everything but the pain pill."

"Harris—" Sunee started.

"If the pain gets bad, I'll tell you." He pushed up her sleeves and flipped over her arms. "What about your pain?"

"I'm fine."

"You didn't tell me you were hurt," Ashe said.

"The airbag." Harris planted a kiss on Sunee's hands.

Kat dished up her food. "Who was this guy?"

"No clue," Harris said.

"When Dr. A wakes up," Ashe pushed his chair away from the table, "maybe she'll have answers."

They went quiet.

"I asked Piper to come to brunch," Ashe said. "She doesn't want to leave her mother."

"Speaking of her mother." Kat bounced a little and wiped her mouth. "I found him."

"Him? The guy who died?" Sunee asked.

"No." Kat tugged on her bag, pulled out a photo and handed it across the table.

It was a photo of his face, but it wasn't him. The man held a big-ass check.

"That's the third child?" Ashe tipped the picture.

"I was flipping through cable channels last night and almost fell over when I saw him playing poker." Kat pointed at the picture. "Meet Andrew 'Drew' Phoenix."

Harris blew out a breath. "I finally got used to looking at Ashe. Now this."

Sunee rested her head on his healthy shoulder. "I need a DNA sample."

"I'll find him and get that for you," Kat said.

Harris leaned back and listened to the conversation flow around the table. He'd been lucky. He'd always had a family.

Now he had more. He had Sunee to light up his life. And Kat was his irritating little sister. Ashe was the brother he'd always wanted. Maybe Piper and this Drew would join their circle of friends.

He held up his coffee mug. Everyone turned to him. The love burning in Sunee's eyes took his breath away. He pressed a hard kiss on her lips. "I know we haven't discovered all the answers, and I think there will be more questions, but I truly believe we will solve this mystery. Together."

They all raised their coffee mugs and repeated, "Together."

Book 2 - CONNECTIONS is available now at AMAZON. Read on to learn how Ashe deals with the mystery of his origins.

CONNECTIONS

CHAPTER ONE

Houston

Ashe Bristol paced the room. The walls were closing in on him. He wanted out of the hotel he'd been living in for too many weeks. He wanted his personal gym and his own space.

That wouldn't happen for at least a week. The closing date on the home he'd purchased kept changing. At least his trade from the Ravens to the Texans allowed him enough time to take care of moving before training camp.

Of course he could have taken his dad up on his offer to stay at his house.

Unfortunately, Coach, his dad, ate, slept and breathed football.

Ashe hadn't wanted the constant pressure. He wanted, no *needed* more in his life.

It was probably insane to buy a home. He didn't know what he'd be doing a year from now. He didn't know if his body would hold up for an entire season.

He wanted one more year out of his knee. Just one. Maybe two if he was lucky. Then he could retire.

He flexed his healing knee. Something popped. The doc said he'd always have popping and could look forward to arthritis and knee replacement in his forties. Great.

Ashe threw on running shorts and a T-shirt. The surgical scar around his knee was red and angry. He'd finished his physical therapy. Now he was trying to get back into shape before camp. As he left his room, he pulled a ball cap low on his face.

There was another reason he wanted out of the hotel and away from the public eye. He and Harris Torrington looked too much alike.

And they didn't know why.

Well, they knew they were genetically related. And that their mothers had both had fertility problems and thus had embryos implanted. Harris and his birthdays were within a week of each other.

And they looked like spitting images of Dr. Andrew and Dr. Elaina Ashland.

Hell, he hadn't known his mom and dad weren't his biological parents. That was a shock.

It would be great if they could ask Dr. Elaina Ashland what she'd done, but someone had tried to kill her, and she was still in a coma. Dr. Andrew Ashland had died thirty plus years ago.

Someone had also tried to kill Ashe's friend Sunee who had run his and Harris's DNA tests. Sunee couldn't explain why he and Harris were more closely related than siblings, but they weren't identical twins. The DNA results didn't make sense. And Sunee was brilliant.

He tugged the hat lower. He had to exercise. He had to get back in shape for the upcoming football season. That meant risking recognition. As Harris.

Outside, he stretched his hamstrings and recited his mantra. *One more year.* Ever since his injury mid-season with the Ravens, he'd been careful. He slowly jogged away from the hotel. With each stride, he willed the tension from his body and concentrated on each step.

His shoes slapped the pavement in a rhythmic pattern. He checked his time and pushed up the pace. Running in Houston in July was like running in a sauna. He could hear his mom's voice telling him he should have grabbed a bottle of water out of the minibar.

He friggin' missed his mom. She might not have had any additional answers to the mystery of how he and Harris were related, but she'd been his biggest supporter. And when his mother had been alive, she'd tempered his dad's football fanaticism.

But after five years in remission, cancer had stolen her away with little warning. One minute she'd been cheering him on as he led the Ravens against Dad's Texans, the next she'd been in a hospital hooked up to tubes and monitors and telling him not to cry.

He swiped at the water in his eyes. It must be windier than he'd thought.

Turning left, he ran smack into a crowd of people spilling out of a theater. He wove in and out of the pedestrians, thinking he needed another route. Unfortunately he didn't know the area well enough.

He worked his way around two couples standing in the center of the sidewalk.

"Hey, Torrington," a man yelled.

Ashe's heart skipped a couple of beats, but he ignored the stranger.

"Torrington," the man yelled a little louder.

The ball cap hadn't fooled this guy. Or the fact that ever since he'd met Harris, he'd been growing out his hair and beard.

Ashe ducked his head, zigzagged through the crowd, and stepped off the curb to get clear. He couldn't get trapped and have this guy realize he wasn't Harris.

As he escaped, the man said, "I swear that was Harris Torrington. What's he doing running downtown? He lives in Eagle's Canyon."

Hell in a hand basket. Ashe scrambled away as if a defensive back had broken through his offensive line.

It was time to get off the street and out of downtown. He didn't want anyone else recognizing him.

That would be hard. In three hours, he had a team press conference.

He'd better come up with an answer as to why he looked like Torrington.

Pick up CONNECTIONS now at AMAZON.

THANK YOU DEAR READERS!

If you loved Harris and Sunee's story, could you take a few moments and review DISCOVERY. It helps other readers find my books.

Here are the links to the review sites:
Amazon
BookBub
Goodreads

Thank you!

ALSO BY NAN DIXON

POETIC JUSTICE - *Romantic Suspense*

DESIGNER CHILDREN - *Romantic Suspense*
DISCOVERY
CONNECTIONS
DECEPTION
REVELATIONS

THE MacBAINS - *Contemporary Romance*
MAID FOR SUCCESS
EDGE OF FRIENDSHIP
HOW WE STARTED (novella)

BIG SKY DREAMERS - *Contemporary Romance*
INVEST IN ME
STAINED GLASS HEARTS
DANCE WITH ME

FITZGERALD HOUSE - *Contemporary Romance with some Romantic Suspense*
SOUTHERN COMFORTS
A SAVANNAH CHRISTMAS WISH
THROUGH A MAGNOLIA FILTER
THE OTHER TWIN
UNDERCOVER WITH THE HEIRESS
TO CATCH A THIEF
A SAVANNAH CHRISTMAS WEDDING (novella)

ACKNOWLEDGMENTS

There are so many amazing people in my writing life. Always first are my critique partners: Ann Hinnenkamp, Leanne Taveggia, Cat Schield and Lizbeth Selvig. And of course my editor Judy Roth. Your advice is so appreciated.

I'm blessed to have the Dreamweavers in my life. They are filled with wisdom.

I have to thank the BBC reporters who did an in depth piece on genetic modification years ago. Your report kick-started this idea as I drove from Ohio to Minnesota and began this series.

And of course I have to thank my family — because they are everything to me. Dr. Dan - any errors are my own!

To my readers—thank you, thank you, thank you!

ABOUT THE AUTHOR

Best-selling author of the DESIGNER CHILDREN, THE MACBAINS, BIG SKY DREAMERS and FITZGERALD HOUSE series, Nan Dixon spent her formative years as an actress, singer, dancer and competitive golfer, but the need to eat had her studying accounting in college. Unfortunately, being a successful financial executive didn't feed her passion to perform. When the pharmaceutical company she worked for was purchased, Nan got the chance of a lifetime—the opportunity to pursue a writing career. She's a five-time Golden Heart[R] finalist and lives in the Midwest. She has five fabulous children, three wonderful son-in-laws, four granddaughters, two grandsons and one neurotic cat.

Nan loves to hear from her readers so stay in touch or contact her through the following social media.

Made in the USA
Las Vegas, NV
10 May 2025